Lindsay's Legacy

Lindsay's Legacy

Janice Jones

www.urbanchristianonline.com

Urban Books, LLC
78 East Industry Court
Deer Park, NY 11729

ISBN 13: 978-1-60162-890-9
ISBN 10: 1-60162-890-0

First Printing January 2012
Printed in the United States of America

10 9 8 7 6 5 4 3 2 1

Distributed by Kensington Corp.
Submit Wholesale Orders to:
Kensington Publishing Corp.
C/O Penguin Group (USA) Inc.
Attention: Order Processing
405 Murray Hill Parkway
East Rutherford, NJ 07073-2316
Phone: 1-800-526-0275
Fax: 1-800-227-9604

DEDICATION

I dedicate *Lindsay's Legacy* to my friend and brother in Christ, Reverend Bobby Thompson Jr. You gave me the name for this novel before I ever wrote the first syllable. I thank you for your continued support of all my writing endeavors. You have been behind me spiritually and financially since *His Woman, His Wife, His Widow* hit the shelves. I praise God for your dedication to me and my ministry.

ACKNOWLEDGMENTS

Thanks and praises are always first due to my Lord and Savior, Jesus Christ. Without you, I am unable to write, and I would actually have nothing to write about. Thank you for trusting me enough to do this for the Kingdom.

To my children, Jerrick and Derrick Parker: Thank you for being great sons. And look at us now—you all have grown to the point that we can now be friends. Remember, though, I will always be Mama first. To my grandson, Jevon Parker: "Gannie" misses you. I can't wait until we can spend more time together.

To my father, Harold Bumpers: Your support of me never surprises me, but it always means the world to me. We just have to work on you realizing that there is a two-to-three-hour time difference Detroit and Phoenix. Daddy, when you call me at 8:00 A.M. just to say hi, it is actually 5:00 A.M. in Phoenix. LOL.

To my siblings, Sherrie Roberts, Darrius Bumpers, Ronald Binns, Linda Gardner & the twins, Darrin (Main) and Darnella Bumpers: Growing up with you all was a whole lot of fun. Being grown with you all is a whole different kind of fun. LOL. Thank you for all of my nieces, and nephews, and godchildren. I love you all to pieces.

To my friends in Detroit: Wendy Roberts, Curtrise Garner, Monique Gaskin, Ashley King, Jimmie Porter,

Acknowledgments

Derrick Parker, David Jones, and William Price: You guys are the best. I know I can always, always, always depend on you all. You have proven it time and time again. We are friends for life, which actually makes you all family.

To my Arizona friends, which really equates to my First Institutional Baptist Church Family: Pastor Stewart, you are my mentor, my father in Christ, and even a friend. Rev. Karen Stewart, also a mentor, a sister, and a great friend. Girl, I will take these earrings off if I have to. LOL. To the entire church congregation, you all have been so supportive. And to those of you who put up with me even when I know you didn't want to, a special thanks to you: Cheval Breggins, Claudia Phelps Wade, Nancy Hooper, Georgia Harris, Geralyn Staten, Rosalyn Ricketts, Renee Roberson, Brandy Oliver, Erika Alexander, Tandie Myles, Michelle Robinson, Renette Gutierrez, Forrest Wade, Roberto Gittens, Carlos Molina, and Kendall Washington. Sonya Kelly and Eric Jones, you two are not members of FIBC, but you are definitely a member of my family. You all are so wonderful. You make being away from my family at home a lot easier to bear.

To my editor Joylynn Jossel, you are the best. I know I got on your nerves with my deadlines. I thank you for your patience and for working with me through it all. To my agent, Janell Ageyman, thank you for your diligence and for keeping my name in your mouth wherever you go. I am enjoying our relationship. To the staff at Urban Christian Books, thank you so much for all that you do to bring our work to fruition and for all that you do to keep the books moving.

And a special thanks and acknowledgment to my best friend Denise Franklin: Nothing that I write would ever get written if it were not for you. You keep me

Acknowledgments

focused. You keep me on point. You tell me the truth when something sucks. You cry with me through the hard times of the characters, and you threaten me when they do something you don't like. You have walked me through every syllable of every book I have written, and I will never be able to fully express how much your love, friendship, and assistance mean to me.

If there is anyone who I have missed, please charge it to my head and not my heart. Know that I love you too.

Prologue

"S-Man, it's on you now. Your daddy was my heart. He was my blood. Because he didn't have a daddy, I took him under my wing. But he was your father. He was your king. He worked hard to take care of you from the time you were a dot in your mama's womb. You ain't never wanted for anything, nothing your whole life. You have lived like the prince you were created to be on the back of your daddy. But your daddy gone now. He dead! Now S-Man, you got to be the king."

Sixteen-year-old Sha'Ron Taylor sat with his uncle Bobby and listened to him as if he were God Almighty who had descended from heaven to engage him in conversation. He said nothing. He simply listened, waited, and wondered as he chewed on the tasteless, cold french fries on his plate.

Robert Taylor, Uncle Bobby as he was affectionately known by family, leaned in closer across the booth that separated him and his great-nephew so as not to be overheard by anyone else in the restaurant. "But before you claim the crown of your daddy's kingdom, you first have to avenge his death."

Sha'Ron bounced back and forth in his thoughts. Yes, he hated Lindsay for killing not only his father, but also having the gall to take out his mother too. He wanted her dead. But he didn't relish the idea of giving up his own life to a prison cell for murder.

He knew Uncle Bobby wanted him to kill Lindsay. This was not their first conversation on the subject. However, Uncle Bobby didn't want to overburden the young lad by harping on the task that needed to be done for the entire two-and-a-half years that Lindsay had been locked up. Now that her release was imminent, the time had come for them to plot and plan. Sha'Ron had secretly hoped that Uncle Bobby would eventually decide to have one of his minions take out his stepmother. No such luck.

"Uncle Bobby, man, you know I ain't no punk. You also know once that trick is dead I will celebrate the anniversary of her death like Christmas. But how do I kill her and get away with it? I'll be the first person the police suspect once she's murdered."

"Of course, I know you ain't no punk. Your worry, S-Man, is natural. It actually shows your intelligence. You get that from your father. It's smart to be concerned and not some hotheaded little kid looking for revenge. That's why we got to be real careful about this. You can't just walk up on her the moment she hits town and gun her down like some raw amateur. Naw, S, this here deed gone take some time. We gone have to work first at getting inside Ms. Lindsay's head . . ."

Uncle Bobby sat back against the booth seat rubbing his chin as a sinister snarl claimed his features. Then he continued his thought.

". . . before you blow it off."

Chapter One

"Lindsay Renee Westbrook. Today is supposed to be a day of joy, happiness, and love. You're going to have to stop all this crying, sweetheart."

The tears continued to flow unchecked. It was a good thing her makeup had not yet been applied; otherwise, it would be ruined by now. Her children were beautifully attired, sitting in the hotel clubhouse with her grandmother, waiting to serve as her attendants. The most important person in the world to her was in his dressing room with his brother, who served as his best man, calmly getting dressed. The ten or so guests that included Cody's parents, his sister, and a few of the people he had met here at Martha's Vineyard sat in the hotel chapel awaiting the ceremony to begin. Her beautiful silver dress hung on the back of the dressing room door. Her mother continuously tried to compose her as she sat creating rivers in her bathrobe. She wanted so badly to get up, get beautiful, and get married, but her feet were held hostage by the lead of guilt and sorrow she felt in her heart.

"Mama, I don't think I can do this. I can't do this without Shyanne."

"Yes, you can, Nay. Shy would want you to be happy, baby. You know that. She is in your heart and in the beautiful memories the two of you created together."

"But, Mama, the only memory that's in my head right now is the memory of how I got my best friend, my sister, killed."

Lindsay thought about the day that Shyanne lost her life. It was her thirtieth birthday, and Shaun had given her a royal beat down as a birthday present. Shyanne went in search of Shaun to deal with him for what he had done to her best friend and found herself caught in the line of fire of other drug men who had come to gun Shaun down. That was actually the most painful day of Lindsay's life, one she would probably relive every year on her birthday.

"I know she would want me to be happy, but I feel bad because she doesn't get to see me in my happiness. All she ever got to witness was my pain and distress while I was with Shaun; pain and distress that caused her death. Then when I think about that, I think about how I killed Shaun to avenge Shy's death. Then I killed Rhonda, and I started to realize that maybe I don't deserve to be happy." Lindsay grabbed more of the nearly empty box of tissues and sobbed even louder.

She was definitely grateful to have been given such a light sentence. Two years for murdering two people had been merely a slap on the wrist in the eyes of most people. As a result of Cody's great skills as her defense attorney, he was able to convince the district attorney not to take the case to trial. Had he taken the case to trial, Cody would have gotten her completely off on a temporary insanity charge for killing Shaun and a self-defense charge for killing Rhonda. The DA saw the validity of Cody's arguments and decided to offer a plea bargain. After all, Shaun was a notorious drug dealer, and Rhonda had attacked Lindsay first.

Lindsay was so sure that she had truly dealt with the pain of Shyanne's death during the two years she spent in prison. If anyone had asked her, she would have been willing to bet her life that she had sincerely forgiven herself for what she believed to be her part in the murder of her best friend. Today, however, all of the guilt, pain, and regret came flooding back as if Shyanne had died just yesterday. *Why?* Lindsay wondered. *Why today of all days?*

"Nay, sweetheart, you love Cody, don't you?"

"Of course, I do, Mama. I love him with all my heart. My fears and doubts are not about whether I want to be married to him. I know I do. I just don't know if I feel worthy enough to be his wife after all the wrong I have done. He deserves a wife who is better than the wretched mess that I am."

Sherrie Westbrook kneeled in front of Lindsay and firmly gripped both of her wrists in one of her hands while she used her other hand to lift the bowed down head of her only daughter.

"Lindsay Renee Westbrook, you listen to me, and you make sure you hear me. I love you with a love that is indescribable. You love Cody with every fiber of your being, and he feels exactly the same way about you. You love your children so very much. Now, you take all that love and multiply it by one hundred and you still have not touched on how much God loves you. He loves you, Nay-Nay, and He has forgiven you. You have suffered the consequences of your actions by serving your time in jail and being away from your children for two years. You have suffered from all the pain you have endured since the day you met Shaun Taylor, including the death of Shyanne."

Lindsay appreciated her mother's words of assurance and love. She needed to be reminded right now how much God loved her. Even more so, she needed to hear and be convinced that He had forgiven her. As Sherrie continued talking to her daughter, Lindsay knew, in complete faith, that the Holy Spirit spoon-fed into her mother's mouth every word she spoke.

"Today is the beginning of a brand-new life for you. You are a child of the King and deserving of every promise in His Word and His Word promises His forgiveness if you repent. You have done that, child. So you stop letting the devil talk you out of what you have a right to, Nay-Nay. Shyanne is also God's child. She's fine, resting in Him, at peace. Take comfort in that, Nay. Please, baby. There is nothing that you can do to bring her back. So wallowing in self-pity and self-imposed guilt will do no one any good. Marry the man that you love and be happy. Be happy, Nay, for your good and to the glory of God, because not even this is about you. It's all about Jesus."

Before Lindsay even knew what was happening, Sherrie began to pray.

"Father God, I come right now in the mighty name of Jesus, praising you, Lord, for your mighty works, for your precious grace and mercy, for your overwhelming love. Lord, I come to say thank you for a beautiful day that we have never seen before and for all the blessings this day holds for us. Master, I come right now asking that you shower down your peace, your wisdom, and your joy. This is the day my daughter is going to marry the man that you created just for her. Lord, give her the assurance that she needs to follow through with the plans that you have for her and Cody and guide her, Lord, so that she is the wife that you purposed her to be. This is my prayer in Jesus' matchless name . . . Amen."

By the time Sherrie released Lindsay's sore wrist, her tears had dried, her spirit had lifted, and she was ready to marry the man her heart desired.

"Okay, Mama. I can do this, for myself, for Shyanne, and for Jesus. Thank you so much for always allowing God to use you to help fix me. I love you, Mama."

"I love you too, baby. Now come on. Let's get you into this dress and all beautiful for your new husband."

For the next forty minutes, Sherrie helped Lindsay apply makeup, put the finishing touches on her pre-styled hair, and helped her into her beautiful, although nontraditional, silver tea-length wedding dress. She then got herself dolled up and outfitted in her lavender sheath dress. The silver and lavender color combination had been Shyanne's favorite colors.

While she and her mother primped, Lindsay was reminded of how she did this for her first marriage with Shyanne. She expected the memory to be painful, but she found it rather to be bittersweet; the sweet being that no matter what mistakes she made in her life, Shyanne had always been by her side to see her through them. The bitter had been that her first marriage had been such a disaster to such a horrid man. But Lindsay refused to allow even that thought to place her back into the funk her mother and God had just coaxed her out of. Together, she and Sherrie put the final touches on their wedding looks and headed out to meet her brother Kevin, the man who would serve as her escort down the aisle to her betrothed.

Sherrie signaled a hotel staff member to go and alert Cody and tell him it was okay for him to make his way to the chapel. She also told her to let everyone know the bride was ready and that the ceremony could begin.

The procession began with Cody's best man, Thaddeus, escorting Sherrie to her seat in the front of the chapel where the ceremony would take place while the song "Nothing Has Ever Felt Like This," by Rachelle Ferrell and Will Downing, played. He then joined Cody at the makeshift altar and arch. Next, Lindsay's grandmother, Linda, was escorted by Li'l Shaun, to the seat next to her daughter. Following Linda and Li'l Shaun

were Margaret and Anthony Vincini, Cody's parents.
All of the members of the wedding party were hand-
somely attired in the chosen colors of lavender and
silver.

Lindsay could see the procession from where she
and Kevin waited for Shauntae, the final person in the
wedding party, to walk the aisle. Much to her surprise,
however, another couple was standing ready to head
down the aisle. When Lindsay looked closer, she realized the male and female, all decked out in the appropriate attire, were Shyanne's parents, Gregg and Tonya
Kennedy.

Lindsay had no idea Shyanne's parents were going to
be at her wedding, and much less of an idea that they
were going to be a part of her wedding party. It took
every ounce of self-control she possessed for her to
not break free from Kevin's grasp on her arm and bolt
down the aisle after her godparents. What a wonderful
surprise wedding present. She knew beyond a shadow
of a doubt that her wonderful, soon-to-be-husband was
behind the whole thing. She would be sure to properly
thank him tonight.

Next and last to proceed down the aisle before the
bride was her beautiful daughter, Shauntae.

Finally, the music changed from Rachelle Ferrell to
BeBe and CeCe Winans's song, "If Anything Ever Happened to You." Kevin looked lovingly at his big sister
and in his eyes Lindsay saw love, respect, and admiration. With his voice he said, "Nay, I am so happy for
you and for Cody. You have been through so much in
your life. You have made some bad decisions and had
to live with them. But you are so strong. I love how you
have rebounded by trusting God and changing your
life." He then bent slightly so he could place a tender
kiss on the cheek of his hero. "Now, let me get you

down this aisle and to the man who is worthy of a lady as special as you are."

Lindsay stood rooted in her spot, staring and smiling at Kevin with a remarkable love of her own for her baby brother. She willed the two tears in her eyes not to fall so she would not mess up her makeup, but they had a mind of their own. "Kevin, you are so wrong for making me cry like this. I'm telling Mommy on you after my wedding, you bigfoot bozo." She figured if she could make the two of them laugh, she wouldn't completely break down. The sibling duo burst into giant smiles. She returned her brother's loving kiss and the two proceeded down the aisle still grinning from ear to ear.

As Lindsay and Kevin slowly made their way down the rose-petal-strewn aisle, keeping time with the song playing, her eyes found those of her intended. She locked in and focused on the beautiful face of the man she knew God had created just for her as everything else around him seemed to have disappeared from the vicinity of the garden theme they chose for their ceremony.

When she and her mother had chosen the music for her wedding, Lindsay had been quite pleased with the songs they selected. As she and Kevin crawled at a snail's pace down the aisle, she was now angry at herself for not having picked an up-tempo song with a fast beat so that she could have sprinted toward her man and still been in rhythm with the music.

Cody looked absolutely perfect standing at the altar awaiting her arrival. His beautiful heart and soul were encased in his magnificent six foot three inch frame. He had not gained or seemingly lost a pound since the day she initially laid eyes on him more than six years ago. All 190 pounds of him were flawlessly poured into the black tuxedo, lavender shirt, and silver vest he wore. He proudly wore his Italian ancestry as his dark olive skin radiated splendidly in the sunlight of the day. With the exception of the few unruly strands that always lay across his forehead, every other strand of the jet-black hair that God had so lovingly placed upon his head was in its proper place. The dark brown eyes that watched her every move as she gradually inched toward him glowed with love for her. The teeth that were the backdrop of his drop-dead gorgeous smile sparkled. Her sexy Benjamin Bratt/Ben Affleck look-alike still had the power to make her body tingle and her heart race.

Finally, after what seemed like a ninety-minute walk, Lindsay made it to the altar where the man of her dreams awaited her. Kevin stood holding her arm as the pastor from the church Cody attended whenever he was at his cottage in Martha's Vineyard began the ceremony, waiting for the proper moment to hand his sister over to her very soon-to-be husband. Kevin proudly announced, "I do," as the pastor asked, "Who gives this woman to be married to this man?" He kissed Lindsay on her cheek, placed her hand in the hand of his future brother-in-law, and took his seat.

The moment Lindsay's hand connected with Cody's, her entire body began to tingle. Her heart began beating so hard, she assumed her wedding guests could probably see her chest thumping as a result of the powerful force slamming inside it. She became so overwhelmed with love for the man that literally held her life in his hands that she had to keep herself from blurting out loud and insisting the pastor hurry up before Cody had an opportunity to change his mind.

The preacher began the ceremony with all of the traditional words and vows. Before they all knew it, he had pronounced the couple man and wife and stated, "Mr. Cody Vincini, you may now kiss your bride."

When the newly married couple broke the kiss, Cody had to literally hold his wife up to keep her from falling to her very unsteady knees. Lindsay declared the very first kiss that she shared with her new husband had been the very best kiss of her entire life. Once she was able to compose herself, she and Cody stood together as their few guests came to greet and congratulate the newlyweds. When Shyanne's parents approached, a wee bit of the guilt from earlier resurfaced. Lindsay held her emotions in check, however. The last thing she wanted to do was upset her second set of parents by blubbering about Shyanne not being there because she had gotten her killed.

Tonya Kennedy hugged Cody first. "You make sure you take good care of our very special daughter. Do you understand me, young man?"

Gregg Kennedy followed his wife and cosigned her declarative. "You need to make sure you listen to my wife, Cody Vincini. If you ever cause our little girl here one ounce of pain, I will hunt you down no matter how far you run to hide and chop off both of your feet, Kunta Kinte-style."

The Kennedys' claim of her being their daughter was nearly Lindsay's undoing. But she held strong to the turmoil swirling within her. Both the Kennedys embraced her simultaneously, each feeding her soul with words of love.

"We are so happy for you, Nay. We love you so much, and your happiness is paramount to us. Shyanne would be so proud of you. I'll be praying each and every night for complete joy and peace in your marriage."

Again, Mr. Kennedy followed his wife's words with sentiments that were a little harder to hear without crying. "Nay-Nay, losing Shyanne was the hardest thing Tonya and I have ever had to endure, but knowing that we still have a beautiful daughter in you makes our loss just a bit easier. We want you to know that we will always be available for you no matter what you need us for. We love you, young lady."

Again, the three shared a warm and tender hug in unison. Lindsay allowed the tears in her eyes to run unchecked. Mrs. Kennedy also cried uninhibited. Lindsay wanted to tell Shyanne's parents how much she missed her; how much she wished she were here to be a participant in this very important day. She refrained, however. She did not want to do anything to shatter the loving moment they were sharing.

After the Kennedys and the rest of the wedding guests had given their congratulations, Lindsay and Cody, along with all of the wedding party, took pictures in various locations around the beautiful hotel where the wedding took place. Immediately following the photo session, everyone proceeded to the reception area of the hotel to continue the wedding celebration.

Lindsay and Cody stayed with their guests for approximately an hour after they had all eaten dinner; then the newlyweds excused themselves and headed for their own private celebration in the room they reserved for their wedding night. Lindsay's mother, grandmother, Kevin, and her children would spend the night at Cody's and her Martha's Vineyard cottage. The Kennedys and Cody's parents had rooms reserved in the hotel for the evening. Tomorrow, all the respective families would fly home. Cody and Lindsay would fly to the tropical paradise of Ocho Rios, Jamaica, to honeymoon for seven days. When they returned from their honeymoon, they would move into the wonderful new home they purchased since her release from prison. Prayerfully, she would leave behind all the debilitating baggage of her first marriage and her old life with

Shaun as she and her children stepped into new lives filled with God's presence and His overflowing blessings.

Chapter Two

"Mom, would you please tell your son to stay out of my room and away from my things? If you don't, I'm going to strangle him," Shauntae yelled her frustration as she entered the kitchen where Cody and Lindsay sat enjoying a morning cup of coffee along with each other's company.

The new family now lived in a four-bedroom, three-bathroom home in the Green Acres subdivision of Detroit, near Seven Mile and Livernois. On the first day of Lindsay's release from prison, she and Cody went house hunting. The couple immediately fell in love with the beautiful home they and her children now shared. Cody made an offer on the house, and blessedly, they were able to close on the home in just thirty days because of the housing market and the economy in Detroit. During those thirty days, Lindsay and her mother planned her small wedding. While she and Cody were on their honeymoon, Kevin and Sherrie took care of having all of the couple's and the children's things professionally moved into the home. Sherrie also handled registering the children in the private school they now attended not far from the house. Cody still owned the condominium he previously lived in, but now leased it to a very good friend of his.

"Shauntae, first of all, stop yelling at me. Second, you don't give me ultimatums. Do you understand?"

Lindsay awaited her daughter's affirmative response before she continued. "Now, tell me the problem you're having with your little brother."

Before Shauntae could plead her case, Li'l Shaun appeared and began giving his side of the story. "Mommy, I only went into her room to look for my gym shoe. I didn't touch her stuff."

"Shaun, why would your gym shoe be in my room, huh? I don't allow you in my room, so your stinky shoe could not possibly be in there." Again, Shauntae was yelling.

Now on the defensive, Shaun yelled back at his sister with an explanation that made perfectly good sense to him. "I don't know. I looked everywhere else for it except in your room, so it must be in there."

"Both of you, stop yelling," Lindsay yelled.

Cody decided to step in before all the yelling gave him a monster headache. In a very calm tone he said, "Shauntae, please help your brother find his shoe. Shaun, stay out of your sister's room unless she gives you permission to be in there."

"Is that it? That's *all* you have to say to him? That will never work. He won't listen to just that." Shauntae was still yelling.

Lindsay and Cody had only been home from their honeymoon forty-eight hours. After having been away from managing her children for a whole two years, Lindsay found herself more than a little out of touch at how to handle a dispute between her teenage daughter and adolescent son. Cody, however, stepped in and handled the situation as if this were something he had been doing his entire life.

"Hey, kids, can we first start off by using our indoor voices? Now, Shauntae, state your case," Cody said calmly in his composed attorney's demeanor.

"Why does she get to go first?" Li'l Shaun demanded.

"I thought I said inside voices, Shaun. And because I said so."

Wow! Lindsay thought. She couldn't have said it better herself. She was truly impressed to see how well her husband worked with her kids, especially considering the fact that he had no biological children of his own, therefore, no real prior experience.

Shauntae began her explanation. "We are supposed to be in a new house, making a new start as a new family, but Shaun still wants to keep doing the same things the same way. When we were living with Grandma, he was always in my room bothering my things, getting on my nerve. Whenever I would yell at him, Grandma would tell me to be understanding because he was probably just missing Mommy. Okay? Now, what's *his* excuse?"

Lindsay's heart tore a bit as she heard Shauntae repeat her mother's reasoning for her baby pestering his sister. She checked her emotions, however, and continued to watch as Cody mediated the sibling dispute.

"All right, Shaun, it's your turn to tell your story," Cody instructed. "Why do you keep going in your sister's room?"

"Her stuff is better than mine," was Li'l Shaun's plain and simple explanation.

Cody merely shook his head. Shauntae rolled her eyes. Lindsay laughed out loud. She took charge at that point. "Shaun, I don't think it's so much the fact that Shauntae's stuff is better. It's just different. Because she doesn't want you to touch it or be in her room, you can't go in there without her permission. Understand?"

Li'l Shaun disappointedly nodded his head affirmatively. Lindsay then addressed Shauntae. "Shauntae, sweetie, will you consider allowing your brother to hang out with you in your room occasionally?"

Shauntae rolled her eyes so far up into the top of her head, Lindsay wondered if she would ever see her daughter's beautiful green pupils again. "Okaaaaay," she replied exaggeratingly, "but I still think he's playing you, Mom. That stuff about my stuff being better than his stuff is just an excuse to still hang out in my room. Your child just hates to be alone. He was this way the whole time you were away, Mommy. The kid needs therapy." Shauntae was really only joking, but Lindsay's heart was once again pierced by her daughter's words.

Deeming the matter settled, the two children walked away to continue getting ready for school. Just before they were completely out of the kitchen, Lindsay heard Li'l Shaun ask Shauntae, "What's therapy?"

While Cody considered the first of the more than three million battles that he and his new bride would have to settle between their children a complete success, Lindsay stood looking sad and confused.

"Sweetheart, what's wrong? I think that ended pretty well. Why do you look so distraught?"

Lindsay joined her husband in sitting at the breakfast table. "Cody, you were wonderful with the kids. You stepped right in and handled the beginning of the fight like an old pro. At first, I didn't have a clue about what to say since I have been so out of practice. But you rescued me as you always do, and you did it as if you'd been parenting for many years."

"Well, I have had two years to get to know Li'l Shaun and Shauntae. You know that your mother allowed me to spend lots of time with them while you were in prison. But none of that explains why you look so out of sorts, Lindsay."

During Lindsay's judicial process, Cody convinced her how much he loved her, that he had never stopped loving her, and he would always love her. By the time she was sent away to start serving her sentence, they had become a full-fledged couple. They got engaged about six months into her prison term.

"I'm just concerned about what Shauntae said about Li'l Shaun needing therapy and how she said he behaved while I was in prison. I think she may be right, Cody. Perhaps the kids and I do need some counseling; them, individually, and the three of us as a family."

Cody at first started to protest about Lindsay's claim because the kids' behavior did not seem in any way unusual to him. He quickly silenced himself, however, as he listened to his spirit's guidance and voiced his next words accordingly.

"In the two years since your incarceration, have you or your mother spoken at all with the kids about the death of their father and your involvement?"

"Not really. When Mama or Granny would bring the kids to visit, I didn't want to mar our time together by bringing up that negativity. I mean, they know why I was in jail, but I selfishly never discussed with them their feelings over my killing their daddy and taking him out of their lives."

After hearing Lindsay's declaration, Cody was indeed glad the Holy Spirit had intervened. He too began to see Lindsay's point upon learning she and the kids never discussed their feelings behind Shaun's death.

"Did your mother ever give you a clue or tell you the kids even asked her about Shaun?"

"No. She said the kids never mentioned him. Mama said whenever the kids would appear sad or whenever Li'l Shaun would behave as Shauntae described, both children would always attribute their emotions to missing me only."

"Well, then, I believe you are right. The kids may need to talk to someone about their seemingly bottled-up emotions. But I think you should take the opportunity to try to get them to talk to you first. See if they'll share with you now that you are home."

Lindsay nodded her head in agreement. While she was actually terrified at broaching the subject, she knew she had to override her fear and do what was best for her babies. Immediately, Isaiah 41:13 in the NIV came to mind. "For I am the Lord your God, who takes hold of your right hand and says to you, do not fear. I will help you."

"Okay. I'll talk to them when they get in from school. You'd better get a move on, my love, if you don't want to be late on your first day back in the office."

Cody and Lindsay both stood up at the table simultaneously. "Remember, beautiful, I'm the boss. Therefore, I can come and go as I please." He pulled his wife as closely into his tall frame as she could get, then wrapped her in his powerfully loving embrace. He bent his head and overtook her mouth with a breathtaking kiss that showed his desire and reason for him perhaps being late to work.

Lindsay knew, as Cody kissed her, that she would never get bored or become immune to the desire her husband invoked in her, no matter how many years the Lord blessed them being together. For a moment, she forgot the kids were still in the house as her body prepared itself to be taken by her husband right there on the kitchen floor. Cody's next words quickly brought her back to a sobering reality as he broke the phenomenal kiss.

"But I will wait until I return this evening to finish this adventure for two reasons. Number one, the kids are still here. Number two, a boss should lead by example. If I want my employees to show up on time, I should practice being on time as well."

Cody pecked Lindsay's lips once more before heading up the stairs to their bedroom to finish preparing to leave for his office. A little disappointed about having to wait to receive satisfaction, Lindsay relented, knowing her man would make good on his promise later that evening.

Halfway up the steps, Cody paused as something Lindsay said just a few moments ago crossed his mind. "So you really think I handled the kids well, huh?" Before she could respond, he continued speaking his musings aloud. "Perhaps we should consider expanding our brood to include at least one more since I'm so good at this dad thing. Think about it. We'll talk more on it later." Cody winked and smiled broadly at Lindsay as he proceeded up the stairs.

His words forcefully knocked the wind from Lindsay's chest. She fell backward into the chair she previously occupied. She never bothered to tell her husband about the child they conceived while she was still married to Shaun or about the permanent tubal ligation she had immediately afterward . . .

Chapter Three

Long after the children and her husband had left the house headed to their respective destinations, Lindsay still sat in the kitchen, pondering, worrying, and fearfully fretting over Cody's request for her to consider the two of them having a child together. It had been nearly five years since the abortion, and this was actually the first time she had thought about it again.

This, topped with dealing with the kids' post-daddy-death drama, was giving Lindsay a migraine headache. Her heart longed for the ability to talk to Shyanne about her new and old issues, but she knew she only had God to turn to now.

Finally after sitting for so long, Lindsay decided to get up, kneel down, and pray. "Heavenly Father, I come to first give you glory, honor, and praise. I come, Lord, to offer thanks for my life, my salvation, my family, and especially, right now, my marriage. Father God, I come with a very troubled heart, in need of your strength and guidance right now. Lord, your Word says that you will never leave us or forsake us. I take that to mean even when we are dealing with the consequences of our own crazy actions. I need you now, Lord. Tell me, Father, how to handle making Cody aware of the awful thing I did all those years ago. Tell me, Lord, how to explain to him that I am incapable of giving him the child he desires. And, Father, while I have your ear, I ask that you help me to deal with the issues that may be plaguing my children behind my selfishness and stupidity as well. Help me, Lord, as only you can. In Jesus' name . . . Amen."

Once she finished her prayer, Lindsay decided to tackle the one issue she could handle right away. She called her children's pediatrician to see if she had any suggestions for a child psychologist. When she dialed the office, she was unable to speak directly to Dr. Morten, but still managed to get the names and phone numbers of two reputable therapists from the nurse. Lindsay decided to call the office of the doctor nearest her home first. Fortunately, she was blessed to be able to catch the doctor who was available to speak with her.

After speaking with Dr. Nancy Hooper, an African American Christian psychologist who specializes in post-traumatic stress with children, Lindsay decided to make an initial appointment for consultation. Dr. Hooper suggested that even after Lindsay spoke with the children and they appeared okay to her, a more professional diagnosis was warranted. The consultation appointment was scheduled for two Saturdays from that day, two weeks away.

Lindsay felt somewhat lighter after completing that task. With part of her burden lifted, she was able and available to hear from the Holy Spirit. She was instructed to call her pastor and schedule an appointment with him to discuss her other dilemma. Lindsay found that God's favor was indeed upon her because she was able to secure an appointment with Pastor Paul Adams that day just after Shauntae was due to get home from school. Her daughter would be able to keep an eye on Li'l Shaun until either she came back from her meeting or Cody returned home from work.

Just after hanging up from Pastor Adams's assistant, the phone rang. The caller ID indicated it was from her brother Kevin.

"Hey, Kevin. What's up?"

"What up, sis? I just called to see how the honey-moon went and how the rug rats were adapting to hav-ing you home full time."

"The first part of your inquiry is easy to answer. The honeymoon was absolutely perfect. But how could it possibly be anything else when I'm married to a man who is as close to perfect as our human condition will allow." After saying this, Lindsay again began to feel the pressure of her predicament with Cody. She wasn't prepared to share her dilemma with Kevin, so she pulled herself together as best she could before she be-gan to cry. No one other than Shyanne and God knew about the abortion.

"Okay. That's great news. So what about the second half of my inquiry? How are you and the kids adjust-ing to being back together? I know it's only been a few days, but I'd like to know how it's going."

Lindsay informed Kevin about her intentions to get the kids into counseling. "Their first appointment is two Saturdays from now," she said in conclusion.

"I think that's a great plan, sis. It definitely couldn't hurt anything. Shoot, maybe you and Cody may even want to think about having another one, once you all get the kinks worked out of the two you already have."

Lindsay nearly fell from the chair she sat in at her brother's declaration. Today was surely her day to pay for her sin. Before she broke down on the phone and caused Kevin to worry and become curious, Lindsay hurriedly ended their conversation.

"Kev, I've got to get off the phone. I . . . got to . . . get prepared to run some errands, and then head out for an appointment with Pastor Adams," she said, hop-ing to keep things as close to the truth as possible. No sense adding the guilt of flat-out lying to her already burdened soul.

"Pastor Adams? What do you need to see him about?" Lindsay now regretted being so honest.

"I'm going to tell him about the kids too. You know I just want to make sure I'm covering all of my bases. Spiritual and psychological." Now she would have to make sure she mentioned the kid thing to Pastor Adams as well as her real reason for seeing him.

"Okay. Cool. Just keep me informed, sis. And be sure to let me know if there's anything I can do to help."

"Okay, I will." That was all she said before quickly hanging up the phone. She didn't want to chance saying something else unintentionally.

Looking at the clock, Lindsay realized she had a couple of hours to kill before she needed to ready herself to leave for her appointment with Pastor Adams. Since her home was already neatly organized thanks to her mother, her grandmother, Kevin, the kids, and the professional movers, she decided to finish unpacking from her honeymoon. She would then go online and look over her options for school for the quickly approaching semester. She and Cody decided she would spend her days going to classes to complete her degree in early education. Classes would start in the middle of January, just a week away. At age thirty-two, Lindsay was going to be a full-time student.

She headed upstairs to her bedroom to finish unpacking. As she put their things away in the closet, in the dirty laundry to be washed, or in a pile for the dry cleaners, Lindsay reminisced about her perfect honeymoon with her perfectly wonderful husband. Her sunny disposition quickly soured as thoughts of the secret she had kept from him resurfaced. She had no idea how telling him the truth after nearly five years would affect him. Cody seemed so happy that morning at the thought of the two of them having another baby. How would he feel when he found out that not only was that impossible, but she had also aborted the seed they conceived together? What if he couldn't handle what she had done and decided to leave her? That thought immediately caused tears to spring to her eyes and fall to her cheeks. She could not bear the idea of Cody no longer wanting her. She would go absolutely insane if he asked her for a divorce because of a very stupid and selfish choice she made all those years ago.

When Lindsay made the decision to have the abortion once she found out she was carrying Cody's child, she thought she was doing what was best for her and her children. Her primary focus at the time was getting her marriage to Shaun back on track once he got out of prison. Shaun would surely divorce her, or worse, if he knew she was having an affair with his attorney. Since she believed she wanted things to work between her and Shaun, Lindsay was certain she would never have to deal with Cody again. There was no reason for him to know about the pregnancy or the abortion. She knew it would only hurt him.

"God, please help me. Tell me what to do," she pleaded as she sank to the bedroom floor.

After lying on her face praying for an uncalculated amount of time, Lindsay finally found the strength to get up and finish unpacking. She then went on to prepare herself to go to meet with Pastor Adams. On the drive to the church, Lindsay continued to pray that God would speak to her through her pastor. While she knew God would not want her to continue to lie to Cody, she also rationalized that He would not want her marriage to end.

By the time she arrived at the church, Lindsay was an emotionally confused wreck. She parked the car and went inside the church, hoping she did not have to wait too long to see the pastor. She was not sure how much longer she had before she would completely fall apart. God's favor was on her side, at least thus far, because she only had to be announced by Pastor Adams's assistant, and then she was ushered right into his office.

"Well, hello, Mrs. Vincini. Welcome back from your honeymoon, darling. You know I'm still a little salty that I didn't get the opportunity to perform your ceremony," he teased with a big smile.

"I'm sorry, Pastor Adams. Cody and I wanted to be married in the place where we shared really great memories," Lindsay said, and just as quickly realized that is when the events that plagued her now first began. It was during their first trip together to Cody's cottage in Martha's Vineyard that she became pregnant with his child while still married to Shaun.

Lindsay began to visibly shake in her stance. Pastor Adams noticed immediately and helped her into one of the cushy chairs seated in front of his desk. Instead of sitting in his chair behind the desk, he sat in the chair next to hers, moving it a little closer so that he could hold both her hands in both of his.

"Father God. I am beseeching you now, Lord, me, your humble servant, Paul Adams. Lord, I am coming to your throne of grace on behalf of your young child, Lindsay, here. I have yet to find out why she is here, but I know that you in your infinite wisdom already know. You know everything about us, Lord. I trust and believe in you wholeheartedly, recognizing, Lord, that you are aware of her desire for our meeting. I'm coming to ask you for your guidance as I talk with her through whatever trouble it is she faces. Help me, Lord, to listen with nonjudgmental ears and to respond in truth, wisdom, and most important, love. These and all blessings I ask in your Son Jesus' name. Amen."

"Amen," Lindsay repeated.

"Okay now, child. Tell me why you are here. Before I sat you down and prayed, you looked as if you were going to faint on me."

Lindsay took a deep breath and began telling Pastor Adams everything; from the beginning of her affair with Cody all the way up to his suggestion today that they have a child.

"Now, Pastor Adams, I am faced with having to tell him the truth after nearly five years of selfishly keeping it from him. My marriage could be ruined. I am so afraid."

Lindsay was audibly sobbing now, but still holding onto the hope that Pastor Adams would speak a miracle into her situation. She was so desperate to believe that he would be able to tell her there was something she could say to Cody that would make him not leave her, still love her, and totally understand why she had inadvertently deceived him.

"Well, well, well, young lady. You do have a trial on your hands." Pastor Adams stood and paced around the small space that made up his office.

Lindsay remained seated as she watched her pastor take several slow, yet, deliberate, steps. She imagined, no, actually assumed, he was putting himself in Cody's shoes. She just hoped that whatever conclusion he came to, it left her and her husband still together.

Pastor Adams soon returned to his seat next to Lindsay and continued their conversation. "Nay-Nay, I must give advice based on the Word of God only. My personal feelings and your personal feelings are not to be taken into consideration."

Lindsay felt her heart sinking further and further into her stomach at hearing Pastor Adams's words. He continued to talk and the small amount of hope for him to perform a miracle evaporated.

"Sweetheart, I must advise you to tell Cody the truth, the whole truth and nothing but the truth. God hates a lying tongue. I know this is going to be difficult for you. For both of you, but I'm going to need you to trust me on this. More important, I'm going to need you to trust God."

Lindsay was crying so hard and loudly now she could hardly hear what Pastor Adams was saying. However, enough of what he said penetrated, and she knew what it was he said she should do.

"God will be with you through this, Nay. If you walk through this obediently, things will eventually work out. Now, I'm not promising that you and Cody will come through this with your marriage unscathed. I'm simply stating that if you handle this honorably, it will all work out for your good in the end, no matter what that looks like."

The last part of his sentence shattered Lindsay's heart to shreds, reminding her of something she heard her grandmother say. *"The Word of God sometimes cuts."*

The tears in her eyes dried, but the burning in her soul remained white hot. The fear she may lose her husband was very, very palpable.

Pastor Adams's next words restored a tiny modicum of hope to her spirit. "Cody Vincini is a good man, Nay. He is a Christian man who has turned his entire life around and given it to God. He has gone through the fire with you and remained steadfast in his love for you. He is also a wise man who loves God. He has to realize he too bears some of the responsibility in this as well.

Sure, he has been left in the dark about some very important particulars, but it took the two of you to create this mess as a whole."

"That is very logical and spiritual, Pastor Adams. I'm just not sure how practical it is. You didn't hear his voice or see his face when he mentioned us having a baby together. Now, I, the woman he loves, have to tell him I killed, literally and figuratively, any chance of that ever happening." Lindsay stood from her seated position and made ready to leave.

"Nay, listen to me. I want you to tell Cody I want to talk to the two of you after you share your news with him. I honestly believe we can work through this with some good spiritual counseling."

Lindsay nodded her head in agreement, but she didn't speak. Pastor Adams spoke a departing prayer, gave Lindsay a hug that was intended to be comforting, then she left his office and headed home.

Chapter Four

Lindsay took the scenic route on her drive home from the church. She took in the still-white snow in some neighborhoods that had fallen last night, lightly blanketing Detroit in its cold beauty. The icicles that hung from the bare trees helped to paint a pretty winter portrait. The church was only a five-mile drive from her home, but Lindsay calculated that she had already been driving for more than thirty minutes. After getting within two blocks of her own street, she decided to take a cruise down Seven Mile going toward the neighborhood her mother still lived in. Shyanne's parents sold their home about a year after their daughter's death and purchased a condo in the Farmington Hills suburb. They found staying in their bungalow with all of their only daughter's memories too hard to do.

As she traveled west on the avenue, she reminisced as she saw old landmarks. She passed the old arcade, that was now abandoned, where she and Shyanne use to ride the bus to hang at. Their favorite pizza parlor, which was just across the street, was still in business. She smiled as she passed the Coney Island restaurant on the corner a couple of blocks farther west. Lon's had the greatest Coney dogs and always had them on special on Tuesdays. One Tuesday, Shyanne ate four Coney dogs and was too sick to go to school the following day. Lon's and the pizza parlor were two of the very few businesses that remained open in her old stomping grounds.

So many memories of the times she spent with her best friend flooded her brain as she proceeded down Seven Mile. Just about every block from Greenfield to Lahser held some memory of an adventure she and Shyanne shared on the mile. Her thoughts were happy, sad, and melancholy all at once. However, this took her mind off the problems she knew awaited her at home.

As she got near Pierson Street, the street where her mother still lived, she almost made the right turn out of sheer habit. However, she caught herself, realizing she could not let her mother see her in this state. Sherrie could read her like a book. She would instinctively know that Lindsay had major turmoil going on inside the pages of her life, and she just wasn't prepared to share that with her now. She wanted the first person she revealed the truth to, to be Cody.

Lindsay decided it was time to go home and face the music. She pulled into the gas station on the corner and turned her car around, heading back in the direction of her home. When she arrived, she saw Cody's SUV parked in his space in front of the garage and her heart did a little flip. She was so nervous about facing him. She started to rationalize her situation and began thinking she didn't have to say anything to him today. She would deal with the children's situation first, then give herself a few days to recover from that before tackling the other issue. Yes. That made plenty of sense. For the first time since being faced with the problem of telling Cody the truth, she felt just a bit better.

Lindsay entered the house to find her children in the family room working on their homework and her husband in the kitchen getting ingredients together to begin preparing dinner.

"Hey, Shauntae. Hello, Li'l Shaun." She kissed both children on the top of their heads as she spoke their names. "Do you all have a lot of homework?"

"No," Li'l Shaun replied.

Shauntae followed with, "Not really."

"Okay. After we have dinner I want the three of us to have a conversation." Neither child responded or rebutted, so Lindsay took that to mean she was understood. She then made her way into the kitchen.

"Hey, handsome," Lindsay said as she approached Cody, giving him a more provocative kiss than the puppy pecks she shared with the kids.

After breaking the kiss, Cody replied, "Hey, yourself, beautiful. Where have you been? I was a little surprised when I arrived home and found you were gone."

Lindsay's wayward nervousness quickly returned. How could she possibly explain going to visit Pastor Adams without telling Cody the whole truth? She quickly decided, however, to just tell him what she told Kevin earlier. That she went to visit him to talk about the kids. But as soon as that half truth entered her head, she realized she actually didn't even mention the kids' issue with Pastor Adams at all. So, in essence, she had lied to Kevin. She decided to ride on that lie for the time being.

"I went to the church to talk to Pastor Adams to get his spiritual insight on the issue with the kids and their father's death. I did make an appointment with a child psychologist today as well, and I plan on speaking with the children after dinner. I just wanted to get our pastor's thoughts as well." *Lord, forgive me,* she silently prayed just after completing her story.

Cody, unbeknownst to Lindsay, sensed the nervousness in his wife. He stared at her for a brief moment, then dismissed her uneasiness as nervousness about having to talk to the kids later.

He continued to prepare dinner while Lindsay helped Shauntae and Li'l Shaun with their homework. The food preparation and the homework were both completed simultaneously. The family sat down together and shared a nice meal along with some interesting dinner conversation.

"How was school today, kids?" Lindsay asked.

"Cool," Shauntae replied.

Li'l Shaun followed with, "Not for me. A girl in my class has been bothering me for a long time. Today she tried to kiss me. On my mouth!"

Lindsay raised a curious eyebrow while both Cody and Shauntae found his story amusing.

"What did you do?" Lindsay asked seriously.

"I moved my head away so she would miss. Then I told her to keep her lips to herself." Cody and Shauntae laughed harder.

"What did she say to that?" Lindsay asked.

"Nothing. She just giggled like those two are doing." This reply garnered even more chuckles.

"Stop laughing at him, you two. Li'l Shaun is obviously bothered by this."

"I think you are just as bothered by it, Mom. You sound just a wee bit perturbed," Shauntae said as she put her forefinger and thumb in a distance of about a half inch apart to emphasize her point.

Li'l Shaun picked up on what his sister was saying and began pleading. "Mom, please don't come to my school. I can handle Imanye all by myself."

Now it was Lindsay's turn to laugh. "Okay, big boy. I will let you handle things with Li'l Ms. Imanye. But one word of warning. You will not hit her, understand?"

"Yes, ma'am."

They all continued with small talk while they finished their meal.

As they were cleaning the table and loading the dishes in the dishwasher, Lindsay spoke to the children.

"Shauntae, Li'l Shaun, when we are done here, I want to talk to the two of you up in my bedroom." Upon hearing Lindsay's declaration, Cody eyed her to see if she wanted him to join them. She indicated she did not with a slight shake of her head.

Upstairs in the bedroom, Lindsay, Shauntae, and Li'l Shaun made themselves comfortable on the king-sized bed. Lindsay sat in the middle as her children flanked her on each side. She did a little extra pillow fluffing and smoothing of the comforter in an effort to buy her a bit of time while she emotionally prepared to broach this very difficult subject.

Shauntae, in typical teenage demeanor, quickly became bored and annoyed.

"Mom, the pillows and blanket are fine. What did we come here to talk about?"

Lindsay stopped fidgeting and began their conversation by first praying. "Father God in Heaven, I praise you, Lord, for this day. I praise you and thank you for my beautiful children. I ask you, Lord, to help me to always keep them safe and protected from all hurt, harm, and danger. And, God, I ask that you guide me through this difficult task. This is my prayer in Jesus' name . . . Amen." In unison, both children repeated, "Amen."

"I brought you two up here this evening to talk about Shaun, your father." Lindsay paused to see if her statement had any visual effect on her kids. Seeing nothing obvious, she pressed forward.

"I want you each to tell me how you feel about your father being dead, and more important, how you feel about me and my being responsible for his death. Which of you would like to go first?"

Lindsay was certain there would be no fight over who would start. She was not wrong. Neither child seemed in any hurry to tell her their feelings on the subject at hand. Finally, however, Shauntae broke the silence.

"Mom, honestly, I miss Daddy. At least I do when I think about him. I know you and he had a lot of problems, but those problems never became my problems. Daddy always treated me good, and I miss him." Shauntae's sentiments tore at Lindsay's heart. She felt so bad for her daughter's loss. She really wanted to weep for the pain she now knew her baby girl felt, but she also knew she had to press forward and hear her son's views on the subject.

"What about you, Li'l Shaun? Do you have any feelings about your father?" Lindsay asked.

Li'l Shaun shrugged his nine-year-old shoulders but didn't say anything initially. Lindsay could tell he was conflicted, probably afraid that telling her the truth would hurt her feelings.

"Li'l Shaun, please, baby, tell me what you want to say. Mommy won't get mad. It's okay if you tell me the truth."

"Okay. I miss my daddy too. I didn't know him a long time like Shauntae, but he treated me good too when he lived with us. He told me he loved me a lot of times, and he called me his little man. He said I was his mini-me."

Lindsay inwardly cringed at the mention of her son being like Shaun. She hoped that meant in physical appearance only. Though she didn't like the comparison, she certainly could relate to how Li'l Shaun could miss his daddy's love.

"Okay. So you both love and miss your father. That is actually good for me to hear. It lets me know that while he and I had our issues, he was still a good father to you both. I'm very glad to hear that." The answers to the second part of her questions were probably going to be a little tougher to take, Lindsay reasoned. Nevertheless, she needed to hear their feelings on this as well.

Lindsay started with Li'l Shaun this time, because she didn't want him to parrot his big sister's answers to such a tough question. "Now, let's tackle the really hard part of this discussion. Li'l Shaun, how do you feel about me being the one who took your daddy away from you?"

Lindsay gritted her teeth and clenched her stomach muscles in preparation for her son's response. She watched his eyes grow as big as saucers. She assumed in fear of hurting her feelings. Eventually he started speaking.

"Mommy, I just don't understand why you did it. I just wish you didn't shoot Daddy, and I wish you didn't have to spend that time in jail. It's okay that you married Cody, because I love Cody too. You still didn't have to shoot him, though." Li'l Shaun's voice raised an octave by the time his speech ended.

Lindsay was hurt, scared, and relieved by Li'l Shaun's very vivid expression of his emotions. Of course, she hurt for what she had done to her son. She was scared that he would resent her forever, and she was relieved that he was mature enough to tell her how he truly felt.

Shauntae, realizing it was now her turn to verbalize her true feelings, became visually apprehensive as well. But she too, like her little brother, forged ahead with her truth.

"Mom, when you shot Daddy, you shot him for your own selfish reasons. I really don't believe you gave me or Li'l Shaun a second thought. I believe if you did, you wouldn't have done it. You say you are glad to hear that Daddy was good to us, but you already knew that he was. Otherwise, you would have taken us away from him a long time before you killed him."

Lindsay bristled just a bit at her daughter's none-too-subtle reprimand. She remained quiet, however, and let her finish speaking her mind.

"You took away our father, Mom. You didn't even care how any of it affected me and Li'l Shaun. Not him being gone forever, or not us having to lose you to jail too. And when Daddy died, it's like the whole other side of my family died as well. I haven't seen my big brother or my grandmother or my aunts since Daddy's funeral. You took away a lot from us, Mom. I know you were not too fond of them, but they are still family to me and Li'l Shaun."

Shauntae was right. She was none too fond of her children's paternal family, the people she dubbed the real live *Addams Family*, no relation to Pastor Adams. In spite of her daughter inserting her crazy side of the family into their conversation, Lindsay still realized that both her children gave very heartfelt answers to her questions. Now it was her time to speak.

"Shauntae, Li'l Shaun, Mommy wants you to both know how very pleased I am with you. Your answers were very intelligent and very honest. And though I was hurt by the things you pointed out about me, I am still very happy that you shared it all with me."

She paused to give each child a hug and prayed that after they vented the way they did, they would not reject her. She was not disappointed. After receiving welcomed returned embraces, she resumed their conversation.

"You two are both right. When I shot your father, I acted very selfishly. I did not think for one second about my babies. I am so sorry for that. Losing your Aunt Shyanne was the most painful event of my life. I blamed her death on your father, even though he didn't actually kill her. It was the things he did that put her in the wrong place at the wrong time. I was so angry inside with him for that. My anger made me lose control, and I snapped. I had no way of stopping myself from doing what I did because at that moment I was no longer capable of thinking correctly."

Lindsay slowed down for a moment to think and choose her words carefully. She did not want to paint herself or her actions as good, in turn, minimizing the kids' rightful feelings of hurt and confusion.

"And even though I did what I did because I was hurt and angry, I was still wrong because of how I hurt you two in the process. Again, I am so sorry. I won't ask you to forgive me now, but I have made an appointment with a doctor for the three of us to receive some counseling. Her name is Dr. Hooper. She is going to help us all deal with our feelings so that one day you both can truly forgive me for what I did."

Li'l Shaun nodded his head in agreement, but Shauntae seemed a bit more apprehensive.

"Mom, you mean we are going to see a psychiatrist? Isn't that for crazy people?" she asked.

Now Shaun's features resonated doubt.

"No, Shauntae. Dr. Hooper is not a psychiatrist. She's a therapist." Lindsay searched for the best way to make her daughter more comfortable. "It's kind of like a massage therapist versus a chiropractor or a back doctor. A psychiatrist fixes people that are broken mentally like a doctor fixes broken bones. A massage therapist works on the pain and tension in a person's body by slowly working it out of them. A psychotherapist slowly helps people work through their pain and tension caused by traumatic instances, like that which our family has suffered. Does that make sense?"

"Yes, I guess so," Shauntae responded. Li'l Shaun nodded again in agreement since his big sister was now cool with it.

"Our appointment with Dr. Hooper is not for two weeks, on a Saturday. So during this week, I will see what I can work out and hopefully by the weekend, you'll be able to see your big brother, your grandmother, and your other family."

Shauntae's eyes brightened, and for the first time since entering the room she smiled. Li'l Shaun got excited too. Probably because he figured he should since Shauntae was excited.

Lindsay ended their conversation for the evening by instructing each child to get prepared for bed.

"I'll be back in a little while to check on you both." She then headed downstairs to her husband, hoping he could offer her some comfort and assistance on how to contact her former in-laws. The thought of seeing Sha'Ron again after having murdered both his parents was very, very frightening. . . .

Chapter Five

Lindsay came down the stairs to find Cody asleep on the family-room sofa with some sort of national news show watching him on the television. She sat on the chair across from the sofa so she would not immediately wake him. She was only allowed a couple of minutes of just watching him at peace before he awakened on his own.

"I sensed your presence," he said as he stretched and sat up, motioning for her to join him on the sofa. "So, how did it go?" he asked once Lindsay was snuggled closely by his side, wrapped comfortably in his arms.

"As well as could be expected, I suppose. The kids were very candid with me. And while it pained me to hear their hurt, I am glad they were willing to tell me the truth. Both of them basically said I handled things poorly by killing their father and taking him away from them."

Lindsay allowed the tears she hid from her children to silently fall from her eyes onto her cheeks. Cody noticed the waterfall starting and held her a little tighter.

"I'm glad the kids were honest with you too. Now we at least know what we are working with. I think this will better help the therapist to assist them. She won't have to start off by pulling teeth to get them to talk."

Lindsay nodded her head in agreement. Still crying, she and Cody sat quietly for a few moments, allowing her time to vent her emotions through her eyes. When she was again able to speak, she filled Cody in on the rest of her conversation with Li'l Shaun and Shauntae.

"Shauntae also feels that I took away her paternal family when I took away Shaun. She said she missed those misfits."

Cody laughed at Lindsay's name for her former in-laws. "Misfits they may be, dear, but they are still blood relatives to our children."

Lindsay liked how Cody referred to the children as theirs and not just hers. This also brought to mind the secret she knew she would soon have to reveal. She pushed down that thought for now and concentrated on the issue at hand.

"Cody, do you think the *Addams Family* is still in the same neighborhood, in the same house? I would like to try to work something out with them so that the kids can see them this weekend, if possible."

Cody instantly became concerned by Lindsay's wanting to contact Shaun's family. There was no love lost between his wife and her former in-laws before she killed Shaun. There would definitely be, at the very minimum, a colossal hatred for her from them now.

"Lindsay, are you thinking about going there to see them yourself?" Cody asked in disbelief.

"Yes, Cody. How else can I reconnect the children with them? I know what you're thinking—"

Cody interrupted before she could finish her own thought. He released her from his arms and now sat adjacent to her, staring her in the face. "Good. Then you know that I am thinking you are absolutely insane. There is no way I'm going to allow you to just waltz over to Patricia's house and say, 'Hey there. Long time no see. Sorry I killed your son, but let's be friends anyway.' No way, Lindsay."

"Don't yell at me, honey. This is difficult enough!"

Cody didn't even realize he had raised his voice until Lindsay pointed it out to him. "I'm sorry, baby. There's just no way you are going over to Patricia's house, no matter where she lives," he stated more calmly this time.

"Okay, Cody. How do you suggest I reacquaint our kids with that side of their family?"

Cody thought carefully before answering his wife. He pondered for several silent moments before coming up with a plausible solution. "I'll go. I'll go to where they last lived to see if they're still there. If they are not, I will use some of my former connections to find out where they are. They won't be too pleased to see me either, I'm sure. But I don't think they will have as much hostility toward me as they certainly will toward you."

Lindsay considered Cody's proposal, soon coming to the conclusion that it may be her only solution. Yet, she was concerned for his safety too. The Taylor clan was not the friendliest or most sensible group of people. In fact, in Lindsay's opinion, they were practically uncivilized. What kind of mother sanctions her son's occupation as a drug dealer?

"Cody, I appreciate you doing this for the kids. I'm still worried about you, though, going over there. You know as well as I do, these folks are everything but saved. I have often said Patricia was a direct descendent of Satan."

Again Cody laughed at his silly wife. "Baby, I won't lie to you. Your concern is warranted. The Taylors are true products of the streets of Detroit. But Sha'Ron had a good relationship with Shauntae and Li'l Shaun. Patricia also showed a lot of love for her grandkids. It won't be easy, but I will feel them out first. Then if they agree to it, I will be the one to play liaison between them and the kids."

Lindsay gave her husband a beautiful smile that glowed from deep within her heart. She was so blessed to have this man in her life. Lindsay was encouraged by her husband's commitment to her and her children. Even with the secret lying heavy on her heart, she could still feel his wonderful love. She hoped he would be this loving when she finally told him the truth about their having a child of their own.

"I trust you, sweetheart. I know you will work this out for the best."

"Let's pray, Lindsay, and ask God for His protection and guidance."

The couple prayed together, and then headed up to their bedroom for the evening. Cody stepped into the bathroom to take his shower while Lindsay went to check on Li'l Shaun and Shauntae. She then went to make sure everything downstairs was cleaned and put in its proper place. When she came back to the bedroom, Cody was sitting comfortably in their bed going over some work from his office.

Lindsay left him to his work while she went to shower. Her personal hygiene taken care of, she joined her man in bed. She kissed him seductively while he was right in the middle of reading a legal brief.

Cody tossed his work aside and began the love dance with his wife. "I love you, Lindsay Renee Vincini." He took his time removing the one-piece nightgown his wife wore. When she was undressed, he slowed the rhythm of their dance. He kissed her lips, her cheeks, her neck, and then whispered in her ear. "Now is probably not the best time for us to consider having another baby with all that's going on with the kids, but it definitely won't hurt for us to practice making one."

On the outside and for his benefit, Lindsay laughed at her husband's joke. Inwardly, she cringed, however, as she thought about the heartbreak she would cause when she told him the truth. . . .

The following day when Cody arrived at his office, he did what needed to be done to get his staff started for the day. He began with the daily morning meeting to brief them on cases and hear their updates on what they were working on. Soon after those ritualistic tasks were completed, he made a phone call to a former client of his and colleague of Shaun's to see if the woman would help him with finding the current address of Patricia Taylor's clan.

"Hello," the woman answered in a voice that assured Cody she was unfamiliar with the phone number showing on her caller ID.

"Hello, Toni Thompson."

"Cody Vincini? Is that the voice of the finest white man I've ever met?"

"Tee Tee. Always with the compliments. You are never going to change, girl. I'm insulted that you no longer recognize my office number, girl."

"Don't be. I just upgraded my phone yesterday, and I haven't gotten around to transferring my contacts. Be grateful I decided that when I do, you are going to be one who is on the 'keep 'em' list. So what's up, Cody? Why you call on ole Tee Tee? I hope it don't have nothing to do with my former line of work. You know I been outta the game for a little while now."

Toni Thompson, also known as Tee Tee, was the first cousin to Rhonda Weber, Shaun's first baby mama and the woman Lindsay killed. She was also formerly employed by Shaun's organization as one of their top lieutenants. After getting busted on a conspiracy and possession charge, her second, Tee Tee served three years in a federal prison. She came out of jail a new woman, however, walking away from the drug game and never looking back. Cody represented her in court and was able to get the original sentence reduced from ten to fifteen to three-and-a-half to seven years. She was actually in prison when Lindsay killed Shaun and Rhonda.

"Not about the game specifically, Tee. I just need to know if Shaun's mother is still in the same hood or if she's moved." Cody went on to honestly explain his reason for wanting to find out where Patricia lived. "You see, Tee, I just think I would have a better chance at putting this little family reunion together. They would probably shoot my wife on sight if she set foot on their doorstep."

"Could you blame them? I respect that she's your wife and all, Cody. But chicky murdered the woman's son, not to mention she took out Sha'Ron's daddy and mama, my own cousin."

When Cody decided to give Toni a call, he had not actually remembered she had a familial connection to one of Lindsay's victims.

"Tee, I'm sorry. I have to admit I didn't even think about Rhonda being your cousin. I offer my apologies on behalf of my wife as well. You may or may not believe me, but Lindsay is truly remorseful over what she did to both Shaun and Rhonda. If she could rewind her life and take it all back she would."

A few moments of silence rested between the two former associates, each pondering their own thoughts. Cody truly regretted getting Toni involved considering that he now realized her cousin had been killed.

Toni mulled over whether she was willing to help a man who had once helped her and been part of her team. "Look, White Boy C." Tee reverted back to the name the crew called Cody back in the day. "I'm gon' tell you that Shaun's people still in that same spot they been at all these years. Patricia ain't going nowhere. She still is and forever will be a hood rat, no matter how old she get." Tee chuckled at the end of her statement.

"Thanks for the information. I appreciate it because you really didn't have to do that."

"Don't worry about it. It's really no biggie since I ain't have to give up no new address or nothing. Oh and FYI, you might also be interested in knowing that Uncle Bobby is grooming Li'l man Sha'Ron to one day take over his daddy's spot. So while y'all over their planning a reunion between the brothers and the sister, also know that Sha'Ron got his foot in the game."

"Man, that's rough. Like you said, Tee, it don't seem like none of them Taylors have changed much at all over the years. Shoot! Sha'Ron can't be any older than sixteen, right?"

"Exactly!"

"I will definitely let Lindsay know. Thanks again, Tee, for all your help." Cody hung up the phone. He immediately began wondering how Lindsay would handle Sha'Ron being in the game and being around the kids. . . .

Later that day after leaving work, Cody decided to pay the Taylor clan a visit. He didn't tell Lindsay his intentions, deciding it best to just forge ahead and report back to her what he found out after his visit.

He pulled up to the house on Piedmont Street which looked exactly the same as it did the last time he was there, which was back before Shaun married Lindsay. He parked his car at the curb right in front of the house. Before getting out, though, he sat there staring at the house, but looking past it, through it, and trying to see into the souls of those who still inhabited it.

Patricia Taylor had been a knock-down, drag-out beauty. Cody's first impression upon meeting her several years ago had been Dang! What a hottie! Even without an ounce of makeup, the fancy clothes most women who looked like her donned, or even having her hair done up in some trendy style, she was gorgeous. Her daughter, Francine, was her mirror image and possessed something that Patricia seemed to lack; remarkable intellect. Patricia's oldest two children were both good-looking people with powerful brains. The third child, Tameeka, was not as pretty or as intellectually bright as her older siblings, but the girl wasn't exactly a slouch in those departments either. And had Patricia, as a mother, pushed Shaun and Francine into doing something positive with their lives, Tameeka would have probably done her best to follow in their footsteps.

Instead, however, Patricia, opted to be a parent who, without a doubt, loved her children, but decided not to put forth the necessary effort, attention, and never-quit attitude toward raising her offspring. She allowed her kids to do as they pleased as long as they managed not to get on her nerves during the process.

Back in the day, the inner workings of a household like Shaun's and other clients like him never bothered Cody. However, since becoming a Christian and actively crusading on the Lord's side, he really began to pay attention to issues such as these. This is why he was a member of the Children, Youth, and Young Adult Ministry at his and Lindsay's church. It is also why he volunteered and mentored young boys in their neighborhood YMCA.

Cody finally decided to emerge from his vehicle, realizing that crying over spilled milk was getting him no closer to completing his task. He walked up the sidewalk through the snow no one had bothered to shovel, continuing up the three steps that led to the porch, and right on to the front door. He rang the doorbell and waited in the cold for a response, not knowing whether anyone was home. But if he remembered correctly, Patricia Taylor hardly ever ventured out of the sanctity of her home.

After less than thirty seconds, Cody saw someone look out the window to spy out the uninvited intruder. A nanosecond later, Patricia snatched open the door.

"What the . . . White Boy C! I just know you ain't done showed up on my doorstep. Not the raggedy bastard that married the trick that shot and killed my son?" Patricia yelled.

Cody was stunned. Of course, it was not by the abrasive and rude manner by which Patricia greeted him at the door. He was expecting and ready for that. No. He was stunned by his host's appearance. Patricia always looked as if she were at least fifteen years younger than her actual age. So to see the woman before him who claimed to be Shaun's mother shocked him speechless. The frail little woman on the other side of the screen door, whose real age should have been about fifty, looked to be at least sixty. The youthful beauty he remembered just a few moments ago was gone and replaced with a haggard appearance worn down by life and perhaps sickness. If Patricia had not verbally announced that she was Shaun's mother, Cody was not sure he would have recognized her on his own. He literally stood there with his hand covering his mouth, which hung wide opened.

Before he realized what happened, someone walked up behind Patricia. "Grandma, what's going on? Who are you yelling at?"

Cody recognized Sha'Ron immediately. He was the mirror image of his dad, all the way down to the green eyes.

"Hello, Sha'Ron. Do you remember me?"

"Don't you speak to that traitor, Sha'Ron. In fact, I'm thinking you should go and get a pistol and blow out his knees." Patricia's words did not surprise nor frighten Cody. His heart simply broke because she uttered the ugly desire to her sixteen-year-old grandson, not caring for a moment that such a decision, if Sha'Ron decided to carry it out, would land him in prison. Nope. Patricia Taylor had not changed a bit.

Seeing White Boy C gave Sha'Ron a quick moment of pause. He was very aware that he married the woman who murdered his parents. But the wheels in his head quickly began to turn again as he realized, somehow, Cody's presence would assist him in his own murder plot. He wasn't exactly sure how yet, but his gut told him that Cody's sudden arrival back on the scene would surely help his cause.

"Grandma, chill. Let's at least hear what this fool has to say." Sha'Ron put on a menacing face and injected a little attitude into his voice so as not to appear too friendly or overly eager to have Cody on their doorstep. It was all just a front, though. Sha'Ron was excited about the doors Cody's arrival could possibly open.

"What? Hear him out? No! I want to *knoc*k him out!" Patricia yelled. She then began to cough violently.

"Hold up a minute, White Boy," Sha'Ron asked of Cody, then left him standing on the porch while he tended to his grandmother. After escorting her to her bedroom and getting her settled, he returned to the front door to find Cody shivering from the cold, but still waiting.

He remembered he was supposed to be speaking to the enemy so he returned the attitude to his tone. "So what up, dude? Why you here?"

"Sha'Ron, man, it's cold out here. Can I either come inside or you step outside and into my car so we can talk?"

Sha'Ron eyeballed Cody for a few brief moments as he seriously considered the options he presented. "Why don't we talk in your car," Sha'Ron stated as if the idea had been his to begin with. "I'll grab my jacket and let my grandmother know what's up."

Cody left the porch and returned to his car. He started it and cranked the heat on full blast. January in Detroit was no punk.

Sha'Ron appeared at Cody's passenger door less than five minutes later. Cody popped the lock and the young man made his entrance into the car.

"I see you still like rolling in style, White Boy," Sha'Ron said as he admired the luxurious tan interior of Cody's off-white BMW 750i.

Cody looked into Sha'Ron's eyes and saw the same look he used to see in Shaun's eyes. The same look he saw in all of his former clients from the game's eye. Even the same look he used to have. The look that said money and material possessions are what determined your status in life.

"It's just a car, Sha'Ron. Sure, it's a nice car, but just a car nonetheless."

"Yeah. Okay. Whatever. I know you didn't come here to lecture me on what's really important in life. So what's up? What you want, White Boy?"

Since Sha'Ron came straight at him with the questions, Cody decided to give him answers in the same manner.

"I'm here because your little sister and brother, Shaun-tae and Li'l Shaun, want to see you. In fact, they want to see all of their family on their father's side. Judging by the way your grandmother greeted me with threats instead of cookies, I'm sure she would have opened up on my wife with a sawed-off shotgun had she shown up. So I'm here on their behalf."

"Still the mouthpiece, huh, White Boy?"

Cody studied Sha'Ron, observing his youthful swagger and unreadable demeanor. He was so much like his father. Cody was sure those fatherlike qualities were both a result of DNA and his great-uncle Bobby's training. The same training his daddy had received.

Sha'Ron eyed Cody in return, seeing a change in him. From what he remembered, White Boy C had been the only white guy he had ever seen who actually even hung out with his father and Uncle Bobby's crew. Yet, he seemed to fit right in with the rest of the thugs. Yes. White Boy was an educated attorney, but he had a very sharp street swagger of his own. Now, however, young Sha'Ron sensed that his edge was no longer as prevalent. Not completely gone, but merely rechanneled, so to speak.

"So my sibs want to see me, huh? How the woman who made me an orphan feel about that?"

"My wife's main concern is what's best for her children. If seeing you and the rest of your family makes them happy, then she's cool with it."

Sha'Ron sat quietly for a moment as he reminisced about Shauntae and Li'l Shaun. Yeah, they were his fam; his blood. They spent a lot of time together too before their mom killed his parents. Yeah, he missed them. Seeing them would actually be pretty cool. It would also be an opportunity for him to start working on his uncle's plan to do to their mom what she had done to his.

"When she trying to put this li'l reunion together?"

"Lindsay was thinking perhaps the kids could come by here this Saturday. If you would be willing, do you think you could get your grandmother and aunts, Francine and Tameeka, along with their kids, together over here?"

Sha'Ron thought about it and realized that most likely his family would not object to seeing two of his dad's other kids. Tawanda and her daughter Shauna were always around, even though Tawanda had married another dude from his father's crew. However, that was not his main focus. He needed to start gathering information on his prey, Cody's wife.

"How about I come to your house this Saturday by myself. I mean, I'll work on getting the rest of the family on board with the reunion and all too. Maybe for a Sunday dinner or something over here. But I think we should start slow for now; with just me and my sister and brother first."

Cody was a changed man, but his street instincts remained sharp. Something about Sha'Ron wanting to come to their home unnerved him. He was certain Sha'Ron had no love lost for Lindsay, which was understandable. So he knew he would have to carefully watch his wife's back, no matter how this all worked out.

"Why don't we start with this, Sha'Ron. You and I, along with the kids, could all go out to dinner somewhere together this Saturday. That way, you can start getting reacquainted with them. You name the place."

Sha'Ron couldn't even be mad at White Boy's intuition and defense. Like he told himself, he still had the edge, just rechanneled. "Okay. That'll work. Let's exchange numbers. You go home and work it out with wifey and let me know what time we can hook up. Oh yeah, I love Red Lobster."

Chapter Six

The following morning as Cody and Lindsay sat at the breakfast table, Cody thought about his visit to the Taylor household the previous night. When he came home late last night, Lindsay just assumed her husband had been held up at the office and never questioned his tardiness. Cody, still uncomfortable about his encounter with Sha'Ron, didn't want to disturb her entire night with his uneasiness, so he kept quiet about the visit. Today, however, Lindsay could see the worry wearing heavily on his handsome face.

"Cody, is something wrong, baby?"

"We need to talk about something, Lindsay. But I think we should wait till the kids are off to school and out of the house."

Lindsay could hear the seriousness in Cody's voice so she offered him no argument. She, instead, would patiently wait until he could fully explain whatever the dilemma was that caused him to look so stressed.

Cody went to the home office and called to let his staff know he would be in later that morning while Lindsay helped the kids get ready to leave for the school bus. Once Shauntae and Li'l Shaun were gone, the two of them settled into the family room on the sofa to talk.

"I went to visit Sha'Ron last night," Cody said directly.

"What! Why didn't you tell me when you came in last night, Cody?"

"I didn't want to disturb your rest last night, honey. I figured it would be best to discuss all the happenings with you while we were both fresh this morning."

Since Cody was in no rush to share how his visit went with the Addam's Family, Lindsay was almost reluctant to know the details. Curiosity won out, however, so she probed for information.

"Okay. So how did it go? What happened?"

"Patricia initially came to the door and went off when she saw that it was me standing on her porch. She practically threatened to shoot me."

"Same ole Hate-tricia, I see."

"Yes and no, baby. She definitely hasn't change into a woman with a lovely personality, but physically, Lindsay, she looked horrible. The Patricia I remember was very beautiful and youthful looking. The woman I encountered looked old, sickly even."

The last part of Cody's statement triggered a remembrance in Lindsay. "Oh my. I wonder if her cancer has returned."

"Cancer? I didn't know Patricia ever had cancer."

"Yes. When I first met Shaun he told my mother and me that he dropped out of college so he could help his mother, who, at the time, was suffering with breast cancer when he quit. You never noticed that she only had one breast while you were ogling her beauty?" Lindsay said a little sarcastically.

"I honestly never paid much attention. Wow! Maybe that's it. So sad."

Sad, indeed, Lindsay thought. While Patricia had never made the list of one of her all-time favorite people, she was still the grandmother to her children. And furthermore, a human being probably suffering with a horrible illness. Lindsay knew she would be adding Patricia to her prayer list.

"Let's get back to our discussion. How did you end up talking to Sha'Ron since Patricia was against you even being there?"

"Sha'Ron was there, and he overheard Patricia yelling at me so he came to investigate. He somehow convinced his grandmother that he wanted to hear what I had to say. This, by the way, happened after she began having a violent coughing fit and he took her to her bedroom to settle down. Wow! Cancer!" Cody too decided that he would begin earnestly praying for Patricia.

"So what did you tell Sha'Ron?"

"I told him Shauntae and Li'l Shaun wanted to see their big brother. He says he's up to it himself, but he's not sure if everyone is ready for a big family reunion just yet. He's going to see if he can work that out. In the meantime, he has agreed to meet me and the kids for dinner this Saturday at Red Lobster."

Lindsay was pleased to hear Sha'Ron was open to seeing her kids, but a little puzzled as to why she had been excluded from the equation. She certainly understood Sha'Ron's desire not to sup with her, but was confused as to why Cody would agree to such a thing.

"You and the kids? Not you, the kids, and I? What's up with that, Cody? Do you think I'm letting them go without me?"

"Lindsay, come on. Be reasonable. Sha'Ron isn't ready to be around you just yet, even if he doesn't realize it. He actually referred to you as the woman who made him an orphan."

Ouch! That stung, but again, his feelings were warranted and his statement totally honest. "What do you mean by, 'even if he doesn't realize it'?" Lindsay asked, suddenly realizing Cody had said those words.

"Sha'Ron didn't seem hesitant about seeing you. But something in my gut, let's call it the Holy Spirit, was not comfortable about that. He actually suggested he come by here to the house to visit with the kids."

"Well, I think that's a wonderful idea, Cody. I think the kids would be more relaxed seeing him after all this time if they were here on their own turf."

"I understand your reasoning, Lindsay. But there is something you need to know before you get so gung ho about inviting him here to our home. Heck, before you give this whole reunion idea your final approval."

"What's that, Cody?" she asked hesitantly.

"Sha'Ron is in the drug game now with his great-uncle Bobby."

Lindsay's hand flew to her wide-opened mouth in horror. She wasn't shocked by Cody's revelation. More than anything, she was disheartened to learn about the destructive path her children's brother was taking.

"How do you know that? Was he bold enough to tell you?"

"No. Do you remember Toni, Rhonda's cousin?" Lindsay nodded that she did. "She told me. She's the person I contacted to find out if the Taylors had moved or not. They are still in the same house, by the way."

"Oh my gosh, Cody. That is horrible. I'm not sure if I even want the kids around him, if that's the case."

"I figured you would feel that way, but I'm not so certain we should let that stop him from at least seeing the kids."

"What! Why shouldn't it?" Lindsay asked incredulously.

"Let me ask you this. What reason would you give the kids for not allowing them to see their brother?"

Lindsay thought about it for a moment, debating about whether she would be completely honest with her children or would she give them the old parents-know-best speech; and if necessary, resort to the old because-I-said-so sermon. She definitely did not want to lie to them. Perhaps in being totally honest, her kids would be smart enough to decline seeing Sha'Ron on their own.

"I think the best thing to do, Cody, would be to tell them the truth. Sha'Ron is involved in a very serious and dangerous game. I would explain to them that I don't want them around that kind of person."

"Then you would sound like a hypocrite, Lindsay. Their father was that kind of person."

"I . . . but . . . that's different."

Cody raised an eyebrow, communicating loudly that he wanted her to elaborate the difference to him.

"Cody, come on. Be serious. I was an adult, and Shaun was an adult. The three people we are talking about now are still children. Two, of which, I'm responsible for. I have to protect them."

"Lindsay, you were not an adult when you started dating Shaun, remember? And you're right. None of them are adults, including Sha'Ron. Maybe this could be an opportunity for us to help him."

"Help him how? This is the only kind of life that boy knows."

"Then this could be a chance for us, as Christian people, to show him something different. Something new."

Lindsay felt like Cody was fighting dirty by throwing her Christian responsibility in her face like this. She was trying to be a good mother and protect her children. God would definitely understand that. Cody was being unfair and unreasonable.

"Cody, I understand your desire to want to help Sha'Ron. I do. But I am not willing to do that at the expense of my children's safety. I know that family. Christ and Christianity are the last things on their minds."

"Then whose job do you think it is to try to change that, huh, Lindsay? God has appointed us to introduce them to Christ, starting with Sha'Ron."

Lindsay stared hard at Cody, trying to see if she could find something in his eyes that told her he was just kidding. She knew she wouldn't see any such thing, but she needed to look anyway. She didn't want Cody to be right, but she knew he was. Still, she pleaded her case, hoping he would back off his position as a saintly do-gooder. She would repent to God later for her un-Christian attitude.

"Cody, please understand I am fearful of what the kids could be exposed to while being around Sha'Ron. You have to remember that my best friend was murdered simply because she was standing in the same spot as Shaun." Lindsay knew she was now playing dirty. She immediately felt the conviction of the Holy Spirit as a result, but she kept quiet and hoped her last statement would quiet Cody's insistence on helping Sha'Ron as well.

"Lindsay Vincini, are you serious? For real? You and I both know better than that." Lindsay tried giving Cody the innocent *"what are you talking about look,"* but Cody kept talking. "Look, sweetheart. I do understand your fears, but God can handle those. We don't have to trust Sha'Ron. We simply have to trust God. He will let us know if, and, when to pull back. Right now, He is telling me to help Sha'Ron. The kids wanting to reacquaint with him is a perfect opportunity to do so."

Lindsay knew she was not going to win this battle against her husband. She decided to try, instead, to look at the positives of this situation.

"Cody, you have to promise me you are going to be there at every gathering between my kids and their brother. You also have to be sure you don't allow the kids to go over to Patricia's house. If the rest of the Addams Family wants to see the children, they are going to have to make similar arrangements as Sha'Ron. Agreed, Counselor?"

Cody thought about Lindsay's conditions for a moment before agreeing. Realizing her request made sense, he said, "Yes, Your Honor."

Though still not totally comfortable with the arrangement, Lindsay gave up the fight and gave in to trusting her husband and God. She also hoped Cody could actually influence Sha'Ron in a positive way.

"Well, I guess that's it. You better get on your way to work, love."

Lindsay stood from the sofa and waited for her husband to do the same. When he did, the couple embraced lovingly and on one accord.

"I'm glad you have agreed to do this for Shauntae, Li'l Shaun, and Sha'Ron as well," he said while he held his wife. The two shared a passionate kiss just before Cody made ready to head to the office.

Sha'Ron prepared to call Uncle Bobby as he drove to school the morning following Cody's visit. He adjusted the volume on the music in his barely used triple black Mustang convertible, purchased for him by his uncle. Wintertime in Detroit did not permit him to put the top down as he so desperately wanted to so he could display his impressive sound system. But when alone in his ride and not on the phone, he kept the speakers working overtime.

"Uncle Bobby, you are not going to believe this. My former stepmom's new husband came to see me yesterday. He wants to put together a reunion between me and my little brother and sister." Sha'Ron went on to explain the details as they were told to him.

"Wow, S-Man! Things are coming together pretty cool. This couldn't be any better if we planned it ourselves. Okay, boy. I just want you to play it cool. Go along with their program. Learn what you can from them, even if you are only going to be hanging with that punk lawyer and the kids. You need to know about them too. Stay focused, S, and keep the goal in front of you." Uncle Bobby hung up. That was always his style: all business; never any affection; never any sentiment. It was forever about making the most of every opportunity that presented itself.

When his father was alive, Sha'Ron remembered the bond they shared; the time his dad spent teaching him about life, but also the time he spent just sharing himself with him. His dad was his best friend. And even though they were men, Sha'Ron remembered that his father always told him he loved him.

Whenever Sha'Ron reminisced about his dad like this, he would always feel like crying. He hated the softness he felt inside. He hated the ache and emptiness in his heart, and he hated his former stepmother for killing his father and making him feel this way. . . .

Chapter Seven

Two days before the sibling reunion, Lindsay sat with her mother in Ruby Tuesday's restaurant having lunch. The pair had spent the better part of three hours shopping at Laurel Park Place Mall in Livonia. Lindsay was assisting her mother with getting her wardrobe together for a vacation to Phoenix she was taking with some friends from church.

Lindsay had been nervous about the kids seeing Sha'Ron ever since she and Cody made the final decision to let it happen. She had been talking her mother's ear off about it nonstop while they shopped. And now that they had sat down and prepared to replenish their strength with a meal, the complaining continued.

"Mama, I just don't get how people can have so little regard for the life of a child. Sha'Ron is only sixteen. Neither Patricia nor Uncle Bobby could care less that they are ruining his life."

Sherrie Westbrook sat silently listening to her daughter complain about her former in-laws. She had been listening to Lindsay for hours go on and on about her fear of allowing her grandchildren to be around their older brother. For the most part, she just nodded and gave the occasional "hmm" or an "oh" as a reply. However, as they were seated and relaxed now and she observed the distress in her daughter's voice, she realized she should perhaps exert her opinion.

"Nay, sweetie, listen. You are obviously very concerned about the kids spending time with their older brother. Sweetheart, knowing what he is involved in makes your fear totally understandable. If you were not afraid, you would not be a good mother. Heck, I am even feeling a little vindication in this because I feel like you are validating my parenting skills. I mean, you remember what you put me through when you were dating Shaun, right?"

Sherrie paused to give Lindsay time to reflect back on the time when mother and daughter had a knockdown, drag-out brawl because Lindsay had decided she was simply done with following her mother's rules. She was going to be with her man at all costs.

Lindsay certainly understood why her mother would find the comparison appropriate, but in her mind, the situations were worlds apart.

"Mama, these are my babies. I have to protect them. Shaun and I were both grown when we made our decision to be with each other. We were old enough to live with the consequences of our actions." Lindsay remembered this being the same argument she gave Cody when they began having this same discussion.

"Oh really? Grown, huh? Because I remember it just a bit differently. I remember it being your seventeenth birthday, which by legal standards, still made you my child."

Lindsay rolled her eyes to the top of her head, realizing she could no longer argue with her mother's logic. But she gave it the ole college try, as the saying goes.

"Mom, yes, I was still legally underage but . . . but . . . but it was different, Mama. Li'l Shaun and Shauntae are just little children."

"Nay, I'm not saying I disagree with you. I totally understand your apprehension." Lindsay sighed gratefully as her mother spoke in agreement with her. "However, I can certainly understand your husband's reasoning as well."

Now Lindsay's eyes grew as big as saucers as she heard her mother quickly change her position over to Cody's way of thinking.

Sherrie noticed Lindsay's look of distress. "Let me explain, Nay-Nay. You say your kids are young. This is true."

Before she could finish her point, the waiter appeared to take their orders. After giving him their selections of both their beverages and entrees, Sherrie and Lindsay resumed their conversation.

"As I was saying, baby girl, your kids are younger than you and Shaun were, but I want you to remember that Sha'Ron is also younger than you were too. I think Cody's heart is in exactly the right place. He wants to make an attempt to help this young man. I think that's honorable. You should be proud of your husband."

"Mama, I am proud of his intentions. I just don't want my kids to have to be part of his plans to save that boy. What if it does no good and Sha'Ron continues on his path of destruction until he lands in jail or in his grave? How will my kids feel then having to face another such loss?"

"Nay-Nay, that is totally in God's hands. Cody will have very little to do with whether his efforts fail or succeed. You both just have to trust God. That is exactly what I had to do when you walked into this same situation at age seventeen. I was worried sick, but I had to let you go and give you to God."

"But, Mama . . ."

"Lindsay, there are no buts here. You either trust God, or you don't."

Lindsay knew she could no longer argue with her mother's reasoning or her faith.

"Hello."

Deep in the musings of her mother's words, Lindsay had not even noticed the woman approach their table. Sherrie was also caught off guard by the beautiful stranger's approach. She assumed that Lindsay was familiar with the woman. Otherwise, why would she have approached their table? The stunned and confused look on her daughter's face gave indication that she was not very pleased by the woman's sudden appearance. Lindsay just sat there staring and speechless.

"Hello to you," Sherrie greeted her after realizing Lindsay was not going to open her mouth.

"Hi. I assume you are Lindsay's mom since the two of you look so much alike. My name is Keva. I'm sure you have heard of me, all wonderful things I imagine," Keva chuckled.

Sherrie immediately recognized the name and totally understood her daughter's shock. Not wanting to be rude, even under the circumstances, she decided to converse with Keva. Lindsay interrupted, however, before her mother even began.

"Keva, I have told you more than once to call me Nay or Nay-Nay. What are you doing here? I thought you lived in Atlanta," she stated very aggressively.

Sherrie prickled at her daughter's tone, but Keva replied as if she had not been fazed by Lindsay's abruptness.

"My family and I moved back here about a year and a half ago. That's why I am so happy to see you here today."

"Excuse me? What do I have to do with you and your family being back in Detroit?"

Sherrie understood all too well why her daughter had such animosity toward Keva. The two women had never done anything other than battle over Shaun since they were made aware of each other. Yet, Sherrie had hoped the bitterness Lindsay felt for this woman, or any other woman from Shaun's past, would have been buried with the dead man responsible for it. Lindsay was a Christian woman who should have known all too well the power of forgiveness and the consequences of not forgiving.

"Nay-Nay, please stop being so rude. Keva approached you in a nonaggressive manner. God and I expect you to respond in kind," Sherrie said firmly.

Lindsay definitely did not appreciate being chastised, especially in front of Keva. She expected her mother to understand why she was being mean to the woman her former husband cheated with and with whom he produced a child. But out of respect for her mother and God, as she so easily threw in, she decided to conduct herself in a more Christian-appropriate manner.

"Keva, have a seat." Lindsay slid over on her side of the bench to make room, and Keva sat down. "I apologize for my rude behavior. Honestly. I guess I allowed some old feelings to resurface and control my actions. I should just put that crap behind me and let it go." Lindsay was still not very comfortable in Keva's presence, but she was determined to act bigger than her feelings.

Sherrie smiled at her daughter's change of attitude.

"Nay-Nay," Keva said carefully, "I understand your reaction to me. It's not as if we were ever bosom buddies. Your mother mentioned God's expectations of us, and I can only agree with her. It's only because of God that I can approach you without the hatred I once felt for you."

Suddenly, Lindsay and Sherrie both realized that Keva had gotten saved sometime between their last confrontation and now.

"Good for you, Keva," Sherrie said encouragingly.

Keva smiled at her in return. "Like I was saying, I moved back to Michigan with my husband and Kevaun awhile ago. We live in Westland now, and I'm about nine weeks pregnant with my second child."

"Congratulations," mother and daughter said in unison.

"Thank you. It seems like we are always running into each other in restaurants while I'm pregnant." Lindsay caught her meaning, and they both laughed. "With that being said, Nay-Nay, I want Kevaun to get to know his sister and brother. Shaun's funeral left my son so confused. Every now and then he asks about your kids and Sha'Ron; the last time being just two days ago. Seeing you here today, in this restaurant right around the corner from my house, made me believe that God orchestrated this meeting."

Sherrie agreed with Keva's faith, but at the same time, was concerned about Lindsay's state of mind. Her daughter had been complaining all day about her children getting reacquainted with their older brother. Now, here comes Keva not only bringing up that sore subject, but adding even another child to the mix.

Lindsay sat thinking, *Is God trying to tell me something?*

"Keva, it's funny you should mention Sha'Ron and your son wanting to know more about Shauntae and Li'l Shaun. My mother and I were discussing this just before you came over here. My kids told me just the other day they wanted to be reunited with Sha'Ron. Of course, they didn't mention Kevaun because they don't know him. With all that has taken place in their lives over the past couple years, I doubt Shauntae remembers little else about Shaun's funeral other than her father being dead and her mother killing another person."

"Right! Kevaun and I made our exit just before that happened. We were fortunate enough to miss all that drama."

Keva and Lindsay sat quietly at the table going over that dreadful day in their minds. Sherrie, who was not present at the funeral-murder scene, tried to think of a way to lighten the mood. Or at least change the subject.

"Nay, tell Keva 'bout your and Cody's plan to reintroduce your kids and Sha'Ron this weekend. Perhaps Kevaun can be a part of that dinner."

Keva raised an eyebrow indicating her interest. "Are you kidding? You all already have a time arranged for the sibling reunion? This is perfect. Only the Holy Spirit could devise something like this."

"I agree. My husband, Cody, plans to take Shauntae and Li'l Shaun to meet Sha'Ron at Red Lobster. I will not be part of the festivities because Cody feels Sha'Ron may not be ready to face the woman who killed both his parents."

"Cody. That is not a very popular name, especially in the circles in which we used to run. Would this be the same Cody who used to be Shaun's attorney?"

Lindsay realized Keva was out of the loop during all that drama. She was not aware of all the things that transpired between the time she took off and her reappearance in her life today.

"One and the same," Lindsay grinned.

"Okaaaaay. Brother-man was fine." Keva chuckled as she used air quotes when she spoke about Cody's looks.

"Here is something else you may be interested in knowing. Sha'Ron is also in the drug game, being groomed to take over his father's empire."

Keva's eyes became as huge as saucers as she processed Lindsay's news. "Oh no! Are you serious? Shaun would have never allowed that to happen. What in the world is Patricia thinking? I'm sure she knows."

Lindsay snorted. "Key word there is Patricia."

"'Nuff said," Keva replied.

"Uncle Bobby is still in the game, and from what my husband has gathered, he is training Sha'Ron the same way he trained Shaun."

"Shameful. So, even knowing this, you are obviously going to allow your kids to go to the reunion dinner."

"I am not that keen on the idea. Trust me. But Cody thinks I should just trust him and God. Cody believes it is his duty to try to help turn Sha'Ron in a different direction. My mother here agrees."

"Wow! How noble of Cody. I see he has made some changes in his life."

"I guess we all have," Lindsay said.

The waiter returned with Lindsay's and Sherrie's meal at that moment. He put the dishes in their proper places and asked Keva, "Can I get you something, ma'am?"

"No. I've already eaten. I'm just sitting and chatting with a new friend." Keva smiled at Lindsay. Amazingly, the tension Lindsay felt earlier evaporated.

"No problem. Can I get anything else for you ladies?"

Mother and daughter indicated they were fine, and the waiter left.

Once Sherrie blessed the food, she and Lindsay began eating their lunch. Between bites, Sherrie said, "Keva, as I told Nay, I understand your reluctance to just place your son in the presence of a young man who is selling drugs. But at the end of the day, Sha'Ron is his blood, just like Shauntae and Li'l Shaun. I'll tell you the same thing I told my daughter. I implore you to trust God and allow Kevaun to become acquainted with all of his siblings."

"I'm not that hard to convince, Ms. Westbrook." Lindsay was amazed that Keva remembered her maiden name. "If Cody is willing to allow Kevaun to tag along on the trip, I certainly don't mind stepping out on faith and allowing him to go."

Upon hearing Keva's quick consent and declaration to trust God, Lindsay began to feel really silly, convicted, if you will, about her persistent disapproval of the reunion. She too loved God. Hearing her mother and her once-upon-a-time archenemy speak about trusting Him so easily made her feel like less of a Christian; a feeling she found hard to swallow. She kept her emotions tucked away, though, vowing to pray and ask God to increase her faith.

"I guess that's settled. Keva, if you'll just give me your phone number, I'll call you as soon as all the details are worked out." Lindsay pulled her cell phone from her purse and programmed the numbers Keva recited into it.

"Is this a cell number?"

"Yes," Keva answered.

"I'm about to dial your phone, then you'll have my number as well." Lindsay did as she said, and Keva programmed Lindsay's name in her phone.

"Thanks a lot, Nay-Nay, for allowing me to join you and for hearing me out. I pray that things between us will be better than before for the sake of our children and so we can glorify God." Keva stood to depart. "I'll leave you two to enjoy the rest of your lunch in peace. Ms. Westbrook, it was nice to meet you. Nay-Nay, I'll wait for your call." Keva then left the restaurant.

Once she was gone, Lindsay simply said, "Wow! Who would have thought that?"

Sherrie's reply was just as simple. "God!"

***

"Wow! Look how God works," Cody said as he finished listening to Lindsay tell him about running into Keva that afternoon.

"Yeah. That's what Mama said too."

"So, I guess that means our little foursome will now be a fivesome, or does Keva plan on joining us also?"

"She and I have not yet completely worked out all the details. I promised to give her a call as soon as you put the final touches on time and location."

Cody saw no need to delay finalization of the time and restaurant location. He pulled out his phone and dialed Sha'Ron's cell. He picked up on the second ring.

"What up, White Boy?" Sha'Ron offered as a greeting.

"Hey, Sha'Ron. I was just calling to work out the final plans for dinner this weekend and to let you know there will be at least one more guest present."

"I'm cool with whatever time you come up with, but who is this new guest you talking about?" Sha'Ron wondered if his murderous stepmother had decided to join them after all.

"Lindsay ran into Keva Simpson today. She too expressed an interest in wanting her son Kevaun to get reacquainted with his siblings. Do you remember Kevaun, Sha'Ron?"

Both disappointment and relief invaded Sha'Ron's brain over the fact that Lindsay had not been the added member to their dinner party. The first emotion he understood completely. The feeling of relief shocked him a little. Why wouldn't he want to face his target? He held the phone pondering his thoughts for a while before answering Cody's question.

"Sha'Ron, are you still there?"

"Oh yeah, man. Phone blanked for a second," Sha'Ron lied. "Yea, I do remember him. My dad used to bring him around when he was little; then he and his moms jetted and I didn't see them again until Dad's funeral. Is his mom coming too?"

"I'm not sure. We have to give her a call to let her know the time. Would you have a problem with her joining us?"

"Naw. I ain't got no beef with her. I remember that she and your wife didn't get along too well, though. They were about to scrap this one time at a birthday party or something. They cool now, White Boy?"

"Let's just say they are trying to mend fences for the sake of you all. So let's say we all meet at Red Lobster on Telegraph near Warren at four P.M. Cool?"

"Bet. Works for me."

"And Sha'Ron, do me a favor. In front of the kids, call me Cody instead of White Boy C, okay?"

Sha'Ron chuckled at Cody's request, thinking, *This punk is a real trip these days.* "Sure, man. Whatever. See y'all at four on Saturday." He then hung up the phone.

"White Boy C?" Lindsay asked with a perplexed look as Cody disconnected the call.

"Just an old street name. Sha'Ron has agreed to four P.M. at Red Lobster. You can call Keva and give her the details."

Lindsay dialed Keva's number and gave her the time, date, and location.

"Thanks, Nay-Nay. I really appreciate you being big enough to do this for me and my son."

"It's for my own children as well, Keva. Are you going to attend the dinner?"

"If Cody doesn't mind keeping an eye on Kevaun, I don't mind leaving it to just the kids. I'll drop him off at the restaurant and pick him up when Cody calls."

An idea suddenly struck Lindsay. "Why don't you and I get together around the same time at a nearby restaurant? After you drop Kevaun off at Red Lobster, you can meet me there."

"That sounds like a plan. Why don't we meet at the Chili's on Southfield and Ford Road?"

"Okay. See you there about four-fifteen." They then disconnected the call.

Lindsay thought about her impulsive decision and wondered what made her do that. Cody slyly wondered the same thing.

"What in the world has come over you? Now you want to *hang out* with the woman you simply wanted to *hang* a few years ago."

"Don't exaggerate, Cody. It has been more than eight years since Keva and I had animosity toward each other. And to answer your question, I have no idea what came over me. The invitation came pouring out of my mouth before my brain had a chance to process it."

"Well, I think it's a great idea since your children will be spending time together. The two of you need to really get beyond the past."

Lindsay wondered if she could so easily let go of the former issues she had with Keva. This was a woman who once upon a time was the source of one of the most painful times in her life. She nearly lost her mind when she found out Shaun had actually cheated on her with Keva and fathered her baby.

But she was a new woman now; a woman with a new life, a new husband, and a better relationship with Christ.

"Well, I guess this will all kick into gear this weekend. I pray there is very little drama associated with the new blended family thing. . . ."

Chapter Eight

Saturday morning came, and Lindsay awoke with a little anxiety. Though she had heard the speeches of Cody and her mama, as well as witnessed the trust of Keva, she was still very nervous about the kids spending time with Sha'Ron.

She got out of bed and kneeled at the side of it to pray. "God, thank you for seeing my family through the night and for waking us this morning. Lord, today is a new beginning for my children. I pray for their safety and for this day to be the beginning of a healing process for them. I pray, Lord, for all the children involved, and for Keva as well. I especially pray, Lord, for Sha'Ron. Please touch his heart, Father, and allow a great change to come over him. I pray also for myself. Help me, Lord, to have peace about this whole situation. This is my prayer in Jesus' name . . . Amen."

Lindsay got up and realized that her rising-out-of-bed moment before had not caused her husband to stir in the slightest. Cody lay sound asleep, seemingly without a care in the world. Looking at the clock, she realized it was still early; only seven-fifteen. However, instead of climbing back into bed, she decided to use the time to get some chores done, starting with the family laundry. As the first load of clothes began to wash, Lindsay went through her moderately sized home cleaning and straightening as needed. All rooms were given attention except the bedrooms because her lazy-boned family was still in snore mode.

Just as Lindsay began transferring the first load of laundry from the washer to the dryer, Shauntae made an appearance in the doorway of the laundry room.

"Good morning, baby."

"Good morning, Mom," she replied as she walked in to give her mother a hug and kiss.

Lindsay contemplated about whether she should bring up the subject of today's events or wait to see if Shauntae would mention them.

"Mom, I am so excited about seeing Sha'Ron today."

Okay, so much for contemplating, Lindsay thought. "Are you, honey?"

"Yes. I can't wait till four o'clock," Shauntae squealed excitedly.

She and Li'l Shaun were unaware of Kevaun's inclusion in the reunion. Lindsay and Cody decided they would explain it all, even telling them about Tawanda's daughter, though she would not be there at dinner.

"Well, baby girl, I hope it turns out to be all you expect it to be," Lindsay said convincingly.

"Thanks for setting this up, Mom. I know it probably wasn't easy for you to allow Li'l Shaun and me to do this under the circumstances, but I am so glad you did." Shauntae hugged her mother again.

"I just want you two to be happy. Wanting to reestablish a relationship with your family is not an outrageous request. It makes perfect sense, Shauntae." Those were the words she shared with her daughter. In her head, she was thinking, *If only you knew the whole truth of how I feel, child . . .*

***

Lindsay worked hard at controlling her apprehension all day in order to not worry the children. However, Cody could read her like a book. "Baby, I need you to calm down. Everything will be okay. I promise. I can feel it in my spirit."

"Cody, I am a stressed-out mess. I'm worried about Sha'Ron being around my kids and being a drug dealer. I'm worried about what he might say to them about me that may hurt their feelings. I'm worried about them seeing Kevaun for the first time in such a long time and whether they'll even remember him. I'm worried about them learning about Tawanda's daughter and me not being there."

Tawanda and Shaun's daughter, Shauna, was just an infant when Shaun died. Lindsay never bothered telling her children about the last child their father conceived while the two of them were still married and Li'l Shaun and Shauntae never asked about her after the day of the funeral.

"And I'm worried about spending time alone with Keva. What exactly will the two of us talk about beyond the kids? I mean, what? Will we swap Shaun stories?"

Cody eased behind his wife who was standing at the island in the center of their kitchen. Lindsay was wiping the granite countertop so hard Cody was certain there would be absolutely no color remaining when she was done. He gently began massaging one shoulder with one hand while he removed the dish towel from her hand with his other hand. He then used that hand to massage the other shoulder.

"Lindsay, relax. Everything will work out fine. I will maintain control of things at the restaurant. As far as you and Keva go, you two talk about whatever you need to talk about in order to make things comfortable for the kids to spend time together. Don't think about the past history of Shaun that you two share. Just think about what is best for our kids. You are very good at that."

Cody gently turned Lindsay to face him. He kissed her lips very softly initially. He then deepened the kiss and turned the mating of their lips into a very sensual tongue dance. He knew his kisses always had the power to totally take away his wife's anxieties and make her forget what caused them.

"What was I talking about?" Lindsay asked as Cody released her from his hold.

Cody simply smiled and said, "I'm going upstairs to make sure the kids are ready to go."

Ten minutes later, the Vincini/Taylor clan headed out the door on their way to reentering and starting anew old relationships that were once either good, bad, or indifferent.

"Mom, I thought you weren't coming to the restaurant with us," Shauntae said as they all headed to the same car.

"I'm not, dear. Cody is going to drop me at a nearby restaurant. A friend of mine is meeting me there." Lindsay knew calling Keva a friend was a stretch, but she didn't want to have to explain the realities to her daughter at that moment.

Approximately twenty minutes later, Cody pulled to the front door of Chili's and got out of the car to open the door for his wife. He then walked with her to the front door, opened it as well, and left her there with a departing kiss.

"Given the time it will take us to get to Red Lobster, Keva should be arriving in about twenty minutes," he said as he jogged back to his vehicle.

"That's fine. I brought along a novel to keep me company."

Lindsay entered the restaurant. She gave the hostess, who seated her immediately, her name and explained that she was expecting someone else. She gave the same instruction to the waitress and told her she preferred to wait for the other party to arrive before placing an order. The waitress placed a glass of water in front of Lindsay and departed. Lindsay pulled out her book, *Bring on the Blessings*, by Beverly Jenkins, and began reading.

Lindsay had become so engrossed in her novel she didn't realize that two females had approached the table until they were already seated. Then she looked up with a greeting for Keva dancing on her tongue. The salutation immediately died on her lips, however, when she recognized the companion Keva had with her.

"Nay, I know I didn't tell you I was bringing company," Keva started explaining. "But I wasn't sure how you would react to the news of me bringing her along for our meeting. I figured, though, that we should all get together since we all have a common interest here."

The waitress appeared just as Keva had spoken the last word. She was so focused on doing her job, she didn't initially notice the combative look Lindsay was shooting across the table at the woman who sat next to Keva.

"Oh, I see there will be three of you instead of just two," the waitress clarified in a perky voice. "Can I start you lovely ladies off with something to drink?" The smile on her pretty face faded quickly as she noticed the malevolent looks on two of the ladies' faces.

Keva's companion gawked just as good as she got. She stared at Lindsay viciously from her seated position just in front of her across the table.

In an effort to slice through the tension, Keva began talking. "Ladies, the nice waitress wants to know what we would like to drink."

"Maybe I should give you all a few moments," the waitress suggested uncomfortably.

"No, sweetie. It will only take us a minute to look at the menu and place our drink and appetizer order. Ladies, let's look away from each other and at the menu for a few seconds, shall we?"

After a brief pause, Lindsay unwillingly pulled her gaze away from Shaun's fourth and last baby mama, Tawanda, to look at the menu. She then looked up when she made her decision.

"I'll have a strawberry lemonade," she said while looking directly at the waitress. She then redirected her gaze back at Tawanda, who had never stopped staring at Lindsay. Nor had she changed her scowling expression.

Keva momentarily looked away to peruse the menu. "I'll have the mango iced tea," she announced when she looked up again. Upon seeing the still hateful expressions on her dining companions' faces, she began to feel as uncomfortable as the waitress.

"And for you, young lady?" the waitress asked Tawanda nervously.

Without looking away from Lindsay or adjusting her frown she said, "I'll have a pomegranate patron margarita. I think I'm gonna need a little alcohol to get me through this meal."

"Will there be anything else for you ladies before I put in your drink orders?" the waitress asked without looking at anyone. She kept her eyes glued to her pad as she anxiously waited for a cue to leave the very volatile space.

"What's your name, honey?" Keva asked.

"Tisha," the waitress responded, still not willing to look at the women.

"Bring us an appetizer sampler platter as well, okay, Tisha? That will be it for now." Tisha quickly exited, glad to be away from the thick tension, at least for a little while.

"Keva, what is going on? Why is she here?" Lindsay asked as soon as the waitress left.

"She, I am assuming you are referring to me, has a name, and you know exactly what it is," Tawanda spat vehemently as she continued to stare at Lindsay.

"Okay, ladies. We are all adults here. Let's just try to be civil. I know there is no love lost between the two of you, but why don't we just try to put the old mess behind us and work together for the sake of our children who are all brothers and sisters."

Keva knew this was not going to be easy when she invited Tawanda along. She had actually bamboozled both ladies. She didn't tell Lindsay Tawanda was coming, and she didn't tell Tawanda Lindsay would be there until they stepped through the door of the restaurant.

"I don't know why she should have any beef with me. After all, she shot my man and killed him. Why should she be mad with me?" Tawanda asked nastily.

"Maybe, just maybe, it's because you were sleeping with my husband and had a baby with him while he was still married to me, stupid," Lindsay said loudly.

The other restaurant patrons who sat near them turned and looked in their direction. Keva immediately became very embarrassed, but quickly realized she hadn't seen anything yet.

"Who you calling stupid, you murderer?" Tawanda yelled in retaliation as she stood to her feet.

"I'm calling you stupid, tramp." Lindsay stood as well so that Tawanda would not have an advantage over her should she decide to try something physical.

Keva could not believe how badly her plan was going. She too stood up in hopes of bringing some calm to the brewing volatile situation. "Ladies, please sit down before the manager comes over here and tosses us out. Or worse, calls the police on us. We're making a horrible scene and disturbing everyone in the restaurant."

Both Lindsay and Tawanda looked around simultaneously to find everyone in the restaurant gawking at them. Some of them even looked frightened. Hearing they had a killer among them could have been the cause for that reaction.

Lindsay sat first while keeping a steady eye on Tawanda, who was, in turn, staring at her just as intently. Keva sat next and began massaging her temples, not bothering to look at either of her companions. After several seconds, Tawanda finally took her seat and broke the staring war between her and Lindsay by instead, taking the still full glass of water that sat in front of Lindsay and drinking from it.

Just as Lindsay opened her mouth to protest, the waitress appeared and nervously placed their drinks in front of them. The restaurant manager on duty also accompanied his staff person.

"Ladies, is everything okay over here?" the manager asked softly.

"Sir, we are extremely sorry. I don't think there will be any more problems," Keva stated as she looked from one female to the next, silently pleading with them to make her statement true.

"That's good to hear. We truly appreciate your business, but if there is another scene we will have to ask you ladies to leave as we have other patrons to think about." Again, the manager spoke in very soft tones, but his message was loud and clear. "Enjoy your meal, ladies." He departed, leaving his still skittish waitress to finish her job.

Lindsay spoke quickly before the waitress had a chance to ask for their dinner orders. "Keva, it seems that both times I have seen you in a restaurant over this past week have been a replay of the first time I saw you in a restaurant. You were pregnant then, and you are pregnant now. And the manager is talking about throwing us out now, and the manager did throw me out then."

"That's because you *threw* a napkin holder at me then. Girls, let's please not go there again. Nobody pick up anything and hit anybody with nothing," Keva said jokingly—and seriously—at the same time. She and Lindsay laughed at the memory while Tawanda sat still steaming, unamused by their private joke.

The waitress also didn't get the humor. She just hoped they didn't start throwing things while she stood there. "Ladies, are you ready to order your meals?" Just as she said that, another server appeared with their appetizer.

All three ladies opened their menu and began searching for entrees. . . .

Meanwhile . . . over at Red Lobster . . .

Cody sat quietly as the children reacquainted themselves with each other effortlessly. He, Shauntae, and Li'l Shaun were the first to arrive. Cody went to the hostess stand and asked for a table for five. He explained to the waitress they wanted to wait for the rest of their party to arrive before they were seated.

Shauntae overheard him and questioned him about who the fifth person was. Before he could respond, Keva walked in with Kevaun. Keva was still strikingly beautiful.

Cody recognized her immediately though the teenager with her had changed immensely. Kevaun had been turning five years old when Cody last saw him at his own birthday party. This was a couple of months before he had seen Lindsay for the first time. Shauntae was at the birthday party, but Li'l Shaun was not yet born.

"Hello, Cody," Keva said as she walked over and placed a kiss on his cheek. "Long time no see, handsome."

"Hello to you, Keva. It has been awhile, hasn't it? So much has changed since I last saw you. In particular this young man here with you. Wow! Look how tall and handsome he is."

Kevaun looked to be the perfect complement to both of his parents. While he was tall like Shaun and had the signature green eyes, he also favored his mother quite a bit as well.

"Cody, are you sure it's okay that I leave my son here with you? This is a big undertaking you are about to get into."

"I think we will all be just fine, Keva. Go on. Go meet Lindsay," Cody assured her.

Keva kissed her son on the cheek and gave him a last-minute instruction to behave himself. She waved at Lindsay's two children and headed back out to her car.

Shauntae stared at Kevaun the entire time her stepdad and his mom talked. He was extremely cute to her, but also eerily familiar, his green eyes telling her a tale she was certain she had heard before.

Then, like an immunization shot, it hit her. She remembered having this same exact feeling on the day of her father's funeral. This was the boy who stared at her in the limousine. This was the boy whose mother had said her daddy was his daddy too.

Kevaun had paid little attention to Shauntae or Li'l Shaun since arriving at the restaurant. He had been made fully aware by his mom that today he would be reacquainted with his two brothers and his one other sister. He met his other little sister, Shauna, a couple of weeks ago for the very first time. His mom had explained that he had spent time with Shauntae and Sha'Ron when they were toddlers and that Li'l Shaun had not been born yet when they moved away to Atlanta.

Cody made the formal introductions. "Shauntae, Li'l Shaun, I want you to meet your older brother Kevaun."

Both of Lindsay's children stood staring stunned and confused. Shaun was confused because he had never met or even heard of this guy. Shauntae was confused because, though she had remembered their connection and figured out the possibility of him being a sibling, she didn't understand how he could be older than her.

"We will get more into the details once Sha'Ron arrives," Cody continued when he saw the confused looks.

Right on cue, Sha'Ron waltzed into the restaurant looking the epitome of teenaged cool. His haircut was tight and fresh, giving the appearance of having just stepped out of the barber's chair. His Sean John denim outfit accessorized with a yellow Polo shirt looked as if he had just removed the tags. The all-yellow Nikes on his feet looked as if he had them painted to match his shirt perfectly.

"Hey, Cody," Sha'Ron said as he approached Cody with an outstretched hand for a shake. Cody was pleased that Sha'Ron remembered their conversation about his name.

"What up, family!" Sha'Ron exclaimed as he made his approach toward his brothers and sister.

He hugged Shauntae first. "Girl, you are so pretty. I have missed seeing the face that looks like my own."

Shauntae beamed with pride as she hugged her true big brother.

"Hey, Sha'Ron. I missed you too."

"Look at my little brother. You ain't a baby anymore, Li'l Shaun." He hugged his youngest brother, then asked, "You remember that handshake I taught you?"

The brothers began doing the handshake they created together, which included an uncomplicated mixture of hand gestures and fist bumps. Their customary greeting for one another came back to their remembrance with ease.

"And you are Kevaun," Sha'Ron said a little more cautiously. "You probably don't remember me because you were only about five the last time we saw each other, but I remember you though. Dang, Shauntae looks more like you than she does me." He hugged Kevaun, and then showed him the handshake he shared with their younger brother. "That is a brother thang. It's only for when we see each other, okay?" Kevaun nodded his head in agreement with a smile.

"Your table is ready, sir," the hostess announced right on time.

"Come on. Let's all go and sit down. We'll talk more at the table," Cody said. The children quietly followed him and the hostess to their spacious table.

Cody sat at the head. Sha'Ron sat just to his left, and Li'l Shaun scrambled to sit next to his big brother. Shauntae settled for the seat directly across from Sha'Ron, just to the right of Cody, leaving Kevaun the seat next to her.

"Your waiter will be over in just a second to get your drink orders," the hostess announced, then disappeared.

Cody was pleased to see that all four children sat at the table with varying degrees of smiles on their faces. Li'l Shaun's was the biggest and brightest as he stared around the table at his brothers and sister.

The waiter appeared within moments and took their orders for beverages, then left quickly to prepare their selections.

"Okay, Cody. I'm dying to know how Kevaun is my older brother," Shauntae asked. She then directed a question at Kevaun before Cody could respond. "How old are you?"

"I'm thirteen," Kevaun replied calmly.

"How can that be possible? I'm thirteen. If we are the same age, why did you say he was my older brother, Cody?"

Kevaun had been made aware of the details of all of his father's children back when he and his mom initially moved back to Detroit. However, Cody explained it to both of them, not knowing that Kevaun already knew the story.

"Shauntae, Kevaun was born in July 1996. You were born in November 1996. Therefore, he is older than you by four months. Do you two understand?"

Shauntae nodded slowly that she did. She understood perfectly that her father had been messing around with both Kevaun's mom and hers at the same time.

Cody was concerned about how Li'l Shaun processed what he had just heard. He looked over to find the boy still grinning, as if he were the most blessed child in the world to have these brothers and his sister, regardless of what order they came.

Cody smiled and marveled at the young child's blissful ignorance and innocence.

"While we are on the subject, I may as well tell you your father has another child as well. It's a little girl name Shauna. She should be three and a half years old."

Shauntae again began calculating the years and realized this child too had come along while her father and mother were still together. Wow! Even though she still loved and missed her dad, she was now getting a better understanding of why her mom shot him.

Sha'Ron spoke up to lend his opinion and experience to the conversation. "Shauna has been a part of my life ever since my dad, I mean our dad, was killed."

Everyone at the table except for Kevaun prickled at his choice of words. Even Li'l Shaun showed a small chink in his happy armor. Sha'Ron kept right on speaking as if he hadn't said anything disturbing at all.

"See, this stuff is new to all of you, but not to me. I guess because I'm the oldest, I've had to learn for the longest amount of time what it feels like to keep getting introduced to new sisters and brothers. After awhile, I just kind of got used to it. You all didn't know about one another or wouldn't find out about one another until something bad would happen between our father and each of your mothers. But because I didn't pose a threat to Dad's character or because he wasn't cheating on me or my mom, none of you were ever hidden from me. I knew about you all from the time each of your moms had gotten pregnant with you all." Everyone sat in a state of extreme quietness after Sha'Ron's speech.

The waiter reappeared to take their orders. Everyone telling him what they wanted to eat was their breach of silence. Once the food orders were given and the waiter went away Cody elaborated on what Sha'Ron said.

"Sha'Ron makes an excellent point. How you all became brothers and sisters is far less important than the fact that you are brothers and sisters. Yes, the adults did make some mistakes, but from their mistakes a family was created. This is a clear example of what the devil meant for evil, God will turn it around for your good and His glory."

Sha'Ron listened to Cody's spiel, thinking, *So White Boy is a Jesus freak now?* He chuckled to himself. Uncle Bobby had warned him about folks who used to be into all kinds of dirt who now felt their mess didn't stink no more because they had turned their lives over to God. Uncle Bobby told him that God was just a mystical myth, an ideology that made some people feel superior to others because they believed in some majestic being who supposedly created the world. Yet these were the same sad people who were raising all kinds of hell and would never lift a finger to help a person in serious need. Sha'Ron listened intently to hear more of White Boy's heavenly hypocritical hype.

"We can liken this to the story of Joseph in the Bible. He also had sibling issues. The devil turned Joseph's brothers against him. They were separated for several years, just like you guys, but God eventually restored the relationship and all of them were blessed as result."

Now that was good, Sha'Ron thought. White Boy was actually telling a Bible story that related to their situation.

"That was a good analogy, Cody. We're learning about analogies in my English class right now," Shauntae said.

"Yeah. I like Joseph and the story of how he loved his brothers, even though they tried to kill him," Kevaun added.

As far as Sha'Ron was concerned, what Kevaun just said proved that the Bible only spoke about unrealistic or ancient nonsense. There was no way a dude in this day would be cool with some fools who tried to kill him—brothers or not. The rule of the streets today was kill or be killed; survival of the fittest. If somebody tried to kill you and failed, you best be sure you get them and take them out before they came back at you again.

He decided he would make it a point to school his younger brother on real life when he had an opportunity in the near future. Shauntae and Li'l Shaun he would educate later in life after he got away with killing their mom.

Yes, she was able to take out his father. But if she had been real smart, she would have known that she should have gotten him too because he was surely going to get her.

Cody realized Sha'Ron had become very quiet and looked rather pensive. "Sha'Ron, what's up, man? You all right? You look a little bothered."

Sha'Ron shook himself from his thoughts and found everyone at the table staring at him. "Oh, naw. I'm cool, Cody. I was thinking about how the story of Joseph related so closely to our story. And about how cool it is to be here with my brothers and my sister despite all that has happened."

Cody heard Sha'Ron's words, but didn't really feel the sincerity in them. He could tell the young man was more than likely just spitting game for the most part. Cody knew his instincts came from both his God-given spiritual discernment and his years of defending people who also talked a good game. He was sure Sha'Ron was happy to see his siblings, but he doubted very seriously if he was actually moved in the least by his Bible story.

"When do we get to meet our little sister?" Li'l Shaun asked, cutting into the musings of his stepdad.

"Well, we have to see about getting in touch with her mother and working something out," Cody answered.

"That won't be a problem at all. I see Tawanda and Shauna all the time. I kick it with our little sister at least a few times a week. My grandma babysits her a lot. The next time we get together, I'll be sure to bring her along with me."

While the kids and Cody seemed to be having a peaceful reunion, the baby mama shindig was not going quite as smoothly. The yelling and screaming had stopped for the time being, but the atmosphere remained quite uncomfortable. As soon as the waitress had returned with their food orders and left again, Keva began explaining her reasoning for staging this dinner meeting.

"Look, ladies, I know there has been some unpleasantness between all of us and all in the name of Shaun Robert Taylor. But he is gone now. What he leaves behind are five children who are the innocent victims of all of our mistakes."

"What mistakes did I make?" Tawanda butted in. "I never had any beef or any confrontation with either of you. From what I understand, you two were the ones that were always scrapping, Keva. And old girl over there ain't nothing but violent. She fought with Rhonda. She fought with you, and then she shot and killed Shaun and Rhonda. So tell me, what mistake did *I* make?"

Both Lindsay and Keva stared at Tawanda in complete silence, as if she had grown another head before their very eyes. Keva was the first to address Tawanda's crazy assessment.

"Are you serious? What do you mean 'what mistake' did you make?" Keva paused to lower her voice as she realized she had gotten a little loud when the patrons again began looking their way. "You were sleeping with her husband," she said while pointing at Lindsay. "You had a baby by a married man. You don't see anything wrong with that?"

Lindsay sat quietly perched in her seat, but her nerve endings were screaming, waiting for Tawanda to answer Keva's questions.

"Oh, please. You say it like I raped the man or something. Shaun and I had a consensual relationship. It started out as strictly a work thing, but once he found out she was sleeping with his lawyer, he came to me for comfort the moment he got out of prison."

So now Lindsay knew the truth. Shaun only started messing around with Tawanda after he found out that she had been seeing Cody. Wow! Keva's voice interrupted her train of thought.

"Either way, Tawanda, Shaun was married. So you were wrong. Lindsay having an affair with Cody was wrong. Me sleeping with Shaun and not being married to him was wrong. All of those wrongs were all of our fault," Keva indicated by sweeping her arm around the table to point at each of them. "But we still have the children to contend with and raise, despite the fact that we all played a part in the wrongs. I just want them to be raised together like the blood family they are. Am I wrong for that?"

Lindsay and Tawanda sat quietly after the gentle admonishing of Keva. Lindsay understood Keva's ideology and applauded her maturity, recognizing that it was a result of her new identity in Christ. She too decided it was time to lay down all the misery of the past and to help lay a better foundation for all of the children.

After Shaun's death, Lindsay had taken the money from his bank accounts, the money stashed in their garage, and the money from the sale of all of their properties and divided it evenly among each of Shaun's children. In hindsight, she realized it was easy to throw money at a situation in an attempt to fix it or make it look like she was being godly in doing so. But getting right there in the trenches and dealing with Shaun's infidelities and the products of those issues would require true grit and true strength from God.

"I'm with you, Keva. You are absolutely not wrong. All of our children should be raised together as family, including Sha'Ron. I mean, if he were my biological son, I would do all within my power to get him out of the drug game. So I will work with my husband to help Sha'Ron as much as possible."

Tawanda apparently did not share in Lindsay and Keva's commitment toward the children. She rolled her eyes so far into the top of her head, the possibility of never again seeing the pupils of them seemed very real. She also sucked her teeth and groaned out her frustration loudly enough for those up to three booths away to hear.

"There you go," Tawanda said, addressing Lindsay. "You trying to be Sister Saintly, gon' save poor little Sha'Ron from himself and all the big bad drug deal-ers. Well, in keeping it real, sweetheart, and having no shame in my game, I am married to one of those drug dealers."

While Tawanda claimed to have no shame in her game, she kept her voice very low while she flashed her left hand with the huge diamond ring on her finger.

"So don't be so quick to judge," she said now talking to both Keva and Lindsay. "Neither of you seemed to have a problem with the dope man when you were both with Shaun."

"And look at where Shaun is now, Tawanda. Dead!" Keva said.

"Well, that's because his wife killed him, not the game."

"But the game killed my best friend. And like so many others before her and after her, she was an innocent victim."

Tawanda's face showed an unreadable expression, almost akin to fear as Lindsay mentioned Shyanne's murder. Keva stared at her puzzled while recognition swept through Lindsay like a freight train.

She remembered that Tawanda was with Shaun the night Shyanne was gunned down in the street. She had actually had a physical altercation with Kevin just moments before Shyanne had been shot by the people who were, in fact, gunning for Shaun.

"You remember it, don't you, Tawanda?" Lindsay asked through clenched teeth.

Water pooled in Tawanda's eyes until the overage of liquid spilled out onto her cheeks. Keva stared, still unaware of the event these two were referring to.

"What's going on? What happened?" Keva asked gently to neither lady in particular. But it was Tawanda who supplied the explanation.

"It was the scariest night of my life," she strangled out. "One minute she was standing there, beating the crap out of the man I loved and I instantly hated her. The next minute, she was lying dead in the street with blood spilling from everywhere, and I unconsciously thanked her for inadvertently saving Shaun's life." Tawanda's shoulders visibly shook under the weight of her muffled sobs.

Silent tears ran unchecked from Lindsay's eyes as she too recalled the worst night of her life. She maintained a control on herself that could have only been powered by God because her flesh wanted to choke Tawanda for what she just said.

"When you think about it, Tawanda, the game really did kill Shaun. You see, the only reason I murdered him was because I felt he was responsible for my best friend's murder. Shy was killed with bullets and hate that was meant for Shaun as a result of his position in the game," Lindsay managed to explain in her grief.

"Tawanda, sweetheart, I don't think Lindsay was trying to put down your man in as much as she's just trying to save Sha'Ron from the same fate his father met. Neither she nor I are in a position to judge you, but we can only advise you based on the harshness of our experiences. And from what it sounds like to me, you too have had at least one rather harsh experience yourself," Keva said.

Tawanda's sobs finally subsided, but she continued to look facedown at the table. Lindsay's tears still poured quietly from her eyes.

At that moment the waitress appeared to do a final check on them and leave them their tab. She was so very confused when she left their table. First, they were screaming bloody murder at each other; now, they were solemn and crying. She could honestly say this had been the oddest experience for her in her five years of waitressing.

"Tawanda, your husband is an adult, and he is responsible for his own decisions. Sha'Ron is still a child. Somebody has to take the responsibility for at least trying to properly guide his decisions. I have just decided today to be one of those people," Lindsay said.

"Me, too," Keva agreed.

"I'm not ready to let go of my husband and my marriage," Tawanda said looking up at each lady.

"We're not asking that of you. We just want your permission to include Shauna in our children's family," Keva responded, looking at Lindsay for her agreement, who silently nodded her head.

"Fine," was Tawanda's one-word acknowledgment.

"Then I guess this dinner meeting proved to be a success despite all the drama and pain. Isn't that just like God? He gives us victory through it all. I will gladly pay the check since all this drama was my idea," Keva chuckled lightly.

And back again to Red Lobster, Cody and all the children were having a great time laughing and learning. The kids were telling each other all about their lives, their likes, their dislikes, and their future plans. They were sharing and caring with one another as loving siblings.

"How many points did you score in the championship game, Sha'Ron?" Li'l Shaun asked in awe after hearing his big brother tell him how he scored the game-winning basket last season that sent his team to the championship.

"Well, Li'l Shaun, it wasn't just me in any of the games. It was all of the team that helped us win. I scored eleven points, and three other of my team members had between ten and twelve points too. Together, we won the championship."

Cody was curiously surprised by how humble Sha'Ron appeared before his brothers and sister. On the day he initially approached the young man about the reunion, he was tough and full of bravado. However, around his brothers and sister, he was gentle and mature. Qualities he obviously inherited from his dad.

Shaun Taylor was a no-nonsense, hard-core street gangsta, but around his children, he was extremely compassionate and caring. For the sake of his kids, he would remove the hard-core veneer and just be open and loving with them.

"Okay, I know Shauntae is a cheerleader and on the church's dance team. Li'l Shaun loves bowling in the winter and softball in the spring. What about you, Kevaun? You look like a man who stays in shape. Do you play any sports?"

"Yep," Kevaun answered. "I play basketball and football. Next year in high school, I'll also try out for the track team. They don't have a team at my middle school."

"Cool. Look at this. All of Dad's kids are athletes. We'll all have to work together to make sure Shauna becomes an athlete too."

"Ohh. I can teach her how to dance," Shauntae volunteered.

Cody's ringing phone in no way deterred the chatter of the siblings. "Hello, Lindsay."

"Hey, baby. We're leaving Chili's now and heading your way. Are you all almost done?"

"Yeah. I think we can just about wrap this up. How did things go with you two ladies?"

"Well, there were actually three of us. I'll tell you all about it later. What about you and the kids?"

"Things here were great. Give you more details later as well. See you in a few moments."

Cody disconnected the call and signaled for the waiter to bring their check. "Okay, guys and gal, we need to wrap this up. Your mothers are on their way over here."

Not mine, Sha'Ron thought silently to himself. At least now, though, in just a few minutes, he would have an opportunity to come face-to-face with the person who killed her.

Cody noticed the shrouded look that appeared again on Sha'Ron's face. He purposely looked at the young man after making the comment about the other kids' mothers to see if it bothered him. Apparently it had. Cody wanted to apologize to Sha'Ron, but he knew that mentioning it would be awkward for everyone.

Cody paid the check, and he and the crew went to stand in the front sitting area while they waited for Lindsay and Keva. Cody wondered if the mystery third person would be with them.

He received his answer when approximately two minutes later he saw Lindsay's face as Keva pulled her car into a parking space.

Lindsay, without even thinking about Sha'Ron's discomfort over seeing her, was the first to jump from the car. Keva got out next and urged Tawanda to come into the restaurant too.

Cody saw the women approach, and his brain began processing two facts simultaneously. The mystery of who the third person was solved as he recognized Tawanda. The second fact was that Lindsay and Sha'Ron were about to be face-to-face. His wife was obviously not thinking.

Lindsay, Keva, and Tawanda entered the double doors virtually at the same time. Kevaun walked toward his mother. Shauntae and Li'l Shaun scampered over to Lindsay. Cody again looked at Sha'Ron who, unable to mask his ire and contempt, stared maliciously at Lindsay. Each adult in the foyer noticed the look of pure evil on the young man's face.

Tawanda immediately took action. "Hey, Sha'Ron. You looking incredibly handsome today." She turned his body to admire his outfit. Once his back was to the crowd, she went around him and gave him a big hug, hoping to squeeze some of the tension from him while he was no longer facing Lindsay.

Lindsay felt awful for the fury she saw in Sha'Ron's eyes that had been directed straight at her. She was not afraid, just ashamed of having been responsible for causing him the pain that propelled the hate.

Before anyone could react, Sha'Ron pulled himself gently from Tawanda's embrace. He mumbled a barely audible good-bye and rushed from the restaurant to his car. He left the parking lot just a little fast, but not necessarily recklessly.

Everyone present felt bad for Sha'Ron. Everyone present knew the reason for his distress, including Li'l Shaun.

"I'm so sorry. I didn't even think about the impact seeing me would have on him when I left the car." Lindsay was truly remorseful about her uncalculated appearance before Sha'Ron.

Cody walked over to his wife and pulled her into a light embrace. "Don't worry about it, love. This is just something we'll have to deal with as time moves forward."

"We had a good time, Mom," Shauntae announced to change the subject and lighten the mood. The other two kids began sharing their joy about the reunion as well.

"I'm glad to hear you all enjoyed yourselves with each other. I want you all to meet Ms. Tawanda. Tawanda is Shauna's mother. She has agreed to let her daughter join you all the next time you get together." Each of the children took their time shaking Tawanda's hand.

Lindsay then formally introduced Shauntae and Li'l Shaun to Keva. Keva did the same between Kevaun and Lindsay.

The whole crew then said their good-byes, promising to be in touch soon to set up another reunion. They then left the building, each headed to their respective two vehicles and their respective three homes.

***

Sha'Ron drove home at a fast but safe pace. He pushed his Mustang as fast as he could and still stayed safe from unwanted legal attention. He was furious. He was certain that if he'd had his gun on him, he would have pulled it and shot her dead right there in front of everyone. He thought he could handle being close to her. But he was not prepared. As they say in the hood, he was not ready. . . .

Chapter Nine

One week had passed since Shauntae and Li'l Shaun had spent the afternoon with Sha'Ron and Kevaun. However, not an hour had passed that whenever the kids were in her presence, Lindsay did not have to listen to them relive that afternoon. She was pleased with the joy the reunion had brought her children, so she didn't mind listening to them go on and on about it.

Today, however, would probably be a day of very different emotions for her babies. Today, they would have their very first appointment with Dr. Nancy Hooper.

Lindsay had no idea how Dr. Hooper would conduct the session, but she was certain that there would be some unpleasantness for her children. She dreaded the pain she knew the therapy would produce, but she also knew this would help the children in the long run. Most important, she knew God would see them through this and on the other side of through would be a blessing.

Shauntae and Li'l Shaun knew they had the appointment this morning. Neither child seemed thrilled at the prospect of having to go. All through breakfast they sulked.

"Mom, I don't understand how sitting and talking with a stranger about our feelings will help us. Doesn't it make more sense to just let it go and forget about it? Isn't that what they are always teaching us in church; that we should just forgive and let it go?"

"Shauntae, can you forget about your father?"

"Of course not," she said as she rolled her eyes at her mother's silly question.

"Honey, Dr. Hooper is going to help you and Li'l Shaun learn how to always remember your dad and help teach you to deal with any guilt or anger or shame that may be associated with his death."

Shauntae finished her breakfast in silence realizing her mother was not going to change her mind about taking them to therapy. Li'l Shaun followed his sister's lead.

The kids looked miserable, Lindsay thought. But everything in her told her she was doing the right thing. She only wished Cody were there to reassure her. Unfortunately, he had left about thirty minutes before to meet with a client who only had Saturdays available.

"Okay, you two, finish up in here, and then get your coats on. We need to leave in about fifteen minutes to make sure we get to the office by nine-thirty. I have to get there a little early to complete some paperwork."

Lindsay and the kids arrived at Dr. Hooper's office at exactly nine-thirty. From the look on the children's faces as they walked from the car to the office entrance, someone would have assumed they were headed to the dentist for root canals or the pediatrician for immunizations.

Soon after Lindsay completed the intake forms and insurance information, Dr. Hooper came to the lobby and called for Shauntae and Li'l Shaun. Lindsay left her seat to go with the children.

"Mrs. Taylor . . ." Dr. Hooper started after looking at the paperwork.

"Dr. Hooper, my last name is Vincini. I remarried." No one had mistakenly called her Taylor since Shaun's death.

"Forgive me, Mrs. Vincini. It's right here on the paperwork if I had bothered to look more carefully. Right now, today, I just want to speak with the kids. Would you mind waiting here in the reception area?"

Lindsay instantly became defensive as she digested Dr. Hooper's words. This elegantly beautiful, dark-hued woman was speaking and thinking crazy if she thought for a second that she was taking her kids anywhere without her.

"Dr. Hooper, this is a very delicate subject matter we are here to seek help about. I think it would be best if I was with my children while you talk to them." Lindsay had explained to Dr. Hooper what the issues with the children were when she initially spoke with her on the phone.

"Mrs. Vincini, I am aware of the issues we are dealing with here. It has been my experience in dealing with children for many years, however, that they are far more open when the parents are not in the room, especially when the parent is the focal point of the issue or issues."

Ouch! That statement about her being the reason the kids needed therapy stung. Hard! Lindsay poked her lip out, but in an effort to not show out in front of her children she checked her hurt feelings before speaking again.

"Dr. Hooper, I understand that you are a professional and have probably seen almost everything under the sun when it comes to children's issues, but I'm sure our case ranks as unique. I'm not saying that it's special, just more than likely different than those you have seen before."

"May I call you Lindsay?"

"No, you may not," Lindsay answered sounding seriously affronted by Dr. Hooper's request. She quickly tried to rectify the situation as Dr. Hooper stared bug-eyed at her.

"What I meant to say is I'm not very fond of my first name. I would prefer to be called Nay or Nay-Nay, short for my middle name, Renee." Lindsay realized that her quick reply was a result of how displeased she was with Dr. Hooper's insistence on speaking with Shauntae and Li'l Shaun without her.

"Nay-Nay. Is that better?" Lindsay simply nodded so that she would not say anything else offensive.

"Nay-Nay, I have seen cases that you cannot begin to even imagine. Trust me when I say this situation is not a new one for me. Please allow me to do my job and more important, allow me an opportunity to help your children."

Lindsay was still not comfortable with Dr. Hooper's suggestion, but realized this was just a consultation. If the kids seemed in any way harmed by their visit she would not bring them back.

"Okay, Dr. Hooper. I will allow you to do this your way. I pray this goes okay for my kids."

"Well, I will start by telling you this won't be easy. But I promise," she looked at her paperwork again to confirm their names, "Shauntae and Shaun will be no worse than before they got here."

Dr. Hooper ushered the children through the door and away from Lindsay without another word. Lindsay sat in the waiting room flipping through old magazines while her children were in their trial session with the therapist.

Dr. Hooper asked Shauntae and Li'l Shaun to sit on the sofa in her office. She sat in the armchair next to the sofa. She preferred this method when there was more than one child in her office. Otherwise, she would have sat behind her desk and allowed the single child to sit in one of the armchairs in front of her.

"Shauntae, Shaun, I am Dr. Nancy Hooper. I'm hoping to speak with the both of you today and try to get an idea from you how you are feeling inside about some things you have experienced."

Shauntae and Li'l Shaun sat completely still while they listened to Dr. Hooper talk. Neither of them said a word so the doctor continued.

"Why don't we start with each of you telling me a little about yourselves. I know how old you are, so I can pretty much guess what grade you are in. Tell me what kind of grades you get. Shauntae, you go first."

Hesitantly, Shauntae began. "I get good grades. Nothing less than a B ever. I'm a cheerleader, and I love to dance." Shauntae ended her assessment of herself there.

"Good, Shauntae. Thank you. Now, tell me about you, Shaun."

In normal fashion, Li'l Shaun pretty much mimicked his sister in tone and posture. "I get good grades too. No Cs or Ds or Fs ever. I play softball, and I bowl."

Dr. Hooper took notice of how Shaun imitated his big sister. She would be careful from this point on to usually address him first for any responses.

"Shaun, tell me what you like to do on the weekends. Let's start with what you did last weekend."

Both kids visibly perked up. They sat up straighter, and their faces instantly became brighter. Dr. Hooper couldn't wait to hear what the children did that caused such enthusiasm.

"Last Saturday we had dinner with our big brother Sha'Ron who we haven't seen in a long time. Our other big brother, Kevaun, was there too, who I have never seen before, but Shauntae hadn't seen in a long time. It was a lot of fun." Shaun ended his spiel with a warm smile.

Shauntae started talking next without having to be prompted. "We went to Red Lobster with our stepfather. My brother Sha'Ron is so cool. My brother Kevaun is really cute. I can't wait for my friends to meet them. We also found out that we have a three-year-old sister too. She wasn't there, but her mother said she can join us the next time we get together."

Dr. Hooper wrote some notes on the pad, jotting down this huge piece of information. *These are obviously the other children of their now deceased father*, she thought to herself.

"Good. It sounds like both of you are quite happy to have these siblings in your life. That is a very good thing." Both children excitedly nodded their agreement.

"Do you two understand what I mean when I say that your other siblings are the products of other relationships your father was involved in outside of the relationship he had with your mother?"

Li'l Shaun looked to Shauntae, indicating he was not quite sure what Dr. Hooper said. Shauntae, however, acknowledged that she knew.

"I understand, Dr. Hooper," Shauntae said. "It means that our father cheated on our mother with these other women. As a result, these other women, Keva and Tawanda, got pregnant. Sha'Ron's mother, Rhonda, was our father's girlfriend before he married our mother, though."

Dr. Hooper saw that Shaun's eyes now reflected comprehension after his sister's very plainly put explanation, so she continued. "Very good, Shauntae. Do you all understand that your mother killed Sha'Ron's mother?"

Both kids nodded silently that they did. "How do you feel about that? Why don't you tell me how you feel first, Shaun?"

After hesitating for a brief moment, Shaun began to speak about his feelings. "I remember she was trying to hurt my mommy and my sister. I remember screaming and telling her to leave them alone. I was really scared by the loud noise from the gun and really scared too when the lady fell on the ground right near my mommy."

"You remember that? You were only four years old." Shauntae was certainly surprised by her brother's recollection.

Dr. Hooper pushed past Shauntae's question to continue her own questioning.

"Okay, Shaun, you were scared. Did you feel anything else?"

"Like what do you mean?"

"You said you were scared. Okay. Did you feel anything else like sad or glad? Did you want to cry?"

Shaun seemed deep in thought, as if he was struggling to process his exact feelings about that ill-fated day. Finally he reported. "I wanted her to leave my mommy and my sister alone. When my mommy shot her, I guess I was glad because she couldn't hurt them anymore. But I was still scared."

Dr. Hooper nodded her head in understanding. Shauntae stared at her little brother with compassion and complete awareness of what he was talking about.

"Okay, Shauntae, it's your turn to tell me how you felt on that day."

"I felt pretty much the same as my brother did. I was very scared when she attacked my mother, and I felt I had to help her. When she turned her attack on me, I was happy that my mother was able to get her to stop hurting us, but terrified that she actually shot her."

Dr. Hooper looked at both children, clearly able to accept their similar stories as factual accounts of their true feelings. She jotted down a few more notes, then continued with her evaluation. "Now that you realize Rhonda was your brother Sha'Ron's mother, does that make you feel anything different? Shaun, again, I want you to speak first."

"I feel bad that his mother is dead, and I feel sad that my mother killed her. I'm glad that my mommy is not dead, though, and that Rhonda didn't kill my mommy."

Honest. Very good, Dr. Hooper thought. "Okay. Your turn, Shauntae."

"I feel very bad for Sha'Ron," Shauntae began without hesitation. "The other day when everyone else's mother arrived to pick them up and his wasn't there I just wanted to cry for him. I also felt guilty because it was my own mother who took his mother away from him. Like Li'l Shaun said, I'm glad our mom wasn't killed, but I wish there was something else that could have happened for Sha'Ron's sake."

Again, Dr. Hooper inwardly applauded the children's honesty, and she reflected such in her notepad.

"Okay, you two, here is a more difficult question for you to answer. Because your mother killed your father, as well as Sha'Ron's mother, she had to go to prison for a couple of years. How did her being away from you all of that time make you feel about her? Shauntae, why don't you start this time?"

Dr. Hooper chose Shauntae to go first despite her belief that Shaun would have parroted all of his sister's previous replies. She trusted this time he would be more apt to express his own true feelings because he had done so before. She hoped her instinct would prove correct.

"I'm not sure how to answer that question, Dr. Hooper," Shauntae said.

"Just tell me how you honestly felt while your mother was in prison. There are not right or wrong answers to anything I ask. I just want the truth about your feelings. That's it."

"Well, I think my grandmother took really good care of my brother and me. Cody helped too. But it was really hard not having my mother there all the time. Going to visit her was hard too. I mean, I liked when we were able to see her, but having to leave her, leaving her behind in that prison, drove me a little bit crazy every time." Shauntae paused to collect her thoughts. She stared off a little as if remembering and reliving the painful times when she said good-bye to her mother while she was in prison.

"It was kind of embarrassing to have a mother who was in prison, not to mention that she was there because she killed two people. Having to explain that to my friends and classmates was not cool. I sometimes just wanted to tell people she was dead. It seemed like the easier thing to do. But I didn't want to speak a curse on her, so I never said that."

Sensing that Shauntae had completed her explanation, Dr. Hooper asked Shaun to state his feelings.

"I love Grandma, and I love Cody. But I really missed my mom. I used to cry a lot at first. I was so sad. I didn't talk about her being in jail with my friends. When people would ask about my mother, I would just say she left and now we live with our grandmother. When she came home, I told them she came back from a long work trip."

"Okay. You two did a great job sharing your thoughts and feelings. Our session today was what we will call a consultation. I needed to hear from you all to find out what's going on inside of you. Now it's up to your mother to decide if she thinks you will return to see me.

If she thinks it's a good idea, then I will see the two of you twice a month. Now, let me get you back to your mother so I can speak briefly with her."

The three of them walked back to the reception area. Dr. Hooper summoned Lindsay while she instructed the kids to sit for just a few moments. Lindsay started in before Dr. Hooper had a chance to utter a word.

"How did it go, Dr. Hooper? Did they tell you anything? Were they open and honest with you?"

Dr. Hooper placed her hands on Lindsay's shoulders to calm and steady her. Lindsay recognized the gesture and took a deep breath. Dr. Hooper then began to answer her questions.

"Shauntae and Shaun were both very open and very honest. They have dealt with quite a lot. I believe they have handled themselves amazingly well under the circumstances. At any rate, I do believe they will benefit from therapy. I would also like to recommend that you and your husband continue to allow and encourage them to spend time with their half siblings. This is very important to both children. If you would like them to continue with me, you can set up an appointment with the receptionist for two weeks from today. We will then keep it at that pace for an initial six months."

Lindsay nodded as the doctor spoke. She was pleased with what she heard, even though the information was a lot less thorough than she would have liked. She understood, however, this was how therapists acted with their clients.

"Do you think I will have an opportunity to sit in with them during your sessions?"

"Certainly. At times it will be absolutely necessary."

"Okay, then, I guess you are their psychologist, Dr. Hooper." Lindsay extended her hand, and the doctor shook it very professionally.

Lindsay made an appointment with the receptionist as instructed; then she and the children headed home. The ride to the house was quiet though neither of the children seemed sullen. Lindsay just allowed them to process their initial therapy session without bombarding them with a million questions. The moment they got into the house the quiet came to an end.

"Mom, I'm going to call Sha'Ron and see when we can all get together again."

"Yay!" was Li'l Shaun's response to his sister's announcement.

Lindsay started to protest because she felt the kids should wait until Sha'Ron called them. She didn't want them to set themselves up for a letdown if he decided he didn't really want to be bothered with his younger siblings beyond last week. She then remembered what Dr. Hooper said about encouraging the relationships with their half siblings.

"Uh, okay. Just let me know what he says so we can plan accordingly," Lindsay replied.

Shauntae raced off to her room to make the phone call. She returned to the family room about fifteen minutes later, just when Cody walked into the house and kissed her mom. She gave both parents an update.

"Hi, Cody. Mom, Sha'Ron said we can get together today if it's cool with everyone else. I'm going to call Kevaun. Sha'Ron says he will get in touch with Shauna's mom. I hope she says yes. I really want to see my little sister. Is it okay for us to go, Mom?"

"Go where?" Cody asked as he was clueless about the conversation his wife and stepdaughter were having.

"Shauntae and Li'l Shaun want to hang out with their siblings today," she explained to Cody. She then readdressed Shauntae. "Isn't this short notice, sweetie? Where will you all go?"

"Sha'Ron says we can all meet at Fairlane Mall and hang out for a while. We can get something to eat and just kick it with each other there. Please can we go, Mom?"

"Please?" Li'l Shaun added.

"Shauntae, give me a few minutes to talk with Cody about this, then I'll let you know. Just fifteen minutes, okay?"

Shauntae looked a little defeated, but decided not to give up hope just yet. She and Li'l Shaun walked up the stairs and both went into her room while they awaited the verdict. Shauntae decided to call Kevaun and at least alert him to the possibility.

Lindsay gave Cody the rundown on what happened with the therapist. "She feels we should encourage the children's interaction with their siblings," she concluded.

"I don't disagree with her. I think they should spend as much time as possible with each other," Cody replied.

"I'm no longer against this, necessarily, Cody. It just sounds like the kids are planning this outing to be without any chaperones. I don't know if they are ready for that yet."

"Are you worried about them being ready or you being ready?"

"Both," Lindsay openly admitted. "I know what the psychologist said, and I trust her judgment. But she doesn't know that Sha'Ron is a petty drug dealer."

"I understand your concern, baby, but it's an open public mall. How much trouble can they get into? And you know the security doesn't play at Fairlane Mall."

Lindsay looked into Cody's eyes, and he could see his wife acquiescing. "We'll drop them off, give them a time limit, and be right there to pick them up. It will be fine, Lindsay."

"Okay. Fine. I'm going to trust your judgment." Lindsay called the kids and gave them the news.

"Yes! Thank you, Mom," Shauntae exclaimed excited.

"Thank you, Mommy," Li'l Shaun repeated as he hugged first his mother, then Cody, and finally his sister.

"What time are you all supposed to meet?" Cody asked.

"Sha'Ron says we can meet right outside of Sears at about four. Is that all right?" Shauntae asked.

"That's fine," Lindsay said. "Cody and I will drop you two off; then we will come back and get you, let's say, around seven."

"Okay. I'm gonna go and call Sha'Ron and Kevaun and let them know everything is cool. I can't wait to meet my little sister."

"Me too," Li'l Shaun said as he followed Shauntae right on her heels as she left the room.

Chapter Ten

At 4:00 P.M., Cody and Lindsay parked close to the Sears entrance of the mall. Lindsay decided to stay in the car so she wouldn't again upset Sha'Ron. She saw Keva walking up to the entrance with Kevaun just as Cody approached with the kids. She then watched them disappear into the mall to escape the cold.

When Cody returned, Keva was with him. "Hey, girl," she said to Lindsay.

"Hey. Good to see you again." Lindsay exited the car to embrace Keva.

"So what are you going to do with these few hours of free time?" Lindsay asked Keva.

"My husband, Cheval, and I are going to catch a movie at the theater right on the other side of this mall. He's over there getting the tickets now."

"Oh. I wish I could have met him. I feel much better knowing that you won't be too far away from the kids."

"That's the plan," Keva assured Lindsay. "So what are you going to get into?"

"It just hit me. My wife and I are going to go home and spend a good quality few hours with each other." Cody smiled mischievously at Lindsay. She returned his grin catching his meaning and liking his thought process.

"All right then! I ain't mad at cha," Keva laughed. "Enjoy. And if you don't have a problem with it, I can drop the kids off after we are all done here. I'll make sure they are home no later than eight P.M."

"That'll work," Lindsay said. "Let me give you our address." She reached into the car to grab her purse to retrieve a pen and something to write on; then she handed Keva the paper and gave her a hug before slipping back into the warm vehicle.

"Okay, you two, I'll see you in a little while." Keva jogged quickly to her own car as Cody pulled from the parking space.

"I wonder if Tawanda is going to bring her daughter."

"Shauna was there already. She came with Sha'Ron," Cody explained. Lindsay nodded her understanding.

"So what do you say when we get home, we start talking about us having another child?"

Lindsay's clear eyes became as big as flying saucers. She choked on her own saliva and fell into a fit of coughs, spitting and sputtering while Cody stared at her in horror. He decided to pull into the first available parking spot to make sure his wife was going to be okay.

"Baby, what happened? Are you okay?" Cody grabbed her right arm and held it high above her head while gently rubbing her chest with his other hand. To those passing by, it probably looked as if he were publicly fondling a woman in the mall parking lot. But Cody was far beyond caring what anyone thought. His only concern was Lindsay's health.

After a few more moments the coughing stopped and Lindsay was able to breathe normally again. Cody had caught her so very off guard with his question. There was no warning, no sign; nothing to prepare her for his request to start planning for another baby. She knew the subject would eventually resurface. In truth, there was nothing she could really do to prepare for it.

Not wanting to lie any longer to her husband, she decided she would finally tell him the truth. She would like to have the luxury of doing it in her home as he suggested.

"Cody, I'm fine now. Thank you. I'm sorry I startled you as I did."

Before she could expound further, Cody asked, "Does the thought of us having another child upset you so much, Lindsay?"

If you only knew, Lindsay thought. She was determined to tell him everything the moment they got home.

"Cody, I was a little taken by surprise by what you said, but, baby, as you said, we will discuss it when we get home."

Cody eyed her a little suspiciously, unsure why his talking about them having a baby would unnerve her so. This was not the first time he had brought up the subject, so why the distress? He would respect her desire to speak further once they reached home as she asked, however, and not bring it up again in the car.

Lindsay did her best to not allow her nervousness to show outwardly. She tried to keep her fidgeting to a minimum, but she had no control over the perspiration that broke out on her forehead and upper lip. What would she say? How would she explain what was going through her head and heart at that time in her life?

Prayer! Prayer is what she needed right now. For the duration of the ride home, Lindsay closed her eyes and prayed about how to best tell Cody news that would crush him and possibly change the way he viewed her forever. . . .

***

When the couple arrived at their home, Lindsay was more nervous than she ever remembered being; and it showed. Cody became so concerned, he wasn't sure if he wanted to have the conversation anymore.

"Lindsay, baby, I don't know why the subject of us trying to have another child discombobulated you so, but clearly it did. Maybe we should talk a little later in the future. You are obviously not ready to talk about this now, let alone begin planning to make it happen," Cody expressed once they got in the house.

Lindsay's shoulders visibly relaxed. Her eyes instantly brightened, and the beginnings of a smile began to show on her face. She couldn't believe she had actually dodged the bullet that could have possibly ended the life of her marriage.

"Cody, no, baby. We need to talk. There's something I need to tell you." *What! Did that just come from my mouth?* Lindsay thought.

Cody sat on the sofa in the family room. Lindsay sat across from him on the love seat. Cody found the seating arrangements to be odd, which further added to his bemusement about this whole situation. He said nothing, however. He simply sat quietly waiting for his wife to shed some light on this dark cloud of confusion.

"Cody, I don't even know how to begin. But I need you to allow me to speak, to just get this all out before I chicken out and change my mind. Please don't interrupt me until I'm done."

Cody nodded his head in agreement while his heart beat to a crazy tune of the fear medley that played within him. He was now very afraid of what Lindsay was going to tell him, though he had no idea what it could possibly be.

Lindsay took a deep breath in an effort to steady her nerves, to absolutely no avail. No amount of oxygen or carbon monoxide was going to help her deliver to her husband the most difficult news she had ever had to share with him. So she forged ahead.

"Cody, back when we were involved in our affair, while I was still married to Shaun, I became pregnant with your baby. Because I believed I still loved Shaun and I wanted our marriage to work, I aborted that baby."

Cody's face registered a level of complete shock and extreme pain. His features contorted into an expression Lindsay had never before seen on her husband's face. She kept talking to stay with the momentum; otherwise, she would retreat and begin lying, doing her best to convince Cody she made up her story and create some crazy reason as to why.

"Because of my spiritual beliefs, I started feeling very guilty and very convicted for having destroyed the life of my baby. So I punished myself even further by taking away my ability to ever conceive again. I had a tubal ligation and had the doctor fix it so the procedure was irreversible. Cody, I can no longer have children."

Cody crossed the room in a flash, pulled Lindsay up by both her arms, and screamed in her face. "I need for you to look me in the eyes and tell me that I did not just hear you say that you aborted my child without telling me *and* that you can never have a baby with me!"

Lindsay dropped her head and began to sob as she nodded her confirmation to Cody's statement.

"No! I said for you to look me in my face." He roughly grabbed her chin, forcing her to face him.

"Cody, I aborted the baby we conceived together. Now I can't have any more children." She choked out the words in spite of the sobs in her voice and the watery pain that poured from her eyes.

Cody stared at Lindsay for what seemed like hours. He held his stare long and brutally hard, never moving a muscle. Lindsay dared not look away from the cruel expression painted on his face. She was frightened of Cody for the first time since knowing him. From somewhere in the recesses of her mind, she remembered the one time Shaun, or any man, for that matter, had ever hit her. She remembered that it was because of something she had done with respect to his child. Now she stood before Cody, who also looked like he could beat her unconscious because of what she had done to his child.

Suddenly Cody moved, and Lindsay jumped. Before she realized what happened, he shoved her onto the love seat and quickly stalked away from her.

Lindsay sat stunned on the love seat in the same position for a very long time. She cried as her eyes and chest burned. She continued to cry even when she believed there was no more water left in her body. She cried until she heard the side door slam and the sound of the garage door being raised. She then bolted upright and ran to the door just in time to see Cody backing out of the driveway.

Lindsay ran upstairs to their bedroom to find her nightmare had gotten worse. Cody had packed a suitcase before he left, letting her know his return would be none too immediate. She flopped onto the bed and cried some more.

Lindsay wanted to call Cody, to ask him where he was and where he was going. She wanted to know if he would ever be able to forgive her and if he planned to stay married to her. She desperately needed to know the answer to these questions, but she was equally afraid of what she might hear in his voice—if he even bothered to answer the phone. What if he told her he was completely done with her, her children, and their marriage? What if she heard hate in his voice? No! She decided it was best not to phone him because she knew she couldn't handle hearing anything other than he was on his way home.

Lindsay lay in bed wallowing in her misery until she heard Shauntae call for her once she and Li'l Shaun returned from their visit with their siblings. Lindsay had been so miserable that she had actually forgotten the children were out or what time they were due to return.

"Mom, we're home. Can you come down? Ms. Keva wants to talk to you," Shauntae yelled from the bottom of the stairs.

Oh no, Lindsay thought. Now was not the time for her to have a conversation with anyone. She did not want her children to see her this distraught. Nor did she want Keva to know she was having such serious trouble in her marriage.

"Mom, are you here?"

"Yes, baby. I'm in my bedroom." Lindsay did her best to keep her voice from cracking under the weight of her sorrow. She decided instantly to get up and put on a fictitious bravado for the sake of her children and the brief visit of her houseguest.

She jumped from the bed and went to her bathroom to do her best to right her face. She then headed downstairs with the express intent of quickly getting rid of Keva. She would decide how to deal with her children after that.

"Hey, you two," Lindsay said as she individually hugged each child. "I hope you had a great time. I want you to tell me all about it as soon as I'm done talking with Ms. Keva."

The kids acquiesced to their mother's request. They took off up the stairs, each headed to their respective rooms.

"Okay, girl, what's up? Your eyes are as red as fire engines and as swollen as my belly will be soon. Do you want to talk about it?"

Lindsay didn't realize how badly she looked. She stood with her mouth gaping wide open after Keva's assessment and seemingly sincere offer to listen to what was ailing her heart. Keva's instinct reminded her of how Shyanne always knew when something was not right with her. Realizing how much she needed and truly missed her best friend was nearly her undoing right in front of Keva.

"Don't worry about me, Keva. I'm fine. Thank you for bringing my kids home. Now go on and get back to your . . . husband . . . before he leaves . . . you." Lindsay's voice cracked and the tears came tumbling down.

"Nay, girl, give me one minute. I'll be right back," Keva said before exiting the foyer. She quickly returned to find Lindsay still standing in the same spot as if the tears that fell from her eyes and landed on the floor caused her to grow roots to that very spot.

"Let's go in the family room and talk." Keva gently pulled Lindsay in the direction she wanted her to walk. She moved like a zombie, seemingly unaware of what was going on around her.

Once they reached the family room, Keva gently positioned Lindsay onto the sofa, then sat down right beside her, holding both her hands.

"Talk to me, Nay. Tell me what has you so broken-hearted."

Lindsay continued for several moments to sit catatonic, not mumbling a word. Finally, though, she began to rub Keva's hands. Keva was happy to see some sign of normalcy, but she didn't want to rush Lindsay into anything. She patiently waited until she was ready to talk.

"He left me, Keva. Cody packed his stuff and left me."

"What? Why? What happened? You two seemed fine just a couple of hours ago," Keva replied in total shock.

"We were fine a couple of hours ago, sort of, anyway. The thing that happened today actually started several years ago. Cody just found out about it today."

"Is it something you can talk about? If it's not, I can just sit here with you and we can talk about nothing in particular until you feel better."

Lindsay looked at the woman who sat next to her gently caressing her hand and saw Keva's face, but the voice came from a heart that reminded her of Shyanne. Before she knew it, she had given Keva the full lowdown on why her husband had left her.

"So there is my drama in a nutshell. I kept the truth from him, I can no longer have children, and he has left me."

"Wow, Nay. That is rough. But listen to me. I don't know your husband very well. In actuality, not at all, but the fact that he orchestrated the reunion with the kids, the fact that he loved you through all of your drama with Shaun, and the fact that he's a Christian speaks volumes about your husband. Sure, he's upset right now, but I think he will come around and forgive you. I can't say, nor will I hazard a guess at when he will return, but I believe in my heart that he will come home."

"I hope you're correct, Keva. I really hope you are." Lindsay began crying again as she silently prayed that Keva's prophecy was true.

Keva wrapped her arms around Lindsay, simultaneously hugging her and rubbing her back. She held on until the tears subsided and Lindsay was able to speak again.

"Thank you so much for listening to me and staying with me. I assume you sent your husband home. If you're ready to go, I'll get ready to drive you home."

"How about I stay here with you? I feel like you are going to need some help getting through this evening if Cody doesn't come home tonight."

"Keva, I can't ask you to do that. What about your husband and child?"

"You didn't ask. I offered. Cheval and Kevaun will be okay for one night. Trust me. It's all good."

As if the matter was completely settled, Keva pulled her cell phone from her purse and dialed her husband. She explained to him that Lindsay needed her to stay. He obviously gave his blessing, and Keva ended the call, telling him she loved him. Hearing Keva share such love with her husband caused more tears to fall from Lindsay's eyes. She controlled herself this time, only allowing her eyes to water. No sobs.

"Nay, girl, I hate you are dealing with this, but I'm here for you. You go ahead and cry, weep, fall apart if you need to. This is a very difficult situation. God is here with us. He will catch your tears while I hold your hand."

Lindsay lay her head on Keva's shoulder and let her grief have its way. For about half an hour she cried. After the storm from her eyes let up a bit, Keva gave her a bottle of water. She rehydrated herself, then went to check on her children. She kissed them good night, then returned to Keva in the family room.

Keva scooted over a little on the sofa to make room for Lindsay, but stayed close enough to extend her hand if needed. Lindsay sat down. The two sat in silence as Lindsay flipped through the channels until she found an interesting looking Lifetime movie. After watching it for a little while, Lindsay reached for Keva's hand and squeezed it. No words were needed. The gesture spoke volumes.

Chapter Eleven

The crisp sun shining through the big windows woke Lindsay from a fitful and uncomfortable sleep. As she twisted she remembered she was on the sofa in the family room, not on the bed in her bedroom. She also realized she was not alone on the couch. She uncurled her body and sat up to find a head full of jet-black hair peeking from beneath the blanketed body of the person who shared her sleeping space. A head and body shaped very differently than that of her normal sleeping companion.

Suddenly everything became clear. The events of yesterday came back to her with a rush. Lindsay wrapped her arms around her waist and began rocking back and forth. The constant, forceful movement caused Keva to slowly wake from her slumber. She sleepily moved her body to where Lindsay sat. Then she wrapped her arms about Lindsay's shoulders.

"Keva, he's gone. I can't believe he left me." There were no tears, but the anguish could be heard in every syllable Lindsay uttered.

Keva continued to hold Lindsay, but she did so in a way to still her moving body. She was trying to get her to focus so she would listen to her.

"Nay-Nay, Cody is very upset right now, but he is also a very good man. I believe in my heart and soul that his being gone is only temporary. He loves you and the kids. He will be back. I'm sure of it, Nay."

Lindsay heard Keva loud and clear, because she truly needed to believe her words. She let them sink in and permeate her own heart and soul.

"Okay, Keva. I'm going to hold you to your word and trust that you are telling the truth." Lindsay unfolded her arms from her waist and placed them around Keva. Keva returned her embrace.

Lindsay looked at the cable box to find that it was 6:45 A.M. "I'm going to make breakfast, then get the kids up so we can go to church. I hope Cody comes to service this morning. Will you stay for breakfast?"

Keva thought about it for a moment then answered. "Sure, I'll stay. You owe me a good, hot cooked meal after subjecting me to having to sleep with your feet in my face." Both women cracked up laughing.

"I'll get you a sweat suit to put on so you can at least change clothes. There are extra toothbrushes upstairs in the kids' bathroom. You can go in and take a shower before they get up, if you want." Keva and Lindsay extracted themselves from their sleeping quarters and headed up the stairs. After getting Keva settled, Lindsay went back downstairs to cook breakfast.

After breakfast, Keva call Cheval to come and pick her up from the Vincini house. She then got ready to return home to her family while Lindsay and the kids began preparing for church.

"Mom, where's Cody? It just hit me that he did not come down for breakfast." Shauntae stared at her mother expectantly waiting for what she assumed would be a very simple answer.

Lindsay felt as if she had never been caught so unprepared in her life. How was she supposed to explain Cody's absence to the children?

"Cody had a client in need of a friend last night so he went to stay with him. You know how giving your stepdad is," Keva quickly replied. Shauntae accepted Keva's answer, and she and Li'l Shaun headed upstairs to get ready for church.

"Thank you so much, Keva, for thinking on your feet like that. I had no idea what I was supposed to say to her. I hate that you had to lie for me, but I sure appreciate you for it," Lindsay said.

"Yeah, I hate lying too these days, but I really didn't know what else to say to her. I'll take that sin to church with me and leave it on the altar this morning." Keva and Lindsay shared a laugh. Soon, however, Lindsay's chuckles turned into small sniffles. Keva was again quick to respond with a tender hug.

"I'm sorry to be such a watery mess, Keva. I'm very concerned about my marriage. But I'm also a little melancholy because you staying here with me last night and supporting me as you have reminds me of Shyanne. You are doing for me exactly what she would be doing if she were still alive. Truthfully, I'm not sure I deserve it. I have made such a mess of everything."

Keva released her embrace on Lindsay and simply held her by both shoulders, staring at her directly in the eyes. "Nay-Nay, come on now. You know better than this. Nothing good is going to come from you wallowing in self-pity or in the pain of the past. No amount of sorrow-filled words can change the outcome of your life's previous events. I need you to start speaking new life into your present situation. I need you to trust God. Start praying, saying, and believing that Cody will come back and that the two of you will work through this because God has ordained your marriage. You hold the power of life and death in your tongue, Nay. Use that power for good."

Lindsay returned Keva's stare while allowing her words to softly, but purposefully, sink into her spirit.

She dried her tears and determined in that instant that she would take control of this mess with her husband with prayer and positivity. She knew also at that very moment that God was with her and wanted to bless her.

"Keva, I know I can never replace Shyanne in my heart or in my life, but I am praising God right now for sending you to me to help me get through this. You are being a wonderful friend and sister in Christ. My debt to you is really big."

It was Lindsay who reached for Keva this time and hugged her gratefully. She did not shed a tear because she fully understood that God was infusing strength into her through Keva.

"Lindsay, and forgive me for using your given name, but, Lindsay, I am honored to be your friend and to serve God in this way by being here for you. It's my way of glorifying Him for forgiving me for all the messes I have made in my life, including all that transpired between us when we met in that old life. You owe me nothing, girl. The chance to make things different between us is payment enough." The two women shared a smile that forged a bond that would from that point on seal a lifelong friendship.

Keva left to go home when Cheval called her cell phone to let her know he had arrived. She had to rush and get ready for her own church service while Lindsay did the same for herself and her children. Just before leaving, Lindsay prayed that she would see her husband when she arrived at church.

Cody woke up with a headache the size of the Detroit River. His mouth was dry, and he felt as if he had a hole in the center of his chest. The hotel room was cold despite the heat blowing from the vent over the bed and the fact that he was still fully clothed. Once he rented the room, he came right in and fell across the bed.

Last night had been one of the worst evenings of Cody's life. Never in a million years could he have imagined that he could be hurt like this by the woman he loved more than air. For a long time he loved her more than he loved God, at least until he knew better. But with God only having a slight edge over his wife, he loved her fiercely. He would have sworn to Jesus Himself that his love for her was also unconditional. Wow.

Cody sat up on the bed contemplating whether he was going to go to church. He knew Lindsay would be there, expecting, hoping, to see him there. He knew his baby well. In all honesty, he wasn't sure he was emotionally prepared to see her just yet.

Cody thought back to the very first time he laid eyes on Lindsay Westbrook Taylor. She was married to one of his best-paying clients. Shaun kept his practice thriving, even though he had not had any personal legal troubles. At least not until the day Cody met his beautiful wife. One minute she was looking into his eyes, her attraction to him obvious. He'd seen the look in the eyes of many of his clients' wives and girlfriends. The next thing he knew, she was throwing up on his shoes. He chuckled as he thought about her humiliation afterward. By the time he left her home later that evening, he was pretty smitten by his client's wife.

Cody wrestled with himself for several months about the attraction he had for Lindsay Taylor. Professional ethics wasn't really his concern. After all, he represented the biggest drug dealers in the city of Detroit. No. It was that he was never the type of man who would intentionally go after another man's woman, even though the opportunities presented themselves to him constantly. There was something about Lindsay, though, something on the inside of her that drew him in and caused him to want to cherish her for life. From day one, Cody had thought her to be perfect; at least until the confession last night.

He knew he still loved her with all his heart, knew that he would probably always love her until God removed his heart from his chest. But he felt as if he could never trust her again. Her deception and her decision not to tell him about the abortion were brutal on his soul.

He tried to see things from her perspective. He tried to understand that she had to be in great turmoil once she found out she was carrying his child while she was still married to Shaun. But the only thing he could feel was the hurt that crushed his heart the day she told him she didn't love him, told him that she loved her husband and that no matter how badly he treated her, she would always love him. She told him that while she was carrying his child, unbeknownst to them both at that time.

Cody felt as if he had given all of himself to Lindsay from the very beginning, at a time when she could only offer him a part of herself. But he accepted what she offered until she pulled it away. But still he loved her. He loved her from a distance, but with no less intensity. When he heard about Shyanne's murder, he almost died too thinking about the heartache Lindsay had to be enduring. He loved her then, not knowing how she already put into effect the events that would lead him to the hotel room last night.

And even still, he loved her. He loved her, but he wasn't ready to see her. He could not go to church.

***

While getting dressed, Sha'Ron contemplated his decision to meet his sister and brother at church. Finding out from Shauntae what church they attended seemed almost too easy. All he had to do was ask in very casual conversation while they were hanging out the other day. But to use her to get a line on her moms was probably not a good look.

On the other hand, he realized a man has got to do what a man has got to do. And make no mistake about it; he was going to be the man that took his former stepmom down for killing his parents.

Sha'Ron had not set foot in a church since his father's funeral. His mom's funeral, which was a week after his dad's, was at a mortuary. He didn't remember going to church before his dad's funeral either. So going to the so-called house of the Lord was new for him. But he was going to make sure he looked good. He was going to look the part of a regular churchgoing young man. He did not want to stand out.

Sha'Ron prided himself on being a stylish dresser. His swag on the streets among his peers was unmatched. He was not about to drop a step because he was going to a church. So he carefully chose a black Sean John two-piece suit, an outfit purchased specifically for the funeral of a seventeen-year-old young hood who Sha'Ron had hung out with. He paired the suit with a tan button-down Rocawear shirt, a black-and-caramel-colored tie, not the clip-on either, and a pair of tan Tims. A quick once-over in his full-length mirror on the back of his bedroom door confirmed that he was going to be able to pull off the church-boy look.

Sha'Ron stopped by his grandmother's bedroom to let her know he was leaving.

"Grandma, I'm going out for a while. I'll be back in a few hours."

"Where you going, boy?"

"Church."

"Church? What you going to church for? Is there a funeral on Sunday?"

Patricia began an uncontrollable coughing fit after having strung so many syllables together at one time. Sha'Ron reached for her water glass and found it empty. He hurried to the kitchen to refill it, then rushed back to the bedroom to help his grandmother.

"Here, Grandma. Drink this."

Patricia attempted to sit up and take the glass from Sha'Ron but she was coughing so hard she dropped the glass and spilled water all over the bed before it was completely in her grasp.

Sha'Ron became visibly agitated. His grandmother's mess was going to possibly make him late since he had to now get her into dry pajamas and change the sheets on the bed. His plan was to be standing in the entryway of the church awaiting the arrival of his siblings, his former stepmom, and her husband. He wanted to startle Lindsay, give her a moment of pause. He had not told Li'l Shaun or Shauntae of his intention to join them for church, so everyone was sure to be surprised. Now his plan was going to be ruined because he would not be able to get there early.

Sha'Ron lifted his grandmother's weak and wet body from her bed and sat her in the chair beside it.

"Hey, Nephew. What's up? What you all dressed up for?"

Sha'Ron had never been so glad to see his aunt Tameeka in his short life. Her entrance into his grandmother's bedroom almost made him want to fall to his knees and thank God.

"Auntie Meek. I'm so glad to see you're here. Grand just spilled water all over herself and the bed. Can you get her changed? I'm on my way to church, and I don't want to be late."

"Church! Boy, when did you start going to church?" Tameeka questioned with a frown on her face.

"I'm just going today with Li'l Shaun and Shauntae. Can you take care of Grandma for me?"

"Li'l Shaun and Shauntae? What about they mama? Is she gon' be there?" Tameeka continued to question her nephew while she began doing as he asked with her mother.

"I want to know the same thing, Sha'Ron. Is . . . that . . . heffa gon' . . . be there? If she . . . is, I outta go . . . too . . . so I can . . . knock her . . . upside . . . her head." Again, Patricia spoke between coughs.

Sha'Ron went to replenish the glass of water while Tameeka lowered her mother back into the chair.

"Sha'Ron, how you gon' be around the stupid chick that killed yo' mama and daddy and not go off, in a church, no less?"

Sha'Ron knew he couldn't tell his aunt or grandmother about his plan to eventually kill Lindsay, although the two of them probably wouldn't give too much resistance. Still he knew that it would be best to keep his and Uncle Bobby's plan a secret for now. So he had to think quickly to keep the two ladies from tripping.

"No. That whack chick won't be there. That's why my little brother and sister asked me to come. They said their moms was out of town with their grandma. Cody is bringing the kids to church."

"Humph. Like Mama said, maybe she should be there so I can go and give her a royal beat down."

Sha'Ron was happy that his aunt and grandmother believed him without asking any additional questions. "Well, she won't be there, so don't worry about it. I gotta go so I can get there on time. Thanks, Auntie, for taking care of Grandma."

"Hold up one second, Sha'Ron." Tameeka left her mother's bedroom on Sha'Ron's heels as he headed for the front door. "I wouldn't mind seeing my little niece and nephew soon. See if you can hook that up with White Boy, all right?"

Sha'Ron nodded his consent as he raced out the door. He drove swiftly to the church, exceeding the speed limit by at least ten miles, hoping he didn't run into any police. The last thing he needed was to be further delayed by a cop writing him a ticket. He was still hoping to get to the church before his evil ex-stepmom.

The parking lot was crowded, which meant the church was already filling up with people. Sha'Ron could only hope Lindsay was like most women; always running late. He parked his car in the closest spot he could find and speed walked across the parking lot.

Sha'Ron got inside the church and found a spot in the modest-sized narthex that would give him a great view of everyone that crossed the church's threshold. People were coming in constantly, and Sha'Ron kept his eyes glued to those double doors. He peered so diligently that he didn't notice the middle-aged woman who approached him on his left side.

"Hello, young man. Such a handsome face, yet I don't recognize you. I would remember seeing someone as good looking as yourself. Are you a visitor here at Tribe of Judah Baptist Church?"

Sha'Ron diverted his eyes long enough for him to answer the woman. "Yes, ma'am." He quickly turned back to the entrance.

"Are you here with your parents?"

At the mention of his parents, Sha'Ron focused more intently on the woman speaking to him. While he knew she had no idea of the impact her question had on him, he stared at her through squinted eyes that spoke of anger. He pondered her question, realizing that it was the absence of his parents that had him stalking his ex-stepmom in a church lobby.

"No. I'm all alone," Sha'Ron answered grimly.

Neither Sha'Ron's tone nor his demeanor went unnoticed by Sister Blakely, the church's head greeter, but she continued talking to the sullen stranger in an effort to welcome him to their church. "Well, young man, you are never alone when you walk with Jesus. What's your name, handsome?"

"Sha'Ron!" Li'l Shaun squealed as he ran to his big brother.

Shauntae joined her little brother in greeting their oldest sibling. "Hey, Sha'Ron. What are you doing here? You didn't tell us you were coming to our church today."

"Well, now, by using a little deductive reasoning, I'm going to venture to guess that your name is Sha'Ron." Sister Blakely laughed at her own joke.

"Mrs. Blakely, this is our brother Sha'Ron. I guess he has decided to pay us a surprise visit today," Shauntae supplied for the greeter.

Mrs. Blakely eyed both Shauntae and Sha'Ron a little suspiciously. She was unaware of the two children having any additional siblings. She knew that Lindsay was newly married, however. *Perhaps this young man was Cody's son, although I can't visibly see any Italian features in him*, she thought to herself. She then looked at Lindsay to see if she was going to offer any explanation. All she saw there, though, was fear and confusion.

"Okay." Mrs. Blakely announced, mystified. "Now that your family is here, I'll leave you in their capable hands. You all have a great time in service." To Lindsay directly, she said, "It's nice to see you, Nay-Nay." She then headed in the direction of the sanctuary.

Seeing Shauntae and Shaun beam in their brother's presence made Lindsay's heart leap. She was glad her children enjoyed being around their brother so much. Seeing Sha'Ron made her heart hesitate. While her kids were obviously quite comfortable around him, she was anything but. The mixed emotions she experienced made her heart temporarily forget its ache for her estranged husband.

Lindsay cautiously approached the area where her children stood with Sha'Ron. She felt as if her tongue were glued to the roof of her mouth and all other empty spaces inside her mouth were filled with cotton balls. She could not speak for the life of her. She had no clue about what she could or should say to Sha'Ron.

"Hello, Sha'Ron. Glad to have you with us today. Have you seen Cody since you've been here?" She was amazed at even herself to have found something to say. Her question brought back her heartache.

"No." His answer was abrupt, rude; filled with contempt.

Lindsay was somewhat startled but not totally surprised by Sha'Ron's anger. While she was awaiting his response, she had formulated in her mind the intention to ask him to sit with her and the kids. Now, however, she knew that was probably the last thing he wanted to hear come out of her mouth.

"Shauntae, Li'l Shaun, come on and let's get ourselves seated." Lindsay eyed Sha'Ron warily for another second; then she headed toward the sanctuary, expecting the kids to immediately follow behind her.

"Mom, can we sit with Sha'Ron today since he came to visit?" Shauntae could feel the understandable tension between her mother and her big brother. So insisting that Sha'Ron sit with them, she knew, was not a good idea.

Lindsay stopped in her tracks and turned to face her daughter. At that moment she also saw the face of Sha'Ron. She, without a doubt, saw unmasked hatred in his eyes as he faced her down.

Lindsay's first thought was to deny her daughter's request. But she just as quickly realized Sha'Ron's anger was directed at her, not her children.

"Okay. That's fine. But after service, I want you to meet me right here in the narthex, understand?"

Both kids agreed before pulling Sha'Ron by the arm into the sanctuary. Before giving his siblings his full attention, however, he gave Lindsay one final glare.

The menacing grimace he shot at her made Lindsay want to reconsider her decision to allow the kids to sit with him. But again, her reasoning revealed that Sha'Ron had good cause to be upset with her. So she would not punish the kids for the bad blood between her and their brother. She then decided to focus her energies elsewhere, like finding her husband here in the church.

Lindsay sat in the pew wallowing in disappointment after she finally allowed herself to accept that Cody was not there. She knew beyond a shadow of a doubt that he had skipped church service today to avoid seeing her. She was so miserable that she barely heard a word of Pastor Adams's sermon. Couple her misery with her concern for her children being with Sha'Ron, a young man who visibly despised her, and her mind was a virtual wasteland for worry. Lindsay was so caught up in her own troubles that she did not even realize that Pastor Adams had given the benediction.

"Nay-Nay, girl, how you doing? How is your mama doing? That's right. She out in Phoenix. Well, what about that handsome husband of yours. Where is he today? And where are your babies?"

"Hi, Ms. Clara. The children are here. They are sitting with their . . . uh . . . with a friend. And Cody had to . . . uh . . . work today."

"Oh. Okay. Well, you and your family have a blessed rest of the day." Ms. Clara smiled and departed.

Lindsay looked up to find several other members coming her way. She really wanted to avoid them so that she could make her way back to the children. She still felt ill at ease with them being around Sha'Ron today. She was also concerned with folks asking her about Cody's absence. She didn't want to continue to tell lies, but she could never let anyone at church know that Cody had left her; especially so soon into their marriage.

Lindsay tried exiting the pew as quickly as she could before anyone could reach her. She was able to maneuver her way back about six pews, halfway to where she needed to be.

"Sister Nay, Pastor Adams would like to speak with you for a moment before you leave."

Lindsay turned to find Pastor's assistant, Tina, giving her the request. She stood confused about whether she should refuse to speak to Pastor Adams. She really needed to get her kids away from Sha'Ron, and she knew that Pastor Adams was going to question her about her and Cody's situation. She decided to compromise.

"Tina, tell Pastor Adams I'll be right with him. I just need to get my kids settled."

As Tina went off to deliver the message, Lindsay started to figure this could be okay. She could first get her kids away from their brother. Then she could use their presence as a reason not to get into a deep conversation with Pastor Adams.

Finally she made it back to the narthex where the kids stood waiting . . . alone.

"Hey, you two. Where's Sha'Ron?"

"He left already. He said he had to go take care of our grandma. He said she's real sick, Mom, and she wants to see us." This information was delivered by her baby, Li'l Shaun.

"Can we go by there and see her soon, Mom?" Shaun-tae added.

"We can talk about setting something up once we get home," Lindsay replied.

"That's when Cody will be home and you have to talk to him first, right?"

Li'l Shaun's question caught her off guard. She was unprepared to answer it, so she did not.

"I have to go and talk with Pastor Adams really quickly. You two follow me."

Lindsay turned and headed toward the pastor's office, hoping the kids didn't start quizzing her about Cody again. The pain of not seeing him at church had her poor heart ready to leap from her chest. But she did not want the kids to know about their drama. Not yet.

She made it back to the pastor's office without further interrogation. Now all she had to do was get in, make her excuses, and get out before he had an opportunity to grill her.

"Hey, Tina, is Pastor in his office?" Lindsay asked.

"Yeah. You can go on in. He's waiting for you. The kids can have a seat out here with me."

Lindsay hesitated a moment. She hoped to take the kids in with her for more effect. She relented, however. She just had to let Pastor Adams know they were out here.

"Hi, Pastor. I really can't stay because Shauntae and Li'l Shaun are out there waiting on me." Lindsay didn't even bother sitting because she figured she would be dismissed in less than a minute.

"Don't worry about the children. I instructed Tina to take them to the kitchen and get them a snack. They'll be fine with her while we talk. Have a seat."

Lindsay's surprise was very visible. Pastor immediately noticed. "Nay, are you okay?"

"Uh, I'm fine, Pastor Adams. I'm fine," she repeated wearily. She then lowered herself very slowly into the seat Pastor Adams indicated with his hand.

Lindsay was unprepared for Pastor Adams's strategy. She thought her plan was foolproof. So she was sure she looked as silly as she felt since her eyes were bucked and her mouth hung open.

"Nay-Nay, why do you look so . . . afraid?"

Lindsay closed her mouth and lowered her head. She was ashamed of herself. She knew Pastor Adams simply wanted to help her in light of what she had shared with him a couple of weeks ago. Considering how badly she felt, she should have been happier to talk to her pastor and have him pray for her. Instead, she chose to act like a child and try to run from his assistance.

"Pastor Adams, please forgive me. I'm just a wreck today. I haven't been behaving like myself. I told Cody the truth last night. He left me." Surprisingly, even to herself, she did not break down and weep.

"Yes, Nay, I had a feeling something was amiss when I didn't see him with you in church. I'm very sorry to hear this, but I don't want you to give up hope. God is still able."

"Thank you, Pastor, for saying that. I'm still holding onto hope. I'm pretty positive my husband will come home soon."

"I called you back here to see if there was anything I could do and to pray with you."

"I'm glad you asked that, Pastor. I think it would be a great idea if you would give Cody a call. I'm not telling you what to say, but I'm sure he would listen to whatever you say."

"That's a good idea. I'll call him after I have my dinner this evening. You just keep the faith, young lady. I know God will work this all out for the good of everyone involved."

Lindsay rose, prepared for prayer, but Pastor Adams wasn't quite finished with his questions.

"Before we pray, Nay, can I ask about the young man that sat with your children today? He's an unfamiliar face."

Tribe of Judah was nowhere near big enough to be considered a megachurch, but it had a pretty good-sized congregation. Yet, somehow, Pastor Adams seemed to always be able to spot a nonmember. He also always knew when his regular members were not in attendance. This always amazed Lindsay. She guessed that was just one of her pastor's gifts.

"His name is Sha'Ron. He's my children's half brother, my late husband's oldest child. He decided to surprise the children and join them for church this morning," Lindsay answered tightly.

"You don't sound as if you're pleased by this young man's appearance here today."

Lindsay closed her eyes and took a deep breath. She then released it slowly. "Pastor, I don't mean to be so sensitive about my former stepson, but in all honesty, his close association with my children unnerves me. Cody found out that Sha'Ron is being groomed to take his father's place in his uncle's drug organization."

"Oh my. That is cause for concern. I can see why you would be nervous and apprehensive."

"Cody thinks we as Christians should help Sha'Ron instead of alienating him. But Pastor Adams, he hates me so much. I can see it in his eyes. I can feel it in his stare. I realize this is not about me but the kids. I also understand his anger, but it honestly frightens me. I actually didn't realize he scared me until I saw him in church today."

"I see. I understand Cody's motives as a Christian man. I also understand your concern and the dilemma you have because he is a sibling to your children. I could discern that the young man was a little rough around the edges just from his appearance and mannerisms. My spirit is telling me you, not necessarily your children, but *you* need to be concerned for *your* safety."

Lindsay looked carefully at Pastor Adams. She noticed the seriousness in his face and posture. She wished now, even more than before, that Cody were with her so he could hear and feel what Pastor Adams was saying.

It was now Pastor Adams's turn to see and feel the new distress in Lindsay.

"Come on, Nay, let's get our pray on." Pastor Adams prayed with Lindsay. After he was done they both felt somewhat better.

"Okay, Nay. As I said, I'll give Cody a call this evening. In the meantime, I don't want you to worry too much about any of this. Remember Philippians 4:6 from the NIV, 'Do not be anxious about anything, but in every situation, by prayer and petition, with thanksgiving, present your requests to God.'"

"I will earnestly try, Pastor. I know God is with me through these trials, so I'll work hard at leaning on His strength. Thank you so much for praying for and for caring about me." The two embraced before parting ways. Lindsay then went in search of her children.

On the ride home, Lindsay tried to think of something as close to the truth as possible to tell the children about Cody's absence. She truly hated lying to them. . . .

Sha'Ron pulled into his driveway still unable to shake the discomfort he felt while sitting through the entire church service. He felt like everybody in the church was staring at him as if they knew he didn't belong there. It seemed as if the pastor was looking at him, knowing he eventually planned to do harm to his former stepmom. It was a very awkward period for him.

He got out of the car finally so he could go in to check on his grandma. Aunt Tameeka's car was gone, so he hoped she had been okay for whatever time she had been left alone. He found her in her room awake and safely watching television.

"Hey, Grandma, I'm back. Do you need anything?" he asked as he peeked in from the doorway.

"Sha'Ron, come in and tell me about seeing that witch at church."

"Granny, I told you she was not there. Now don't you get stressed out even worrying about her. I went there to spend more time with my brother and sister. Forget about Nay-Nay."

"I'm surprised she let you see 'em at all. She always did think she was better than everybody. I'm surprised she ain't turned my grandchildren against all of us." After so much speaking, the coughing started again. Sha'Ron went to the kitchen to get her some water.

"Grandma, I told you not to get yourself excited over her. I'll handle her. Don't worry. Isn't it time to take your medication?"

Sha'Ron carefully put the cup to his grandmother's lips and slowly allowed her to drink from the cup so as to not have a repeat of this morning's fiasco.

Patricia took a few sips, then zeroed in on her grandson's comment. "What . . . do . . . you . . . mean . . . you will . . . take . . . care of her?" She took a little more water.

Sha'Ron didn't realize what he let slip until his grandma repeated it to him. "Grandma, I didn't mean anything, okay. Please stop upsetting yourself worrying about her."

"She killed . . . my son, Sha'Ron . . . I hate her. I . . . really . . . hate . . . her."

Sha'Ron listened to the venom in grandmother's voice and felt the depth of her pain. In his own heart he believed his father's death to be the cause of his grandmother's cancer returning. He didn't know if it made sense medically or not, but it was just after the funeral that she had taken ill again.

"Grandma, I know how you feel about her, but you can't allow her to make you sick."

"Baby, I'm going to my grave with the hate I have for her in my heart. I know I ain't got much time left, but even if I were to live for a hundred more years, I would spend each day of each year hating her. So I'm for sure gon' hate her in these last days." Patricia spoke those words without one moment of pause. Sha'Ron had not heard his grandmother speak that clearly in months. The sheer hate that she spoke of filled the small bedroom and fueled his own anger and determination to avenge his father's death. He just hoped he would be able to accomplish his goal before his grandmother left the earth. . . .

Chapter Twelve

Cody sat in the hotel restaurant looking at the menu for what seemed the one-thousandth time, still unable to decide what he wanted to eat. He truthfully was not the least bit hungry, but he needed to get out of the hotel room. The walls began to feel as if they were closing in on him. He decided to come and get himself some nourishment. He had not eaten a thing since lunch the previous day.

His mind told him he needed food to maintain his health and strength. His heart said there was no room in his body for food because of the unbearable pain that had been with him since he last saw his wife. It clung to every fiber of his being, leaving no room for any other logical natural body reaction. All Cody felt was hurt; not hunger or sleepiness or even anger; simply pain.

However, in an effort to break the monotony of staring at the walls in his room, he decided to attempt to drown the pain in his heart and pay a bit more attention to his head.

When the waitress returned for the third time since she had served him a glass of water, he decided to order. "I'll have the grilled chicken salad, no cucumbers, please, with ranch dressing. Thank you."

The waitress didn't even bother asking if he wanted anything else since it had taken him so long to come up with this order. "Okay, sir. Thank you. I'll be back quickly with that order."

"Oh, and miss, could you also bring me a shot of Hennessy along with another glass of ice water?"

"Certainly. Right away."

It had been quite awhile since Cody had anything to drink stronger than a glass of wine. Tonight he needed something to burn away the pain in his chest. The waitress returned quickly with his drink. He swallowed the shot in one gulp just as quickly as she placed it on the table. His phone rang just as he began to feel the heat of the drink in his heart. A look at the caller ID revealed that his wife had finally decided to call him, no doubt to ask for his forgiveness and beg him to return home.

"Lindsay," Cody answered flatly.

Lindsay could hardly believe he answered the phone, especially on the first ring. Sure, he sounded aggravated that she had bothered to call, but hearing his voice, even a voice filled with contempt, made her heart soar. She took a deep breath, breathing in her husband through the phone lines, temporarily unable to speak a word.

"Lindsay, are you there?"

"Yes, Cody. I'm here. I . . . uh . . . I just wanted to share something with you that Pastor Adams said to me today."

Cody immediately began to feel as if this was some kind of ploy, a simple excuse to give Lindsay a reason to call. "You called to tell me about Pastor Adams's sermon?" he said with a little sarcasm and animosity.

"No. It's more personal than that. Pastor Adams said he believes I should be concerned for my safety as it relates to Sha'Ron."

"What? How and what does Pastor Adams know about Sha'Ron?" Now he was positive this phone call was a scheme of hers.

"Today, Sha'Ron showed—"

"Hold on, Lindsay. My other line is ringing." Cody checked the phone to find an unfamiliar number listed on his screen, but decided to answer it anyway. "This is Cody Vincini."

"Cody, this is Pastor Adams. How are you, son?"

What the . . . Cody thought. *Okay, this could not be a coincidence.* "Pastor Adams. This is a surprise. I've actually got Lindsay on the other line. If you just hold for a moment, I'll let her know I need to call her back."

"Certainly. I'll hold."

"Lindsay, it's Pastor Adams on the line, but I think you knew that. I'll call you later." He disconnected the call without waiting for her reply.

"Pastor Adams, I'm back. To answer your question, I'm not the best, sir. But I'm sure you know that. I'm sure that's the reason behind your phone call." Cody's tone was flat and even. No emotion. He was putting into practice his professional voice inflections. He had no intentions of lying to Pastor Adams. He just didn't want to get too deeply involved in an overly emotional conversation with him about Lindsay.

"You're right, son. I spoke with Nay-Nay today. She told me about your leaving. I'm concerned about that, very much so. But before we get into that, I want to first talk to you about Nay's former stepson, Sha'Ron. I believe she told me that was the young man's name."

Cody was pretty positive that Lindsay would not be able to manipulate Pastor Adams with any false ploys or schemes. So he realized immediately that she had been speaking the truth when she began telling him about Pastor Adams talking to her about Sha'Ron.

"What about Sha'Ron, Pastor?"

"Did your wife tell you he surprised her here at church today?"

"No. She started to tell me something, but you called before she could finish." Cody immediately became concerned for Lindsay's safety. Sha'Ron was not the type of kid who would suddenly decide to give Jesus a try.

"Well, she told me that neither she nor your kids were expecting him, but he was here when they arrived today. The young gentleman stuck out in the congregation like a sore thumb. A very well dressed sore thumb, but out of place nonetheless. I kept an eye on him before and after my sermon from the pulpit. And while he didn't do anything bizarre, he seemed quite uncomfortable; kind of jumpy."

"I see, Pastor." Cody sat processing Pastor Adams's concern while also trying to rationalize it. "The young man is very rough around the edges. He hasn't spent much, if any, time in church. So I'm sure he was nervous. You know you wield some serious sermons from that pulpit, sir. The boy was probably feeling the heat of hell in his seat on the pew." Cody chuckled lightly, but his mind was seriously analyzing the situation between Sha'Ron and Lindsay.

"I'm sure that accounts for some of the anxiety I perceived. But a bigger part of it seems to stem from anger. Anger, no doubt, aimed at your wife because she killed his dad."

Cody's emotions began to run the gamut at Pastor Adams's statement of observation. An instant and very instinctive surge of protectiveness for his wife filled his bones. But how could he protect her if he wasn't even sure he could be around her? He also felt a wee bit inadequate because he had failed to recognize any predatory behavior in Sha'Ron. Sure, he was obviously aware of the boy's anger, but he had not discerned any signs of retaliation. Cody also felt trepidation at the thought of returning home for any reason other than he planned to work things out with Lindsay. Right now, he was still unsure about his stance on that. He didn't want to go home only to end up resenting her.

"Pastor Adams, I honestly didn't think Lindsay was in any real danger from Sha'Ron, but I don't, and won't, doubt your instincts. It's my responsibility to protect my wife."

Cody paused as the waitress came and served his meal. She noticed he was on a telephone call so she quickly made her exit after Cody had given her the thumbs-up indicating everything was okay.

"Cody, are you still there, son?"

"Yes, sir. I was just receiving my food from the wait- ress." Cody continued to talk as he prepared his salad for eating. "Like I said, Pastor, I know my responsibil- ity is to protect my wife, but, sir, I'm not so sure about the state of our marriage right now." Cody again be- came silent as he took a quick moment to ask God to bless his meal.

Pastor Adams took advantage of Cody's quietness. "Yes, son, I also want to talk to you about that. Cody, I know you are disappointed in what Nay-Nay did those years ago. When she came in a few weeks ago to talk to me about it, I was a little shocked and disappointed myself. But unlike you, Cody, my disappointment was in the both of you."

Though Cody knew he should not have been shocked by his pastor's declaration, he was. He actually had not realized that Lindsay had shared the information about her deception with their pastor. But it was her decep- tion, not his. So why Pastor Adams would be disap- pointed in him was puzzling.

"I'm sorry, Pastor, but I don't understand your dis- appointment in me."

"Cody, you were a willing participant in having an adulterous affair with a married woman. You are only focused on the end result of the selfishness created by the two of you."

"Pastor, believe me when I say I have gone over in my head my part in this psychodrama between Lindsay and me. I understand that we would not be in this place in our marriage had I not even slept with her. But, Pastor, I never ever lied to Lindsay. I have never done anything to her but love her. I would have also loved any baby that the two of us would have had together, be it the baby she aborted or the child we could be trying to conceive right now." Cody had not realized he'd raised his voice until he received a strong look from the patron seated across from him to his right.

"Cody, please calm down. It will do you no good to fluster yourself. I understand you want to keep dwelling on what Nay-Nay said to you just yesterday, but I'm gonna be blunt with you here, brother."

Pastor Adams quickly changed the tone of his voice to that of a homeboy versus a pastor. The difference did not go unnoticed by Cody. He sat up straighter in his chair in the restaurant and prepared to hear the down and dirty from *Paul*, instead of a stern lecture from Pastor Adams.

"It's easier to keep blaming your wife for the situation the two of you are in than to take 50 percent, if not more, of the responsibility for it. Yes. She had the abortion. Yes. She withheld that information from you. And yes. She was wrong for all of that. But she did what she did to try to salvage her marriage. Now you may not see the man she was with at the time as much of a husband, but the bottom line is, the brother was her husband.

"The Bible says in I Corinthians chapter seven that if a Christian man has a wife who is an unbeliever and she is willing to continue living with him, he must not leave her. And if a Christian woman has a husband who is an unbeliever and he is willing to continue living with her, she must not leave him. For the Christian wife brings holiness to her marriage, and the Christian husband brings holiness to his marriage. Otherwise, the children would not have a godly influence, but now they are set apart for Him. So you see, Cody, whether she realized it or not, your wife was doing the biblical thing by trying to stay with her then husband. You, on the other hand, knew she was married, and married to your very own client, no less. You also knew she was a Christian woman although she was not behaving like one when she was lying up with you. And that was all good with you. Brother Cody, now that you are a saved man, you understand these two things, I'm sure. Number one is that even though God forgives us for our sins and transgressions, there are still consequences for our actions. Number two is, because God forgives us, we are to also forgive others as a condition of our pardon from Him."

Cody now felt as if he needed to warn Pastor Adams to calm himself because he was the one who had raised his voice at least an octave. He had preached, lectured, and thoroughly chastised Cody in good fashion.

"Uh . . . Pastor Adams, sir, I hear you loud and clear. I understand my part in what happened and the end result. My issue with Lindsay is her lying and hiding it from me about the baby. She knew all along that we would never be able to have a child together. She could have—should have—told me that during our courtship."

"Okay. I hear you there, Cody. Lindsay could have told you about what she did before she married you. But that would not have changed what she did. The fact would have remained that she did, in fact, abort the baby the two of you conceived during your affair. The fact would still remain that she would be unable to give you a child now. Let's assume she had told you the whole story before she married you. What would you have done then?"

Cody took a moment to seriously ponder the pastor's question. He actually had not even thought about what he would have done if he had known about the baby before they got married.

"To be completely honest with you, Pastor, I don't know what I would have done. All I have dealt with since finding out the truth is the pain of her lying about the fact that she killed one of my children and now she can no longer give me a child of my own."

Pastor Adams gave a little snort. "Humph. Sounds like you are still shifting and assigning blame. Here is another question for you, Cody. Tell me what would you have done if Lindsay had told you that she was pregnant with your child even though she was still legally and obviously emotionally married to another man. I want you to think carefully about your answer. Then I want you to verbalize it to me."

Cody's answer was evident to him, but after hearing the way Pastor Adams posed the question, he thought he should rethink it before he answered too quickly. Deciding that his answer remained the same, he responded.

"Pastor Adams, I loved Lindsay as much then as I do now. I would have been more than happy to be the father of her child and a joyful participant in our child's life." Cody thought his answer to be honest and responsible. Surely Pastor Adams would see that his answer would have been the right thing to do.

"Grow up, boy. Cody, you are being very pompous and naïve in your view of that time and those circumstances. You are seeing things with some sort of fantasy vision. Knowing that her former husband was a drug dealer, do you really think he would have allowed you to have a happy-go-lucky relationship with your love child? What? Were you supposed to have every other weekend and one-day-during-the-week visits? Share birthdays and Christmases? Think about it, Cody. You allowed Lindsay to be in a very bad position. I am in no way agreeing with or condoning the decision she made to abort. But I will be transparent and tell you I understand why she made it."

Cody sat in his seat as quiet as the proverbial church mouse. He had no idea Pastor Adams would come at him this hard. As the young folks said today, Cody was not ready.

Not sure what he should say next, Cody continued to sit quietly staring oddly at his barely eaten salad.

Pastor Adams was well aware that his delivery of his way of seeing things was something that was probably new to the young man. The ensuing silence did not surprise him in the least. In fact, he had become accustomed to the way folks acted after hearing one of his "*keeping it real*" lectures.

"Cody, I think it's time you start looking at this realistically. I know it's hard because your flesh and emotions are involved. The truth of the matter is this: you need to run home to your wife and beg her forgiveness for your behavior. I would also like for the two of you to set up an appointment with our pastoral counselor. Perhaps your marriage would benefit from having another objective party to help you both sort through this."

After a few more seconds of silence, Cody finally was revisited by the power of speech. "Pastor Adams, you painted a very vivid picture. I'm still sorting through all the colors and hues in my mind and in my heart, but rest assured that I do see a totally different picture now."

"All right, son. If I don't hear from you or Nay-Nay in the next couple of days, I will call you and check on you. Son, I want you to get in touch with God tonight and have an in-depth conversation with Him. Then I want you to sit back quietly and listen for Him to guide you on this. If I were a betting man, I would win a mint betting that He tells you to go home to your wife."

"I'll definitely be in prayer about everything, Pastor. Thank you for taking the time to talk to me this evening. Good night."

After disconnecting the call, Cody stared at his hardly eaten salad as if he thought he could find the answers he needed in its mashed together contents, as if he could find God there. With no revelation coming forth, he decided to go back to his room and do as Pastor Adams suggested and pray.

Chapter Thirteen

"I doubt if night number two without my hubby will go as smoothly as night number one. I'm not dry begging you to come back or anything," Lindsay snickered, "but your being here to comfort and console me made his absence a little more bearable." Lindsay had been on the phone with Keva for the past thirty minutes filling her in on Sha'Ron's surprise church appearance, her conversation with Pastor Adams, and her very brief conversation with Cody.

"Don't worry, Nay. You'll get through it. Understand this is just a trial that God will bring you through."

"I know this, and I trust Him. It's just dealing with the pain of it until He gets me to the other side of through that I don't like," Lindsay again chuckled.

"You know what? You are a lot better than I think you realize. You can at least laugh in the midst of your sadness."

Lindsay realized that Keva was correct. She actually had begun to feel better after her conversation with Pastor Adams. However, she would truly miss her husband's presence tonight. That is, unless he decided to come home tonight since she knew he too talked with Pastor Adams. She could always hope.

"So, have you told the kids anything yet?"

"Not yet. I was somehow able to avoid any questions on the drive home from church. I'm sure our dinner conversation will be a bit more challenging."

"Well, don't stress about that either. God will give you the words to say. By the way, what you cooking? Say something good and I might just come back and stay with you tonight." It was now Keva's turn to laugh at herself.

"Girl, I'm too emotionally drained to cook. I'm about to call Domino's to place a delivery order of pizza and wings."

"Well, I guess you will be sleeping alone tonight, my sister, if your man don't come home." Both women laughed this time.

"Thanks again, Keva, for calling to check on me. I really appreciate you, girl. But I've got to get my children fed and in bed. This is far later than we normally eat, so I better get off this phone."

"No problem, Nay. I'll give you all a call tomorrow. But if you need me, don't you hesitate to call me."

"I won't. Good night."

Lindsay disconnected the call and immediately dialed the number to order food for herself and her children. Less than thirty minutes later, she called her kids down to eat. Li'l Shaun ran to the kitchen table as if he hadn't eaten in months while Shauntae strolled down in her normal fashion, with her phone attached to her face.

"Okay, lady, say good-bye to whomever you are talking to and join your brother at the table for dinner," Lindsay said.

"Tandie, I'll see you at school tomorrow." Shauntae hung up the phone but never let it leave her hands. "Pizza on a Sunday night, Mom? This is different."

Lindsay knew the questions about Cody's whereabouts would start any minute. Up to now, the Holy Spirit had not told her what to say to the kids about her marital situation. So Lindsay nervously sat down in the chair between her kids and silently prayed that the right words would come once the questions started while she served the pizza and wings.

Before a word could be uttered from either child, Shauntae's phone rang.

"Shauntae, no phone calls at the table while we're eating."

"It's Sha'Ron, Mom. I'll tell him I'll call him back after we eat." Shauntae answered the call.

Lindsay stiffened as she remembered Sha'Ron's stare and Pastor Adams's observations. She would give Shauntae exactly one minute; then she would insist that she hang up. She'd had more than enough of Sha'Ron for the day.

"Oh no! How bad is she?" Shauntae's raised voice startled both Lindsay and Li'l Shaun. "What hospital is she in?"

"Shauntae, what's going on?" Lindsay asked her visibly excited child.

"Okay. I'll let my mom and Cody know. Okay. Bye, big brother." Shauntae jumped from her seat and looked at her mother with a monumental fear in her eyes. "Mom, Grandma Pat had a massive stroke. Sha'Ron says Grandma will probably die tonight. Can we go to the hospital? Please? Sha'Ron needs us."

Lindsay's heart sank. She and Patricia had never been friends. They had actually never gotten along at all. But she didn't wish her dead. She looked at Li'l Shaun to find that he was a little shaken. He couldn't possibly remember too much about his paternal grandmother. He hadn't seen her since Shaun's funeral. He was more than likely reacting to Shauntae's distress.

"Shauntae, sweetie, I know you're worried about your grandmother and your brother, but I don't want you to make yourself sick. Please, sweetie, sit down and tell me everything Sha'Ron said."

Shauntae sat as her mother suggested, but she was far from calm. "He said Grandma had a stroke. Because she was already very sick with cancer, the doctors don't think she will survive. They are at Sinai Grace Hospital."

The pressure suddenly became too much. Shauntae broke down and began sobbing. "Mom, I really want to go to the hospital," was all she could get out with her crying.

Lindsay's somber heart now cracked as she watched her daughter break down. She really wanted to comfort her, but she knew her child well. The only consolation would be for her to agree to take Shauntae to the hospital. That prospect, however, was not something she wanted to do, considering the animosity Sha'Ron already felt for her. Couple his grandmother's dying with the hate he had over the death of his parents and Lindsay knew the mixture could produce a very volatile young man.

Shauntae continued to cry uncontrollably. Lindsay reached around the table to hold her hand and rub her back. Li'l Shaun also got up from his seat to try to console his distraught sister.

"Mom, can we go to the hospital? That would make Shauntae feel better." Apparently Li'l Shaun knew his sister well too, Lindsay thought.

Lindsay put her personal feelings aside and decided to take her kids to the hospital. "Okay. You two grab your coats. I'll go upstairs and get my purse."

Once upstairs, Lindsay called Keva from her cell to let her know about Patricia since she was Kevaun's grandmother also. "Keva, hey. Girl, I'm on my way to take the kids to Sinai Grace Hospital. Apparently Patricia has had a major stroke. With her advanced cancer, the doctors are not expecting her to make it much longer."

"Oh my goodness. Lord knows I'm not a big Patricia fan, and I'm sure she feels the same about me. But I certainly don't wish this on her or her family."

"Yeah, I feel the same way. I just thought I would give you a call to let you know since she is Kevaun's grandmother too."

"Kevaun doesn't even remember much about her. He was so young when we moved away, and he hasn't seen her since the funeral."

"Again, I hear you. I'll call you later if it's not too late to give you an update. If it is late, I'll call you tomorrow."

"Cool. Talk to you then. I'll be praying."

Lindsay went back downstairs, and she and the kids headed out the door. She thought about something just before she left the house. "Kids, wait for me in the car. I'll be right out."

"Hurry, Mom, please," Shauntae begged.

Lindsay quickly called Cody's cell. When he didn't answer, she left him a message giving him the details about Patricia and what hospital she was in. Then she and the kids drove to the hospital.

Both children sat in the car quietly on the ride to the hospital; Shauntae up front with her eyes closed tightly. Lindsay assumed she was praying. Li'l Shaun sat in the back staring out the windows at the passing scenery.

Lindsay worked hard at concentrating on the road as she drove, but her mind wandered to what she would encounter once she got to the hospital. She was sure that both Tameeka and Francine would be there with Sha'Ron. She also assumed Uncle Bobby would be there if he was in town. With the exception of Sha'Ron, she had not seen any of these people since Shaun's funeral. She was sure, however, that they all hated her as much as Sha'Ron did.

Lindsay had always been tough by description. She feared no one and would fight at the drop of a dime back in the day. But that was before her deepened relationship with Christ, before Shyanne, her fighting partner, had been killed, and before she had killed Shaun, the beloved brother, father, son, and nephew of the people she would possibly face at the hospital.

Lindsay was about to come face-to-face for the first time with enemies she didn't think she could actually battle and win. She now understood what it felt like to be going into a battle with fear and trepidation. Despite her fear though, she wanted to do what was right for her children. This may be their final chance to see their grandmother alive.

She began praying silently for God to cover and protect her and her children as she continued to drive the short distance to the hospital.

Lindsay considered dropping the children off at the emergency room door, and then going to park the car. She quickly changed her mind, however, deciding that she needed to be with her children every step of the way.

After paying the attendant and parking the car, she and the kids headed into the hospital to find out where they needed to go. "Hi. My name is Lindsay Vincini. I'm here to see my children's grandmother, Patricia Taylor," Lindsay explained as she approached the information desk.

After searching through the computer, the front-desk receptionist gave her the information she needed. "Ms. Taylor is in CCU, the Critical Care Unit. Take this hall here until you get to the end. Make a left and take the first bank of elevators to the fourth floor. Follow the signs from there to bed number four."

"Thank you." Lindsay walked with the children as far as the elevators; then she sent them up on their own, giving Shauntae the instructions the receptionist had given her. She knew she would be most unwelcome up with the rest of the family. She returned to the emergency room waiting area, sat down, and prayed.

Approximately thirty minutes later, Lindsay looked up to see her teary-eyed children returning.

"She's gone, Mama. Grandma Pat died just a few minutes ago," Shauntae announced.

Her poor child was heartbroken. Li'l Shaun's tears had dried, but his saddened eyes tore a hole in her own chest, and she too began to weep as she gathered her babies to her bosom and held them.

Death was such a common event in the city of Detroit that none of the other waiting room occupants even flinched at the sorrowful scene in the middle of the room. It was as if they all at some point or another had been right there in that very spot, and they totally understood the small family's need for silence and solitude. The room had become eerily quiet.

"No, you don't!" Tameeka screamed, tearing large holes in the serenity of the quiet waiting room. "You don't get to grieve my mama's death. You killed her. You killed her just like you killed my brother."

Before Lindsay had a chance to react, Tameeka charged in her direction, arms flailing, and landed an open-handed swing to her right cheek. The noise from the blow was just as deafening as her scream.

Lindsay was so caught off guard by Tameeka's attack she didn't have a moment to think of defending herself. She just stood there speechless, holding her throbbing cheek. Shauntae had to take up the charge of defending her mother.

"No, Auntie. Please don't fight my mom," she screamed as she struggled to push Tameeka away. Li'l Shaun immediately came to the aid of his sister as he grabbed Tameeka by her leg in an effort to stop her from advancing again on his mother.

Just as the two siblings were able to get one out-of-control aunt away from their mother, Francine came into the room. "Tameeka, why did you leave from upstairs like that? We still have to . . ." Her voice trailed off as she saw how disheveled and frantic her sister looked. She then noticed the source of her sister's enraged appearance. Francine became instantly furious as well. She stood shaking in place, incensed at her former sister-in-law's gall.

"I cannot believe you have the nerve to even be here. You really do think you are tough, don't you?" With each word, Francine took a menacing step toward Lindsay. By the end of her speech, she stood just inches away from her nemesis.

Lindsay was not going to be caught slipping twice. This time, she was braced and ready to defend herself if Francine decided to do something other than just talk. She understood the sisters' grief, and they could say whatever they felt, but she was not going to allow them to physically assault her again.

"Hit her, Frannie. Stop talking to that witch and knock her butt out," Tameeka screamed.

"Don't!" That one word was all Lindsay said, but that one word seemed to be like gasoline doused on a raging fire. Suddenly, all hell broke loose in that previously tranquil waiting room.

Francine started swinging. Lindsay started swinging in defense. Tameeka broke loose from Shauntae and Li'l Shaun in an attempt to get in the fray with her sister against Lindsay. The kids were screaming, trying to protect their mother, grabbing flying arms wherever they could. The receptionist was so focused on watching the chaos she neglected to alert security.

Lindsay and Francine tussled and tumbled throughout the lobby. Just as Tameeka got close enough to the fighting pair to get in the brawl, she found herself being lifted into the air by her waist by a pair of nearly colorless hands. At the same time, Keva came into the room and attempted to get between Lindsay and Francine. With the help of the children, they were finally able to pry the dueling women apart. A lone but armed security officer finally entered the ruckus and endeavored to bring the entire fracas under control.

"All right! I want everyone to stop swinging and screaming. As a matter of fact, don't anybody move until I point to you," the officer yelled in a booming voice. Everyone in the waiting area froze as they heard the thunder in his command. The movement of his feet and the ringing telephone at the reception area were the only sounds that could be heard.

"Sir," he said, talking to Cody, "I want you to put the young lady on her feet. Young lady, when he puts you down, I want you to come and sit in this seat right here."

"Put me down now, White Boy," Tameeka screamed at Cody.

"Young lady, I'm the only one giving orders in here. There will be no further name-calling, either."

"I didn't call him a name. White Boy *is* his name," Tameeka replied indignantly. But she sat obediently as the officer instructed.

The officer then looked in the direction of the crowd that consisted of Lindsay, Francine, Keva, Shauntae, and Li'l Shaun. Looking directly at Francine, the officer said, "Miss in the red blouse, I need you to come and sit in the seat across from this young lady."

He shifted his position in the room to stand between the two chairs. He wasn't sure just yet who was in alliance with whom and who were foes so he stood there in case these two decided to start throwing blows at each other.

Cody addressed the officer. "Sir, that is my wife and her friend there." He waved his arm in the direction of Keva and Lindsay. "These are our children. May I go to them?"

The officer looked at Lindsay. Her blouse was ripped, and there was a trickle of blood on her slightly swollen bottom lip. He then looked at Francine whose appearance looked similar and surmised these two women to be the main tusslers.

"Sir, take your wife and the rest of your family over to that side of the room. Do not move until I come over there to talk to you all."

Cody and his crew moved to the location of the lobby directed by the officer.

"Okay, ladies, what's going on here?" the officer asked Tameeka first.

Sha'Ron entered the waiting area at that moment. He looked around and saw his aunts sitting near the security officer. He noticed Aunt Francine's torn blouse. He continued to scan the room and saw his former stepmom in a similar condition and concluded these two must have been in some sort of fight. His anger leaped above the pain in his heart. Everything in him wanted to charge at Lindsay and choke her until she was as dead as his father, his mother, and his grandmother. The only thing that kept him rooted in his place was the large gun he saw on the security officer's hip. He elected, instead, to impale her with cold cruel eyes, screaming volumes of hatred and death. Just about everyone in the room could see it as well, including the security officer.

"Who is that?" he asked Tameeka before she had a chance to answer his first question.

"That's my nephew, Sha'Ron. Sha'Ron come over here and sit down."

Sha'Ron reluctantly tore his gaze away from Lindsay and joined his aunts and the security guard. The officer could feel the hate oozing from the young man's pores. There was obviously some very serious and very ugly history going on between these two groups of people.

"Okay, let's get back to my questions. What's going on here?" the officer asked.

Tameeka spoke first. "My mother just died a few minutes ago." She paused as she choked on a sudden sob. Getting herself together, she pressed through to continue talking. "My mother just died. She was sick with cancer and had a stroke. That trick over there is the reason she was so sick and stressed out. She killed our brother, my nephew's father, two years ago." Tameeka jabbed her forefinger in Sha'Ron's direction. "And now she has the nerve to show up here like she has a right to be here. Me and my sister just snapped and attacked her when we saw her." Tameeka broke down and could no longer speak. Francine finished answering the officer, though she too was in tears.

"Officer, my mother was diagnosed with breast cancer several years ago, but she beat it. When my brother was killed by his raggedy wife over there, my mother relapsed. Her two kids are our niece and nephew, and this is our brother's oldest son. She also killed his mother."

The officer's head was spinning by the time the two sisters finished talking. He took a glance at the woman they were talking about. Nothing about her suggested cold-blooded murderer. Even just coming out of a fight, the woman was beautiful. He almost envied the man who sat holding her hand and had introduced himself as her husband.

"I'm Officer Antoine Wade. I'm very sorry about your mother . . ." Looking at Sha'Ron he said, "and your grandmother. I understand the anger under the circumstances as you have explained them to me. But I can't just allow you all to be up in here fighting. I'm going over there to talk to them. Then I will get them to leave so you all can finish handling your business here. Again, I'm sorry about your mother and grandmother." Officer Wade left the grieving trio to one another while he went to talk to the other party of this dueling drama.

When the security officer walked away, Sha'Ron looked into the eyes of his aunties. The sadness, pain, and anger he saw only strengthened his resolve to deal deadly with the root cause of all their grief. He shot a glance across the room at his family's nemesis and promised to put an end to her reign of terror on them very soon.

"Come on, Aunties. We need to go back upstairs and finish some paperwork." The trio stood up and headed back up to where Patricia's body lay.

"Did either of you hear back from Uncle Bobby yet?" he asked them as they walked in the direction of the elevators.

Tameeka simply shook her head.

"Not yet. I think he's out of the country. I left two messages. He'll call soon," Francine answered.

They all walked out of the waiting room without looking at the other folks.

"Hey. I'm Officer Antoine Wade. I just came to talk to you all about the fight." He looked directly at Lindsay and asked, "What is this about you having killed several members of their family?" He lowered his voice as he asked the question.

"Officer Wade, my name is Cody Vincini. Lindsay here is my wife. I am also her attorney."

"Mr. Vincini, this is not an official interrogation, so there is no need for you to be anything here other than a husband. I'm just trying to get her side of the story on the fight."

"I'm okay, Cody." Lindsay gently rubbed Cody's thigh to let him know she was capable of speaking to the officer. "Mr. Wade, I used to be married to their brother. I did shoot him after several years of emotional abuse. I snapped and killed him after the accidental murder of my best friend."

Officer Wade stared bug-eyed as he learned of another death associated with today's drama. It was crazy situations like this that made him consider taking early retirement from the police department.

Lindsay continued. "Sha'Ron, my former stepson, called my daughter to let her know their grandmother was close to death. She wanted to come and be with her brother and see her grandmother for the last time. So I brought her and my son down here. The two sisters attacked me when they saw me. This is the first time we have seen each other since my ex-husband's funeral more than two years ago. I understand their hurt and their anger, but I had to defend myself. That's how the fight started."

"Well, surprisingly, the stories seem to match. I won't call the Detroit Police Department out here on this if you all just agree to leave now while they are finishing their business regarding the deceased."

"No problem, Officer. We'll leave now. We are truly sorry about our part in all of this," Cody assured the officer.

The party of five got up from their seats and moved toward the exit of the hospital. Lindsay paused be-

tween the exit door from the hospital and the one leading to the street. "Shauntae, take the keys and you and
your brother get in the car."

The adults waited until the kids were out of earshot.
They had seen and heard way more than any child
needed to for one night.

"Keva, what in the world are you doing here? I thought
you said you were not going to bring Kevaun down
here," Lindsay said.

"I didn't. After I talked to you, it dawned on me that
you were going to be down here with the Addams Family all by yourself. Looks like I got here just in time."

Lindsay hugged Keva. "Thank you so much for thinking of me once again."

"No problem, again. I'm just glad I got here before
things got too bad," Keva replied as she affectionately
returned Lindsay's hug.

"Girl, I have got to get back home and soothe things
over with Cheval. He was not very happy about me
coming here to a potential fight scene in my pregnant
condition. I've got to go home and do some kissing up
to get my husband to forgive me since he'll be able to
see that I'm okay."

"Oh, no, Keva! I forgot you're pregnant. Cheval is
right. You should not have come."

"I will tell you like I told him. I had to come. I care
about you, Nay. I knew God would protect us all, including my baby."

Keva left. As Lindsay watched her leave she had to
stifle the urge to cry. Her emotions were overwhelming
her on so many different levels. She was very happy and
grateful to have someone like Keva to care about her.
She also felt a bit grieved as Keva's concern reminded
her again of her dead best friend. The thought of death
brought her back to the present and the ugly scene that
just played out in the hospital in front of her children.

This was a complete mess, Lindsay thought. One she would have to try to talk through with the kids before she put them to bed tonight. The only bright spot to this whole thing was Cody's presence. She didn't know what his intentions were beyond that very moment, but she was happy he was there.

"Cody, thank you for showing up also. I'm sure you came for the same reason as Keva."

"You're right. I got out of the shower and got your voice mail message. I nearly went crazy."

It was Cody's turn to wrap his arms around his wife in a hug. "Sometimes I wonder if you are braver than you are smart. What were you thinking coming here by yourself, knowing you would come face-to-face with the people who hate you the most in this world?"

Lindsay didn't even mind that he was scolding her. All she cared about was being in her husband's arms again. She responded to his question.

"I honestly did think about the repercussions, but Shauntae's grief overshadowed my logic. I would have felt terrible if I had prevented her from seeing her grandmother one last time before she died because of my drama."

Cody pulled out of the embrace, which, by the way, felt wonderful to him, in order to look in Lindsay's face.

"But look at the drama she had to see you in, again, because of this family." Cody softened his voice to barely above a whisper. "It's a good thing these kids are in therapy. They're going to need it."

Lindsay realized Cody was not trying to criticize or berate her. He was doing what he always did, helping her to understand the gravity of the situation. Even though he was pointing out the very ugly in this mess, she discerned his continued concern and obvious love for her. In reality, she never ever doubted how he felt for her, even after he left.

"As sorry as I am about what the kids have been through this evening, I'm just as sorry to have dragged you into this mess."

Cody stared at his wife and realized he would never stop loving her. He would never stop caring for her. He would never stop protecting her. Therefore, there was no use in staying away from her. Her drama would always be his drama; her life, his life. Her children, even though they would be the only children they ever had together, would always be his children.

"I'm coming home tonight, Lindsay. I'll follow you all there. I'll go back to the hotel tomorrow to check out and get my things."

"Okay," was Lindsay's only response. She hugged her wonderful husband, then hurried to her car to get to her children, who were, undoubtedly, an emotional wreck. She was glad to know she would at least have her husband there with her as she worked to get them through this ordeal one night at a time.

Sha'Ron, Tameeka, and Francine all left the hospital at the same time. Sha'Ron got a ride to his house with Tameeka. He had come to the hospital in the ambulance with Patricia. Francine followed them to her now deceased mother's home.

The somber trio entered the home together. Not a word had passed among them since they left the hospital when they had discussed riding arrangements to the house.

Tameeka went straight to her mother's bedroom, lay on the bed, and cried hard. Francine and Sha'Ron followed her. Francine sat on the bed with her sister and cried as well as she rubbed her sister's back. Sha'Ron stood just inside the doorway. He allowed his tears to flow too, but he didn't join his aunts. He just stood there watching them on the bed, all of them sharing the same grief. They grieved for Patricia, and they also grieved for Shaun.

Sha'Ron had also lost his mother, but he was not close to her. He had been raised by his father and his grandmother. Now they were both dead. As far as he was concerned, they had died at the hands of the same woman. She had to pay.

"Do either of you believe in God?" Francine asked.

Neither of the room's other occupants said anything for several moments. Finally Sha'Ron gave his opinion.

"I sat in church today and listened to some preacher talk about how God loves us, but there are still consequences for our bad actions. He said the penalty of sin is death, but that God's love for us is so deep that He gave His only Son to die for our sins so we don't have to pay that penalty ourselves. So either the preacher lied about there being a God, or if there is a God, He didn't love Daddy and Grandma."

Sha'Ron leaned against the wall, then sank to the floor after stating his case. He started to cry again, and he allowed himself to do so without inhibition or hesitation. He was glad that Uncle Bobby was out of the country because he needed to cry. His dad allowed him to cry whenever he needed to. Now he was crying because he no longer had his father and his grandmother was gone too.

"I don't believe in God. I hope losing my mother to a painful, dreadful disease isn't supposed to make me a believer now," Tameeka said.

She continued to hold her mother's pillow as she cried teardrops bigger than summer raindrops, quickly soaking the pillowcase. She and her mother had not always gotten along, but since Shaun's murder, she, her mom, and her sister had grown closer. Shaun was the hero to all of them. When he was killed by the witch he had married, they all bonded, not necessarily by a familial love, but more by the common hate they all had for Lindsay.

"I've been going to church for a few months with a coworker. I believe in God. I believe God loves us all, including Shaun and Mama. I believe there are consequences for your actions. And I believe that we can still believe in God and not be perfect," Francine said genuinely.

"I asked Mama a couple of weeks ago if she believed in God. She told me she did. She said she believed in God and she believed in Jesus. She said she was taught about God when she was a little girl and went to church occasionally with a neighbor. I need you two to believe me even if you don't believe in God. I need you to believe that Mama is with God now that she is not with us anymore. I don't know about Shaun, but I hope he is with God too. I hate Lindsay as much as the two of you do, but I have to believe that because she believed in God and Jesus, she somehow convinced Shaun to believe when they were together. I don't know a lot about this yet, but I know we don't have to be perfect to spend eternity with God. Mama was not perfect. Shaun was not perfect. But I have to believe they are with God. I can't stand the thought of anything else now that they are both dead. I have to believe they are now together again."

Francine lay down next to her sister and cried the same tears that she did. The Taylor family sat in Patricia's room, mother and grandmother, and shared a grief that was palpable, a grief that seemed to have life and breath. They were being revisited by the same grief spirit that had come by a couple of years ago when Shaun died. They were all drowning in the same tear storm. At that time, they were unsure of who was Shaun's killer. Now, however, they knew that the same person was responsible, directly and indirectly, for both deaths.

Chapter Fourteen

Both Cody and Lindsay agreed that the kids should stay home from school. Shauntae was very hard to consol once they returned home. She teetered between grieving Patricia's death and being upset about Tameeka and Francine attacking her mother. There was also the guilt of having been out of touch with her grandmother for more than two years. On top of that, she was upset with Lindsay as well.

Li'l Shaun fed off his big sister's negative energy. He had his own issues with seeing his mother attacked, but Lindsay was sure everything else he felt came from Shauntae's stress.

Once Cody and Lindsay finally got the kids settled enough to fall asleep, the married couple found their way to bed as well. Both were physically, mentally, and emotionally drained. They agreed that they would discuss their issues the following day. They mustered just enough energy to make love out of the sheer necessity of needing to reconnect after their one-day estrangement.

Lindsay was the first in the family to awaken. She decided to clean the mess left in the kitchen last night before the emergency departure. Cody was the next member out of bed. He snuggled behind his wife as she stood at the sink rinsing last night's dishes.

Silent tears fell from Lindsay's eyes as she thanked God for bringing her husband home. She turned to face Cody, giving him a full-frontal hug.

"Thank you for coming home, Cody. I don't know if you forgive me or not. I'm just so glad you're here. Please give me an opportunity to make it up to you. Please."

"It was made painfully obvious to me yesterday that you don't owe me much of anything. According to Pastor Adams, I'm just as much to blame for this, if not more, than you are."

Lindsay pulled out of the embrace. "Pastor Adams said that to you?"

"Yes. Your pastor scolded me good. After I talked to him, I talked to God, who told me that Pastor Adams was right."

Lindsay started to ask for a further explanation but wisely decided against it. She realized the why and how were unimportant. The important thing was that Cody was home. Now she would just continually pray and ask God what she needed to do to keep him there forever.

"Pastor Adams wants us to start sessions with the church's marriage counselor. I'll call today and set our first appointment," Cody informed her.

"Speaking of counseling, I think I'll call Dr. Hooper to see if I can get an emergency session set up for Li'l Shaun and Shauntae. Their next regularly scheduled appointment is not for almost two weeks."

"That sounds like a great idea."

Cody helped Lindsay finish putting the kitchen in order; then the couple sat in the family room to continue talking.

"Lindsay, I have to apologize for not recognizing that I put you in danger with Sha'Ron. I was arrogant in my desire to save him, and I was blinded to his hate and the possibility of him having evil intentions toward you."

"It's okay, Cody. I don't want to talk about the wrong or mistakes we did. I just want to know what we are going to do about it now. Shauntae and Li'l Shaun love him. I don't want to just cross him out of their lives because he and the rest of his family hate me so much. I honestly believe the Taylors truly love my kids because they are a part of Shaun. I think their attack on me would have been far worse on me if it were not for the presence of their niece and nephew."

"I don't have all the answers right now, baby. I guess we're going to have to pray and be very careful from now on. You'll never ever be around any of them again, especially Sha'Ron, if it can be avoided. Don't even think about going anywhere near Patricia's funeral. If we can't work out another way for the kids to go, then they simply cannot go."

Lindsay hated the thought of forbidding the kids from attending their grandmother's memorial. Shauntae would probably never forgive her if it came to that.

"I hear you, baby. I just pray that we'll work something out. Perhaps Keva will attend. We could send the kids with her."

Cody smiled at his wife. "The two of you are really becoming close, huh? I'm glad to see that, especially considering the history between you two. Your relationship with her is truly an act of God at work."

"She has definitely been a godsend. She stayed with me all night when you left. Then she came running to my rescue last night. She reminds me so much of Shyanne in so many ways. I just pray that I have the opportunity to be as good a friend to her as she is to me. With Shyanne, it seemed as if I was the one always receiving, never giving."

"I'm glad you have her. I'm sure things will even out."

"Thank you for being a cheerleader for our relationship. Don't you have to get ready for work, Counselor?"

"No. I'm taking today off. My family needs me."

Shauntae came down the stairs just as Cody slid across the couch to kiss Lindsay. Her sad eyes were still swollen from crying. She slowly moved across the room from the kitchen to the family room at the pace of someone five times her age. Yesterday's incidents had surely taken a toll on the otherwise very beautiful teenager. She seemed to have aged overnight.

Lindsay was very happy that God had sent Cody home before she had to explain his absence to her children. That would have been far too much for them to handle.

Lindsay got up from her seat and met her daughter in the middle of the floor. She hugged Shauntae as her body went limp. Lindsay half-walked, half-carried her to the sofa.

"Last night was horrible, Mom." Cody slid over on the sofa. Both adults embraced Shauntae while she continued to grieve.

"Cody took the day off work, sweetie, so we'll both be here with you and Li'l Shaun all day. I'm also going to call Dr. Hooper to see how soon we can get an emergency appointment for you two. Is that okay with you?"

Shauntae shrugged her shoulders indicating she did not care one way or the other.

Li'l Shaun came bounding down the stairs at a much greater rate of speed than his sister had. He ran to the couch and joined the family in comforting Shauntae. Lindsay wrapped her arms around him and pulled him into her lap. Aside from the grief that shadowed them, the group looked ready for a family portrait.

"Have you talked to Sha'Ron, Shauntae?" Lindsay asked.

"No. He hasn't called me. I haven't called him because I don't really know what to say to him. And right now, Mom, I'm very upset with Aunt Meeka and Aunt Frannie for what they did to you. They didn't have to act that way."

"Don't be too hard on them, honey. They were very grief stricken over their mother's death. They were angry and hurt. I know what that feels like. I don't think they would have attacked me, at least not in front of you two, if they were thinking straight."

After explaining Tameeka's and Francine's actions, Lindsay realized how much she had grown personally. She actually held no animosity toward the sisters for their attack because she believed what she said to her daughter.

"Why don't you call to check on your brother? I'll call Dr. Hooper to see how soon she can see you two."

"Okay, Mom."

"It still seems like it's not real, Shauntae. I've been in Grandma's room about three times already this morning expecting her to be there."

"Who's there with you, Sha'Ron? Do Aunt Tameeka or Frannie still live there?"

"Aunt Meeka is here, but she doesn't live here anymore. She just stayed last night. Auntie Frannie went home to be with her kids."

"Then who is going to take care of you now, Sha'Ron?"

"I'm a man, girl. I can take care of myself." Sha'Ron answered with much more bravado than he actually felt. "Besides, Uncle Bobby will be back later today. He'll help me and tell me what to do."

"Okay, big brother. I just called to check on you. Call me when you all know when Grandma's funeral will be."

"I will. Like I said, my aunties are waiting for Uncle Bobby to get back in town. Then we'll start making arrangements." A thought popped in Sha'Ron's head. "Is your mom going to bring you to the funeral?"

Shauntae became unnerved by her brother's question. Something in his voice almost suggested he was hoping that her mother did plan to attend their grandmother's funeral. Suddenly the scene that played out at their dad's funeral came to mind. Shauntae realized that a similar scene could take place if her mother went to Patricia's funeral.

"No!" The word exploded from Shauntae's lips more forcefully than she intended, but she meant what she said.

Sha'Ron noticed the irritation and mild hostility. He let the whole subject drop. "Okay. I'll call you later today or tomorrow to let you know what's going on."

Sha'Ron hung up, realizing that he had scared his sister with his question about her mother. He thought about what killing the witch would do to her and his little brother; how much it would affect them, tear their world apart. And as much as he hated their mother, even more so since last night, that disturbed him just a bit.

While he was ready to see Lindsay's life end, he wasn't so sure he was smart enough to come up with a plan to take her out and not get caught. He would definitely talk with Uncle Bobby about this when he returned. He hated his former stepmom now more than ever, but he didn't know if it was enough to risk life in prison.

Sha'Ron decided to check on his aunt who was still in bed in his grandma's bedroom. He walked in to find her wide awake, sitting up, holding a Bible.

"What's that?" he asked.

"It's a Bible. Boy, I know you know what a Bible looks like."

"Yeah, I know what a Bible looks like. I meant to say where did you get it?"

"It was right here in Mama's nightstand. I guess she did believe like Frannie hoped."

"Whatever," Sha'Ron replied. "What time did Uncle Bobby say his plane was landing?"

"At twelve-thirty this afternoon. He said he has his car parked at the airport so we don't have to pick him up. He's coming straight here."

"Cool. Do we have to call the funeral home to make an appointment, or do we just show up?"

"Uncle Bobby said he'll handle everything when he gets here. He just wants us here when he arrives. Frannie said she and the kids will be here by 1:00. Do you think Shauntae and Li'l Shaun want to come over?"

Sha'Ron thought about it before answering. "Naw, they don't need to be here. I'll just tell them what gets decided." Sha'Ron did not want them anywhere near when he and his uncle discussed their mother's demise.

"What time is it now?" Tameeka asked.

"It's ten-thirty."

"Well, I guess I'll run home, shower, and change. Are you going to be okay, Nephew, while I'm gone? Or do you want to come with me?"

"I'll be cool," Sha'Ron assured her with more confidence than he felt.

"All right. I'll be back in a little while. I'll bring a few things with me so I can stay for a few days."

"Okay." Sha'Ron was certainly happy to hear that.

***

"Dr. Hooper says this situation is urgent, so she's going to stay after-hours. She wants me to have Shauntae and Li'l Shaun there at 5:00 P.M."

"I'll go with you. After the appointment, we can all go out to dinner and catch a movie. We need to try to enjoy ourselves. This has been a very difficult weekend."

Lindsay loved the idea. Shauntae, if no one else, definitely needed cheering up.

"But what about school tomorrow? This will end up being a late evening."

"I think we can all afford to take one more day off. I'm sure the school will excuse the kids for bereavement."

"You're right. We need some family time. I'll call the kids' school . . . Oh no. School! I totally forgot I was supposed to start classes today. Oh my goodness. So much has been on my mind this past week I let it all slip away. It's eleven-thirty. My first class was supposed to start at eight-forty-five."

"Oh," Cody said dispassionately.

"Oh?" Lindsay repeated to Cody, a little surprised by his lack of interest. "I think I'm going to drop the classes this semester while I still have a chance to get our money back. I'll just wait to start next semester." Lindsay sat down, disappointment showing in her features.

"Honey, why don't you wait before you drop the classes? Just take this first week off and see how things go. Perhaps by next Monday things will have smoothed themselves out."

Lindsay decided her husband's advice was valid. She would wait. If the way things were progressing between her and Cody was any indication to how things would work out, she would be more than ready to go to classes and get all A's by next week.

Shauntae came to their bedroom and knocked on the door. "Mom, it's me. Can I come in?"

"Of course, sweetie," Lindsay replied.

Shauntae entered and sat on the bed between her mother and stepdad, forcing the two to unwillingly put distance between themselves.

"Mom, Cody, what is Sha'Ron going to do since Grandma has died? Who's going to take care of him? I'm so worried about him." Shauntae started to tell them about her feelings when he wanted to know if her mom was coming to the funeral, but she decided against it. She did not want to worry her mom or make Cody angry.

"His aunts can take care of him, Shauntae."

"I don't know, Mom. When I talked to him this morning, he said he was a man and could take care of himself. He said Uncle Bobby would help him, but I think he plans on living in that house by himself."

"Shauntae, he's not old enough to live by himself. The state won't allow him to live alone."

"How will the state know as long as he continues to go to school every day? How will anyone know?"

Lindsay was becoming a bit exhausted by Shauntae's constant need to find things to worry about. She had seemingly started to become a chronic fuss bucket.

"Shauntae, you are too young to be stressing yourself out like this. Tameeka and Francine will not allow Sha'Ron to stay by himself. You don't need to worry about him. He'll be fine, I promise."

"Okay, Mom. It's just so sad that he seems to be alone. No mother. No father. Now no grandmother. I feel sorry for him."

Cody thought about how hard life had been for Sha'Ron and how he was being forced by those around him to grow up so quickly. Cody felt sorry for him too.

But if he ever tried to hurt his wife, Sha'Ron would be the one to end up sorrier than he ever had been in his short little life. . . .

"Call him again, Francine. It's three-thirty. It doesn't take anybody three hours to get here from the airport," Tameeka ranted. She was stressed, and her nerves were on edge. She had run out of patience waiting for her uncle to show up so they could go and make funeral arrangements for her mother.

Uncle Bobby had always been a controlling tyrant as far as Tameeka was concerned. He loved to show his power and make people do what he wanted them to do by using intimidation and money to control them. He would make people sit around and wait for him simply because he could. He had the money and the connections. So folks just waited for him and on him all the time, including his family.

Robert and Patricia Taylor were the only son and daughter of Carmella Taylor. Their father, whose name their mother would never tell them, was a married black man. Their mother was his white trophy mistress.

Bobby was two years older than Patricia. By the time he was eleven, their father had stopped taking care of their mother. The small family ended up evicted from the nice home their father paid the rent on and was forced to live in a rough housing project on the east side of Detroit. After being there for three days, Robert fell in with a local drug gang and his lifelong career in pharmaceuticals began. Bobby had become the man of the family by age twelve, paying the rent and bills. Their mother had succumbed to the pressure of the drug life as well, but she was on the other end of the spectrum. She started using heroin when Bobby was thirteen. She eventually kicked her habit and lived until about two weeks after Shaun's death when she died of a massive heartache. But because of her addiction, Bobby took on the responsibility of taking care of his little sister. He became addicted to power, and at age fifty-three, he still wielded that power like a Samurai wielded his very sharp sword.

But this was just disrespectful. This was his only sister's funeral. She was dead, and they needed to prepare to have her properly buried. Uncle Bobby was being ridiculous now.

"His phone is still going straight to voice mail. I think something's wrong. Uncle Bobby is a trip, but he has always taken care of Mama." Francine sounded a little worried.

Tameeka was still upset, so she wasn't trying to hear it. "Whateva. I say let's go. We can go, make the arrangements, and just tell him how much it's going to cost."

At that instant, Francine's phone rang. She answered quickly, assuming it was Uncle Bobby, finally.

"Hello."

"This is Frank Harris. I'm Robert Taylor's attorney. Is this Francine Taylor?"

"Yes. What's up with my uncle?"

"Mr. Taylor was arrested at the airport when he departed the plane. The warrant stated he was being charged with murder, conspiracy to commit murder, conspiracy to sell and transport drugs, and international drug trafficking."

"What!" Francine's scream got the immediate attention of Tameeka and Sha'Ron.

"What's wrong?" Tameeka asked.

"What happened?" Sha'Ron asked.

"What do we need to do?" Francine asked the attorney.

"There is nothing you can do. He has not gone before a judge yet, but those charges will not allow bail of any amount. The district attorney seems to have a very good case; wiretaps and video surveillance. I'm going to have my work cut out for me, but I'm going to do my best. It will be a few days before you will hear from your uncle."

"But our mother, his sister, just died. Will he be able to attend the funeral?"

"I highly doubt it, but I will see what I can pull off. Just make the arrangements and give me a call. Your uncle is still paying the bills. Don't worry about that. By the time you all get back to me with the amounts, I should have more information for you."

Francine disconnected the call but held the phone, staring at it as if it were the actual object of all the stress she and her family had endured for the past two-and-a-half years.

"Frannie, you're pale. What the heck has happened now?" Tameeka asked.

"Uncle Bobby is in jail." Francine explained everything to them as Mr. Harris had explained it to her.

"This is *not* happening. This is *not* freaking happening. *Not* today. Shaun is dead. Mama is dead, and Uncle Bobby is about to go to prison for the rest of his life, so he may as well be dead too."

Tameeka stormed from the dining room and back toward the bedrooms. Sha'Ron just sat silently in his chair wondering what would happen next.

"Come on. Get your coats and let's go. We still have a funeral to plan for our mother," Tameeka said angrily.

Francine and Sha'Ron sat staring at Tameeka for a moment as if she had lost her mind.

"Come on! We can't help Uncle Bobby, so sitting here feeling sorry for him or for ourselves is not going to help anybody. My mama deserves a proper burial. So let's go and plan one for her before the funeral home closes."

Tameeka left the dining room and headed out the door as if she would go without Francine and Sha'Ron if they didn't get it in gear. Obviously they believed she would because they grabbed their coats and followed her quickly.

The Vincini family was in the car leaving Dr. Hooper's office. They decided to have dinner first at the Olive Garden Restaurant; then they would see whatever PG-rated film they could find at the theater.

Dr. Hooper explained to Lindsay and Cody that grief and even anger after death are normal. But the extra drama like the fighting and the paternal family's hatred of their mother moved the negative emotions of these kids to dangerous levels. Dr. Hooper's first suggestion was that she talk to the kids on a weekly versus bi-weekly basis for the time being. Second, she suggested that they keep things at home as healthy, normal, and happy as possible. The kids needed a little extra care in order to balance the chaos they would experience up to, and even beyond, the funeral. Third, Dr. Hooper suggested the kids attend the funeral, but Lindsay should stay as far away from the Taylors as possible. The kids did not need to witness any more of that negativity. Lastly, while the adults could not control what the Taylors said about Lindsay, they were not to say anything negative about the Taylors in front of the kids.

Lindsay thought about how good God is as the family drove to the restaurant. The Holy Spirit had already given Cody and Lindsay guidance on how to best deal with the children. God also gave them the insight to prearrange their outing even before they saw Dr. Hooper.

"Mom, should I call Sha'Ron to check on him and the funeral arrangements?" Shauntae asked.

"Sure, sweetie."

Shauntae placed the call, but by the time Cody parked the car at the restaurant, she was visibly shaken. She disconnected the call with her big brother after never uttering a word between "hello" and "talk to you later."

"Mom, there's more bad news. Uncle Bobby got arrested today when he got off the airplane. Sha'Ron said the charges against him will probably land him in prison for life. He won't even be able to go to Grandma Pat's funeral."

Lindsay and Cody looked at each other shocked. Neither was very upset or surprised at Uncle Bobby's arrest, but they were both thinking that it could not have come at a worse time.

"I'm not that upset about Uncle Bobby, Mom. I hardly knew him. I'm just worried about Sha'Ron."

"I'm sorry about this for Sha'Ron too, but, honey, Uncle Bobby is a big drug dealer. You can only get away with doing bad for so long before it catches up with you." After Lindsay had spoken, she hoped her words hadn't qualified as the negative Dr. Hooper had said they not speak against the Taylors.

"I understand. The funeral will be Friday at 10:00 A.M. at Swanson Funeral Home on Six Mile Road," Shauntae said solemnly.

"All right, we'll make arrangements for you and your brother to be there with the family."

"I think we need to pray before we go into the restaurant," Cody said. "Let's bow our heads and close our eyes." Everyone complied. "Father God in heaven, we come before you, Lord, with praise and thanksgiving on our lips. Lord, we come to give you thanks, Lord, for how you have kept this family through all of the tragedy of these past few days. We are praying, Lord, for our children who have had bad reports and witnessed depressing actions. Lord, they have had to deal with death and devastation in their family. I come, Lord, praying that you give them divine comfort for their spirit and souls. Help Lindsay and me to be for them what they need us to be. I come praying, Father, for the Taylor family as well. They too are being persecuted on every hand. Touch them, Lord, as well. And, Father, I pray that they find the miracle of the free gift of salvation in all of this pain and suffering. We ask that you bless this food we are about to partake of. Remove from it all impurities and allow it to strengthen our minds, bodies, and spirits in Jesus' name . . . Amen."

The family said in unison, "Amen."

Chapter Fifteen

Sha'Ron had just changed his clothes. He had put on the suit he wore to church last Sunday to wear to his grandmother's funeral. Then he realized that the funeral was not going to be in a church and his grandma was never a very formal type of person. So he dressed for the memorial in a style more befitting of who she was.

He threw on a pair of Rocawear blue jeans, a yellow, long sleeved Rocawear Polo shirt, and a pair of yellow and white Air Force Ones. He looked at himself in the mirror and smiled for the first time since his grandma died.

"I've got you, Grandma."

As Sha'Ron emerged from his bedroom, both Tameeka and Francine stared at him a little oddly.

"Boy, what do you have on? This is your grandmother's *funeral*, not your girlfriend's house party," Tameeka exclaimed.

"I'm representing my grandma. She was not all flash and glam. She was neat and understated. She never fronted for anyone."

"Don't give him a hard time, Meeka. It's not that important. At least he looks neat."

Both Tameeka and Francine looked the part of grieving family in their black dress and black skirt suit respectively.

"Whatever. How are Shauntae and Li'l Shaun getting over here so they can ride with us in the family car? And why do they still call him Li'l Shaun? Can't they just call him Shaun?"

"Tameeka, calm down. Keva is bringing Kevaun, Shauntae, and Li'l Shaun over here, remember? And don't worry about what they call him. Let's not make mountains out of molehills, not today."

"Whatever."

Francine decided to just ignore her sister. She assumed this was just a part of her grieving process. She was probably anxious to get this whole thing over with.

"Shauna is riding in the family car too, right? Tawanda better not be late like she always is. And there is not enough room for her in the car."

"Whatever, Tameeka."

The doorbell rang. Sha'Ron opened the door to find Shauntae, Li'l Shaun, Keva, and Kevaun on the snow-covered porch. Sha'Ron opened the screen door and let everyone in.

"Sha'Ron, why haven't you shoveled that porch and walkway?" Keva asked.

The entourage entered the house kicking snow off of dress boots and high-heeled shoes. Everyone in this party was dressed in traditional funeral gear.

"Don't come in here giving my nephew orders, Keva. He is not your child. He never was. His daddy never married you," Tameeka griped.

Keva bucked her eyes at Tameeka's very rude comment. Back in the day she would have cussed Tameeka out even in front of the children. She truly considered doing so now, but praise God, she was a different person now. Francine was not as tolerant of her sister's rudeness, however.

"You know what, Tameeka? Maybe you need to go and lie down until we are all ready to leave. I'm thinking you are not feeling very well this morning."

"Whatever, Frannie. You ain't my mama. My mama is dead, remember?" Tameeka made that her parting snide remark as she went to do what her sister suggested.

"I'm sorry about that, Keva. Tameeka has been on one all morning, in actuality, she's been on one all week."

Francine approached Keva for a warm hug. The two ladies used to be best friends when they were teenagers. In fact, Francine was a key factor in hooking up Shaun with Keva while he was involved with Lindsay.

"It's cool. I know she's grieving," Keva replied.

Everyone found a seat around the living room and dining room as they waited for Tawanda and the limousine to arrive. The kids seem to gravitate toward one another, leaving Francine and Keva in the dining room out of earshot of the kids.

"So tell me how you and the evil queen Lindsay became such fast friends? Last I remember, you two hated each other. Every time you were in each other's presence there was bloodshed."

"That was a long time ago, Frannie. I would hope that all of us have matured since then. Nay-Nay and I have children that are siblings. We need to get along for their sake."

"I hear you. But I don't know if I can ever forgive her for killing my brother. Shaun may not have been perfect or a perfect boyfriend or husband, for that matter. But I don't believe he deserved to die."

"Frannie, you're right. Nay did not have the right to kill him. But she did. And she did her time. Believe me, she is sorry. She's lost a lot too. Her best friend was killed during that whole mess."

"Don't defend her to me, please, Keva; especially not today." Francine became instantly angry.

Keva understood Francine's disposition. Not wanting to escalate the tension she simply said, "Fine. Let's just drop this whole conversation. Let me call Tawanda to find out where she is. I'm going to ride to the funeral with her."

The doorbell rang as Keva dialed the first three numbers. Francine got up to answer the door.

"Dang! Why ain't nobody shovel the dang snow?" Tawanda complained as she entered the house and handed her daughter to Francine. Francine, Keva, and all the kids laughed.

Tameeka came stomping out of the room at the sounds of joy. "What the heck is so funny? Why are you all out here having all this fun on the day we bury my mama?"

"Tameeka, hush and go get your coat. It looks like the limo just arrived. Everybody, let's get ready to go. Tameeka, please bring that Bible you found in Mama's nightstand."

"No. You get it." Tameeka left the room to get her coat and returned without the Bible. Then she walked out the front door.

"Oh, that girl." Francine went to the room to retrieve the Bible herself. She returned and everyone filed out of the house and into either the limo or Tawanda's car to head to the funeral home.

They all arrived at the funeral home, followed protocol, and viewed the body as a family of children and grandchildren. Sha'Ron took it the hardest at the casket and again when they closed the casket. He broke down and cried uncontrollably in front of his younger siblings and cousins. He allowed himself this moment of weakness, and it actually felt good.

Shauntae sat closest to Sha'Ron on the chapel pew. She cried as well, both for her grandmother and the pain her brother felt.

Suddenly she looked up and saw a man standing at the casket wearing an orange jumpsuit that said Wayne County Jail on the back. Immediately she recognized the man as Uncle Bobby. He was locked in chains at the wrist and ankles, and he looked shabby, unshaven, and frightening.

"Sha'Ron, come here, Nephew."

Sha'Ron wiped his eyes and stood up to join his uncle at his grandmother's closed casket. Two armed security guards stood just off to the side in the chapel.

"Uncle Bobby, what are you doing here? Your lawyer said you wouldn't be able to make it."

"Man, don't worry about all that. What you doing crying over there like a little girl? You better man up, boy." Uncle Bobby said that loud enough for the other family members to hear him. Then he lowered his voice when he dispensed his next advice. "How you gon' be a soldier with them tears in your eyes? You got a task to complete, soon. I'm wondering if you can do it now since you over there acting like a female."

Sha'Ron stepped back and eyed his uncle carefully. He was locked in chains, facing the possibility of life in prison with no parole, yet he was still trying to clown him and treat him like a punk. Sha'Ron's already raw emotions exploded in anger.

"What, dude? You standing there in somebody else's clothes, with yo' little nannies watching you from over there, and you calling *me* a female? I cried because I loved my grandma and she died. That's normal. Standing there in your clown suit with your matching clown jewelry is not. Kick rocks, jailbird. I got this. I'm gon' do this my way from here on out." Sha'Ron stormed out of the chapel.

Shauntae stood to follow him, but Keva stopped her. "Let his aunts handle this."

Shauntae started to defy her. Her big brother needed her. But she knew if she disobeyed and disrespected Ms. Keva, her mother would knock her out.

Francine and Tameeka both followed Sha'Ron out of the chapel. He was waiting inside the limousine, wishing he had driven instead so he could leave.

"Sha'Ron, you have to come back inside. The funeral is not over yet," Tameeka said.

"I'm good. I said my good-byes. I'll just wait in the car. Leave me alone."

"All right now, boy, we know you're upset with Uncle Bobby, but you won't be allowed to disrespect us. So watch your tone," Francine said.

"Look, my mama is dead. My daddy is dead. My grandma is dead. My uncle is a jailbird forever. I'm thinking I've run fresh out of relatives who can tell me what to do. So leave me alone!" Sha'Ron said even more emphatically this time.

Tameeka moved as if she were about to get in the car to attack Sha'Ron for being disrespectful, but Francine stopped her.

"Come on, Tameeka. Let him have this one. He's hurting and grieving. He'll apologize when things calm down, I'm sure." Francine's words were more of a declarative than an assumption.

The two women left Sha'Ron sitting in the limo and went back into the funeral home chapel.

Sha'Ron sat in the car thinking about the scene Uncle Bobby represented. Seeing him all shackled and enslaved threw him for a loop. Then to have him looking powerless yet still trying to throw his weight around was infuriating. How could someone who would never see the light of day again unless someone else died tell him what to do? No. He would have to figure out how to kill the witch on his own. He would actually start plotting today. He would follow Keva when she took Li'l Shaun and Shauntae home to find out where Lindsay lived. It was time to get this party started. He had lost too many people he loved. Now it was time for payback.

At the burial site Sha'Ron remained in the limousine. He did not want to be in the presence of his uncle. Now that the cars were pulling up to the house and he was assured that Uncle Bobby was back behind bars, he couldn't wait to get out of the car. He felt like it had become his prison since he ran from the chapel.

He looked up and down the street for Tawanda's car, but he didn't immediately see it. No worries though. Keva's car was still parked across the street, so they had to come back eventually.

Sha'Ron followed the small crowd into the house. His grandmother didn't have many friends or any family outside of her brother, her children, and grandchildren. There were about twenty-five people total at the funeral, and that included Uncle Bobby's attorney and the two security guards that were assigned to him.

Francine and Tameeka had the repast meal catered. Francine asked one of her coworkers to stay at the house to wait for the food to arrive and show the caterers where to set up. So just about everyone from the funeral home came by to have something to eat. Sha'Ron stayed in his room until he heard Tawanda talking when she came into the house.

"I'm sorry we weren't right behind y'all. I had to stop and grab Shauna another outfit from the house. She done wrecked the one she had on when she opened her Sippy cup."

Sha'Ron came from his room and mingled with his family all while keeping an eye on Keva. He wanted to make sure she didn't leave without him being able to follow her.

About an hour and a half later, he heard Keva call for Shauntae, Kevaun, and Li'l Shaun to get their coats.

"Francine, we have to get going. I want to get home to my husband and get these two home to their mom. If you need anything give me a call, okay?"

"Thanks for bringing the kids, Keva, and for paying your respects to my mom." Francine then addressed the kids. "All right, handsome nephew and beautiful niece, don't let it be this long before we see you all again. I'm going to make sure you all spend lots of time with my kids. You all are family, and family needs each other."

Francine gave each child a long hug and a peck on the cheek.

Tameeka followed suit.

"You all make sure you keep in touch with me too, okay? I love my nieces and nephews; all of you." Tameeka waved indicating she was including Francine's kids, Shauna, and Sha'Ron, as well.

Keva gave Daiquan and Destiny, Francine's two children, a hug and a kiss. She also attempted to hug Sha'Ron.

"I'll take a hug, but I'm walking out with you all. I've got a run to make," he said.

"What run, Sha'Ron? I don't think you need to leave right now," Tameeka said.

It was decided between the sisters that Tameeka would give up the apartment she was renting and move home to take care of Sha'Ron. While he kept insisting he could take care of himself, he was glad his aunt would be at the house with him.

Sha'Ron started to inform her again that he was not taking orders from her, but he figured it would be simpler to be nice. "Auntie, I'll be back in no later than an hour. I just need to get out of the house for a little bit. I'm going to run over to Marcus's house for a moment."

Francine interjected for her nephew. "Tameeka, let him go. He probably does need to get away for a little while."

"What's up with you, Frannie? You have just been letting this boy do whatever he wants to do and say whatever he wants to say all day. He's going to be living here with me. He's going to have to get used to respecting me and answering to me."

"Auntie Meeka, I understand that. I just need to get out of here for a little while. I promise I'll be back in an hour." Again, it was all about catching flies with honey versus vinegar.

Keva and the kids left with Sha'Ron right on their heels. The kids all said good-bye to their big brother, and everyone got in their respective vehicles. Keva headed north on Piedmont. Sha'Ron headed south, made a quick right, and then got behind Keva about four car lengths. Keva turned right on Joy Road, and then she hit the Southfield Freeway, heading north in the direction of Jefferies Freeway. Sha'Ron was hoping she would take the freeway. It would make it easier to stay inconspicuous.

Once Keva hit Livernois and Six Mile and made the left, Sha'Ron hung back and just watched to see how many streets she drove down before she made a right. He then followed up to the street she turned on and watched her go two blocks. He couldn't count exactly how many houses she was from the corner, but he had enough of an idea of where his prey lived. . . .

***

"Thank you, Keva, for taking my children to the funeral. How did it go?" Lindsay asked.

"It was a small affair that was pretty uneventful until Sha'Ron went off on Uncle Bobby."

The women were standing in the foyer, but when Lindsay heard that tidbit of news, she ushered Keva into a seat in the living room. The kids were in the family room.

"Tell me what happened."

Keva repeated almost verbatim the conversation between Bobby and Sha'Ron, at least what she heard from Uncle Bobby's part.

"Girl, Sha'Ron was so angry you could see him shaking. It was really kind of scary."

"Wow! A funeral is never just a funeral in that family, is it?"

"That's not funny." But both women cracked up. When the laughter died down, they got serious again.

"Nay, I know we have talked about Sha'Ron being dangerous and you being very careful. I just want to reiterate that. That young man was very angry and very hurt. I have a bad feeling in my spirit about him. So I repeat, please, please be very careful. Don't take anything for granted, okay? Where's Cody?"

Lindsay listened to her friend with her heart and her own spirit. "Cody's at work. I hear you. I am listening, I promise."

"Good. Now let me get out of here." The ladies got up and headed to the family room.

"Come on, Kevaun. It's time to go home."

"Yes, Mom," he said. To his sister he said, "He's going to be okay. We have to keep praying for him. I'll call you later. See you, Sis. Bye, Shaun."

Lindsay watched and listened to the scene and felt good. She then gave a sidelong glance at Keva and felt very good. Considering the situation and circum-stances under which these relationships began, it amazed her that they could even be here in this place emotionally now. The NIV Bible verse, Romans 8:28 came to her spirit just then. "And we know that in all things God works for the good of those who love him, who have been called according to his purpose."

"This is good, huh?" Keva whispered.

"It is," Lindsay smiled.

The Vincini family walked Keva and Kevaun to the door, and everyone hugged good night.

Chapter Sixteen

The following day, the day after the funeral, the Vincinis had no plans outside of the house. Cody worked in the office to catch up on some things as a result of his two days off earlier in the week. The kids worked on makeup assignments they received from their teachers to cover the days they were out of school, which were Monday, Tuesday, and Friday. Even Lindsay sat in the family room perusing through her books for her economics and sociology classes. She'd picked up the books last Tuesday when Cody convinced her not to give up her classes when she missed the first class on last Monday. The kids didn't have their next therapy appointment until after school on this coming Monday.

This was the quietest and most peaceful their household had been all week.

On that same day, Sha'Ron had decided he would venture from his home. He sat on Shiawassee Street parked about four doors down from his former stepmom's house. He figured out the exact house when he saw White Boy's BMW in the driveway. He traded cars with his boy, Jamarion. He was driving a money-green Jeep Cherokee instead of his souped-up Mustang, which would have been easy to identify.

Sha'Ron looked at his watch. It was 12:30 P.M., which meant he had been sitting watching the house for an hour. While he sat there, he only had one thought running through his head: to prove to his uncle he was not a punk. He had not formulated a plan on how to kill Lindsay, but he knew he would do it and do it soon.

Sha'Ron stared around the street at the big houses that sat on this block. The neighborhood was quiet. The cars on the street and in the driveways were all stylish and well kept, even if they weren't all newer models. White Boy and the witch seemed to be living the perfect little *Cosby Show* life. They were married, happy, and living large. This all seemed so unfair to him. This was the woman who had come into his life when he was just a baby and destroyed his family. Now she had a new family and was living like a rock star. This was definitely not justice in his eyes.

Sha'Ron saw a car coming from the opposite direction slow down and pull into the driveway behind White Boy's car. He watched as the two people emerged from the vehicle; the driver, a man, the passenger, an older woman. From the distance, the people looked familiar to him. Then it hit him. It was Lindsay's mother and brother. *One big happy family. Yeah, this chick, without a doubt, has to go,* Sha'Ron thought as he pulled away from the curb and left.

The quiet peace of the Vincini home was altered by the ringing of the front doorbell. Lindsay put her books down, actually happy to be taking a break, and answered the door.

"Mama, Kevin! What are you two doing here? I didn't know you were coming over."

"Kevin surprised me this morning by coming over to take me to breakfast, so I figured we would stop by and surprise you," Sherrie supplied, happy to see her daughter.

"Oh, I see. You come by to see me *after* you eat."

"Nay, you come with a lot of mouths to feed. I can't afford to take all y'all out," Kevin kidded.

"Whatever, boy. You making all the loot, Mr. Junior Vice President. Come on, y'all. Let's go into the family room." The three of them walked from the foyer to the back of the house.

"I do a'ight. But your kids are greedy, Nay. It takes a lot of food to fill up Shaun's huge head. And your daughter's feet are so big. I know that's where every morsel of food goes. No, I ain't trying to cancel my 401(k) just to feed your raggedy kids."

"Cody, baby, K.J. is in here talking about our kids," Lindsay yelled into the office. Apparently Shauntae and Li'l Shaun heard her too because everyone converged into the family room.

"Grandma!" both kids yelled simultaneously.

"Hi, babies. You all came in just in time to stop your mama and uncle from fighting." Sherrie gave her two children a look that signaled the game of the dozens was over because the kids were in the room.

"Punk," Lindsay said under her breath.

"I heard that, Lindsay Renee Westbrook Vincini," Sherrie said.

Both Lindsay and Kevin knew it was time to stop because their mother had resorted to using full names.

"Mama, you are going to teach me how to tame my wife like that," Cody said.

Everyone laughed.

"Me too, Grandma," Li'l Shaun said. Everyone laughed again.

"I missed my grandkids when I was in Arizona. I brought you two a bunch of stuff back too. But you have to come spend the night with me to get it. So tell me when you're available."

"Yes!" Li'l Shaun said eagerly. He loved spending the night with his grandma. She always let him do whatever he wanted and eat whatever he wanted. Grandma's answer was always "Yes, that's fine, baby."

Shauntae was just as enthusiastic. During the two years she lived at her grandma's while her mom was in prison, she had made some great friends. She couldn't wait to see them again.

"Can we go today, Mom? We've got a few days to make up our schoolwork. Please, can we go?" Shauntae pleaded.

Lindsay looked at Cody, and he nodded his approval. "Sure. You can stay with Grandma tonight, just as long as she agrees to bring you all to church in the morning."

"Of course, I will. I want you two to go upstairs and pack a bag. I need to talk to your mom and Cody. I'll let you know when we're ready to leave. Oh, and make sure you bring your schoolwork with you."

The kids scrambled away to get ready to hang out with Grandma.

"Mom, what's up?" Lindsay asked.

Cody and Lindsay shared the love seat. Kevin and Sherrie sat on the sofa.

"Your brother has a good-news-bad-news situation to share with you. Go ahead, K.J. Tell your sister what's up as she asked."

"It's not at all bad. Brooke is pregnant, and we're getting married. Your mother is just exaggerating. She's a little peeved that Brooke got pregnant before we got married."

Lindsay chuckled at her mother and brother. Sherrie always treated Kevin like a baby while she allowed Lindsay to live her life and learn from her mistakes. Their mother was also not very crazy about Kevin's girlfriend of two years, Brooke, because she felt Kevin was being controlled by her.

"Mama, K.J. is twenty-nine years old. He'll be thirty this year. You're acting like he's a sixteen-year-old kid who knocked up his high school girlfriend. What's the big deal?"

"She's *pregnant*, Nay," Sherrie emphasized.

"Okay. But they're getting married. He's doing the right thing."

"That's what I'm talking about. Why didn't they get married *first?* I feel like she trapped him into marrying her. She leads him around like a little puppy."

"Mama, no. Trapped him? Are you serious? How can you say that? I was pregnant before I got married. As a matter of fact, so were you. How can you be so judgmental?"

"That's what I said to her. I thought she was going to slap me right there in the restaurant," Kevin said seriously.

"That's why you took me to a public restaurant to tell me about your little girlfriend being pregnant. So I wouldn't slap you. But don't push it now, mister; we are now on private property."

Cody stifled a laugh, but Lindsay was a little aggravated. Of course, her mother was just kidding about striking Kevin . . . probably. But she was very serious about trying to run his life.

"And I don't need you reminding me of the mistakes we made, missy. We were both very young, and neither of us was trying to trap anybody. We were just naïve and in love. Brooke is old enough to know that when you have unprotected sex, you are *trying* to get pregnant."

"Oh, I see. Her being older than we were makes her automatically manipulative. Love has nothing to do with it. And K.J. has nothing to do with it either, right? She got pregnant all by herself."

Cody and Kevin sat quietly while mother and daughter debated about Kevin's girlfriend/fiancée and her pregnancy. They were not consulted for their opinions, so they sat and just listened.

"So, Nay, you're telling me you're okay with them having this baby out of wedlock?"

"Mama, it's not for me to be okay with it or not. K.J. is a grown man. Brooke is a grown woman. They have to be accountable to God for their own actions. I'm not saying it is right. I'm just saying neither you nor I are in a position to judge."

Kevin finally spoke up. "Thank you, big sister, for being brave enough to fight your mother on my behalf. I truly appreciate you and your courage."

"Boy, you are not acting like you're grateful talking like that. Sounds like you're trying to get me a beat down."

"Actually, no, that is far from the truth. I remember the last time I had to witness Mama beating you down. Cody, did she tell you about that? It was ugly. I thought my mama was going to kill her." Kevin shook his head as he recalled the dreadful scene.

"Shut up, K.J., before I turn my allegiance and start agreeing with your mother about your girlfriend being a controlling, manipulative tramp." Everyone including Sherrie cracked up laughing.

Once the laughter died down, Sherrie said, "Let's switch, children. You tell me how things are going with you, my darling daughter. How are the kids handling their other grandmother's death?"

Sherrie was out of town when the mess between Cody and Lindsay started. She knew nothing about their one-day estrangement. God worked things out quickly so there was no need to fill her in on that. Therefore, Lindsay would just talk about the kids.

"Patricia's death was pretty rough on Shauntae. Li'l Shaun didn't remember much about her. He simply reacted to his sister's stress."

Lindsay wasn't sure if Kevin had told their mom about the fight at the hospital. Since Sherrie had not mentioned it yet she was pretty sure she didn't know.

"When I took the kids to the hospital after Shauntae got the phone call from Sha'Ron, I was attacked by Francine and Tameeka."

"What? They put their hands on my baby? Are you all right?" Sherrie sat up straighter in her seat on the sofa. She instantly became furious.

"Ma, I'm fine. It was a week ago. The worst thing is the kids saw it. Because of all the stress and drama, their therapist suggests they come in weekly instead of biweekly for a little while."

"Wow! Is there anything I should know as far as the dos and don'ts with the kids?"

"Dr. Hooper just says we need to do all we can to keep things peaceful around them. Even a little overindulgence, something I know you do anyway, is a good idea. But, Ma, I don't want them around Sha'Ron for the rest of this weekend. I'm going to tell them that before they leave, but I need you to back me on this one."

"No, no. You don't have to worry about me. I agree with you. No Sha'Ron."

Lindsay wondered if she should tell her mother and brother about everyone's heightened concern for her safety with regards to Sha'Ron.

"Mama, K.J., Lindsay has been placed on high-security alert. We are being very careful to keep her away from Sha'Ron as well. Everyone is concerned that he may try to do harm to her. I think you two should know so you can watch out for her when she's with you," Cody butted in.

Well, I guess that answers that question, Lindsay thought. She shot her husband a dirty look.

"I saw that look, young lady. Cody was right for telling us. It's not about you worrying us. It's about us being aware so we can do what we can to watch out for you," Sherrie said.

"Sis, we love you. We want to make sure you stay safe. Don't be mad at Cody for telling us," Kevin chimed in.

Cody pulled his wife close to him on the love seat and embraced her. "She's not mad at me. She's not allowed to be. Dr. Hooper said we have to keep things peaceful for the sake of the kids." Lindsay smiled at her hubby, then snuggled in close to him.

"Let us leave and take the kids with us so y'all *married* folks can have some privacy." It was now Sherrie's turn to shoot her son a dirty look.

"Ma, let it go. I'm getting married in about two months."

"Wow, that soon, little brother? Brooke doesn't want a big wedding?" Lindsay inquired.

"Naw. We're just going to have a small ceremony in the little chapel at church. I'm going to fly Granny in for the ceremony. That will be the most extravagant thing we do."

"That's cool. I'm sure Granny will love that. First, my wedding at Martha's Vineyard, now she gets to travel back home for your wedding. I can't wait to see her. I'm still not over the fact that she left us and moved down to Florida."

Kevin jumped from the sofa. "I'm going to get the kids."

He trotted upstairs to where his niece and nephew were. When they came back down, packed and dressed to leave, Sherrie got up from her seat and put her coat on as well.

"Shaun, Shauntae, you two have fun with your grandma tonight. But I don't want you to plan to go anywhere else. No visiting with Sha'Ron for the rest of this weekend, understand?" Lindsay insisted.

Both kids nodded that they did. "It's cool, Mom. I think we kind of need a break from each other for a few days. But can I visit with Nichole and Isis?" Shauntae asked.

"If you're talking about your friends from the neighborhood, that's between you and your grandma."

"We'll work it all out when we get to my house. Maybe the girls can come to my house tonight for a sleepover," Sherrie suggested.

Just as Lindsay predicted, overindulging the kids would not be a problem for her mother.

Everyone walked to the front door together.

"I'll go out and start the car," Kevin said.

"Don't worry, daughter, dear, I'll take wonderful care of my grandbabies. Cody, you take care of my baby."

Cody stepped behind Lindsay and wrapped his big strong arms around her. "Don't you worry, Mama. I will guard her with my life."

"Good. I love you both. Enjoy your privacy. I'll see you at church tomorrow."

"We love you, too. Bye, Mama," Lindsay said.

"Hey, li'l sister, what you got going on today?" Sha'Ron asked Shauntae via cell phone.

"Hey, Sha'Ron, I'm on my way down the street to hang out with my friend Nichole."

"Okay. Why don't you and your girl meet me at the mall? We can get something to eat and see a movie. I'll buy both of you a LeBron James basketball jersey."

Shauntae considered what her brother said. She felt kind of bad for him. She knew he was probably lonely or needed to get away from Grandma Pat's house. But even if her mother had not forbidden it, she really didn't want to hang out with him today anyway. Like she told her mom, she needed a break from that drama.

"I can't today, Sha'Ron. Me and Li'l Shaun are spending the night with our grandmother. I already have plans to hang out with my friends in the neighborhood."

Sha'Ron could hear in his sister's voice that she really didn't even want to see him. Normally, she would get excited and think of ways to persuade whomever she needed to let her see him. Today, there was no fight in her. She didn't even want to try. Her mother had poisoned her mind and probably his little brother's mind against him.

"Oh. Okay. Cool. Enjoy yourself with your friends and your *other* grandma. I'll talk to you later, Shauntae."

Shauntae felt even worse after Sha'Ron disconnected the call. She knew he was being intentionally snippy with the grandma comment.

Wow, she thought. This was getting more complicated than she ever imagined it would. In the beginning, all she wanted was to reconnect with her father's side of the family. Since her initial reunion with Sha'Ron, she had lost her grandmother to death, she watched her aunts attack her mother, and saw her uncle locked in chains. So much for them all being one big happy family.

The evil witch, as his aunts always referred to her, had gone way too far now. She had stolen the minds of his sister and brother; probably Kevaun too since it was apparent she and Keva were new best friends. But there would be nothing else. Sha'Ron vowed he would not allow Lindsay to take one more thing from him. Nothing!

Chapter Seventeen

Monday morning came quickly, and Lindsay was not mad about it. For her, it signaled the beginning of not just a new week, but also the beginning of getting past the last few weeks.

Though she and Cody had only been separated one night, that one night was horrible. The weeks leading up to her finally telling him the truth had been nerve-racking. So, in essence, that drama had lasted more than one night.

Then there was the horrible drama of Patricia's death and all her children had to deal with and witness as a result of it. Heck, her kids were already in therapy because of the drama she had with their father. Yes, Shauntae and Li'l Shaun had been privy to way more than any thirteen and eight year olds should have to deal with.

But she felt today was a turning point for her whole family. Even her little brother was getting married and had a baby on the way. Yes, today was the beginning of a new season; one of complete healing. They still had a long way to go and a lot of processes to get through, but they were at least moving in the direction of progress; great progress. Yes. Today was the first day of the rest of their lives.

"Thank you, God," she said as she sat up in bed.

"Thank you, God," Cody repeated as if he knew every thought in her head and was cosigning them.

"Today's a new day, baby," Lindsay shared with him.

"I hear you, love, and I agree. But let's start it by being clean with fresh breath. We have to get up and get showered. I'll take my shower first while you get the kids up. Then you can shower while I check on them and get them to the kitchen for breakfast. Then you can—"

Lindsay cut him off midsentence. "I know how this works, Mr. Vincini. This part is not new."

The couple kissed with the unspoken promise of starting all of their mornings together this way.

Once everyone was up, showered, dressed, and fed, they all left the house at the same time going to their respective destinations: Cody to his law office, Shauntae and Li'l Shaun to the bus stop heading for school, and Lindsay on her way to college and her first day of completing her degree.

At the end of her second class, Lindsay waited to talk to her professor to find out if she had missed an assignment last week. Her economics professor said he and the class simply used the first session as an icebreaker.

When the final student had filed out of the classroom, Lindsay approached her professor. "Professor Monroe, I want to apologize for missing last week. Was there an assignment given that I need to complete?"

"Actually, we did have a homework assignment that was due at the beginning of class. If you can give me a good reason for missing last week, I will allow you to complete it by Thursday. E-mail it to me and you'll receive full credit."

Lindsay chuckled, not the least bit worried about her reasons being good enough. She told Professor Monroe the complete truth, including the reason for her one-day estrangement from Cody. By the time she was done, the woman was sitting there with her mouth hanging open. Lindsay laughed out loud at her expression.

"Professor Monroe, all of that was a result of remnants from my past. But I declared and thanked God this morning that today is the beginning of a brand-new day; a brand-new life."

Lindsay received her assignment and went home. She checked her phone and discovered she had a voice mail from Kevin

"Hey, sis, give me a call when you get this message. I'm only working half day today and Brooke is off. We were hoping to get with you today since we know you don't have anything going on. We wanted to go over some things for our ceremony." Lindsay returned her brother's call promptly.

"Hi, sis," Kevin answered.

"What do you mean I don't have anything going on, big head? I have a very full life, thank you very much. As a matter of fact, I'm leaving school right now."

"Oh yeah. You did mention going back to school to *finally* get your degree. Anyhoo, what's up? Can we get together about 1:30 or 2:00? When I get off work we can meet at Southern Fires downtown. My treat as long as you don't bring your kids."

"Shut up. I'll meet you all at 2:00. See you in a little while."

Lindsay decided she would run home and prep dinner for this evening for her family; then she would leave to meet her brother.

Sha'Ron had not been stalking Lindsay long enough to have established any specific patterns. He only knew that Shauntae and Li'l Shaun rode the school bus to school. So she didn't take them to school. He didn't believe she had a job, so he didn't think she would have to get up and out too early in the morning. Therefore, he didn't have to get up and out too early to watch her. Today would be the first day of his official surveillance and logging process. This way, he could get a line on her comings and goings.

He designated a spot about four doors down from her house on the opposite side of the street in front of an empty house for sale for his observation spot. He'd been there about thirty minutes when he saw the witch ride past him in her maroon GMC Yukon SUV. Sha'Ron jotted the time in his log book at 11:55 A.M. Lindsay only pulled the truck into the driveway as far as the front door. On the last two days that he watched the house, he realized that her truck was kept in the garage while White Boy kept his BMW in the driveway, up close to the side door. The way she parked her car gave Sha'Ron reason to suspect she would be leaving again soon. He decided to wait her out and see where she was going.

Sha'Ron kept a loaded .45 automatic gun on the passenger seat of whatever friend's car he was driving that day. He switched vehicles each time he decided to watch the house. It was easy to get someone to loan him their car, especially since he would allow them to keep his sports car in exchange. Today he was rolling in a tan '05 Chevy Malibu. It was actually the car of one of his friends' mom, who had no problem risking his mother's wrath for the opportunity to drive Sha'Ron's pretty car.

Ditching school today was not a problem either. Sha'-Ron used his ensuing grief as a reason to miss school again. He had his friend's older sister make the call, pretending to be his Aunt Tameeka.

In an effort to pass the time, he decided to clean out the text messages in his cell phone. His process was usually to read each of the sent and received messages and save those he thought to be pertinent. He would get rid of those that were inconsequential and in any way incriminating.

While scrolling through his texts, he saw a series of messages between him and Shauntae and read them carefully.

> Sha'Ron: Hey li'l sis. How r u this eve?
> Shauntae: Hey big bro. I'm good. What abt u? Good 2 hear from u. I thot u were mad @ me.
> Sha'Ron: No. Y wuld I b mad @ u?
> Shauntae: Idk (I don't know). Mayb it was just me.
> Sha'Ron: Yeah. I guess. So u havn fun?
> Shauntae: Yeah. I luv hangn w/my grandma. She does not no how 2 say no. Lol. My grandma is so cool. I rember Grandma Pat was cool like tht 2.

Sha'Ron never responded to his sister after that. She never said anything else either. He reread the text series over and over again. He appreciated Shauntae's acknowledgment that his grandma was cool. It crushed him, though, that she had another grandma to love and kick it with. Yes, he knew a little about his mother's mother, but they never really developed a close relationship, not even after Lindsay had killed his mother. Patricia Taylor had loved him, taken care of him, and she never told him no either. She was the coolest.

Sha'Ron began to feel that ache that made him cry. The only other time he felt that ache was when his stepmom killed his dad. He cried a lot right after his father's funeral. His grandma had allowed him to cry. She cried too.

But whenever his uncle Bobby was around, he had to stifle his tears and *man up 'cause only girls are allowed to cry.* He had to be a man, a man who avenged his daddy's death, not cried about it.

Fine. He was going to avenge his daddy's death and the death of his mother and grandma as well, but he was going to cry too.

Forty-five minutes after Lindsay had gone into the house she came back out, got in the truck, and started it up. Sha'Ron heard the sound of the ignition start. That brought him out of his tear-laden recollection.

Lindsay began to back out of the driveway. Sha'Ron quickly started his car and drove up to the house with intentions of cutting her off as she came out of the driveway. However, Lindsay stopped suddenly. She got out of the truck, quickly jogged back to her front door, and went into the house.

She left her truck running so Sha'Ron knew she would be back shortly. He stopped the Malibu in the middle of the street and waited for Lindsay to reemerge from her beautiful house here on Everything Is Lovely Street. *No,* he thought. *She does not have the right to live happily ever after when she has destroyed so many other lives, including mine.*

Lindsay came running, almost sprinting, out the front door back to her truck.

"Stepmother!"

Lindsay heard the booming voice of her former stepson call her just as she got to the door of the truck. She looked and saw him standing in the middle of her street with a big silver gun in his hand.

She froze like a deer caught in bright headlights. That's when the first bullet hit her in the right shoulder.

The force of the impact twisted her entire body to the left. She slumped against the truck, but she did not fall. The next bullet hit her painfully in the upper shoulder on the opposite side of her body, which caused her to lurch forward, but before she hit the ground, the third bullet hit her in the back. She fell to the ground and could no longer feel a thing. . . .

Chapter Eighteen

Just over a week ago, Shauntae was in this same hospital emergency room waiting while her mother went to find out where she and her brother could find their grandmother. Now it was her grandmother screaming at the same receptionist to help her to locate her mother. "Irony" was one of her vocabulary words about two weeks ago. *How appropriate I learned it,* she thought.

"Ma'am, please stop yelling at me. It won't make the computer unfreeze any faster. All I have to do is reboot it. Then I'll have your answers for you."

Sherrie started to yell again, but she realized the ghetto receptionist was right. The only thing she was getting from trying to talk to her was frustrated. She instead pulled out her cell phone and tried to call Cody again. This time he finally answered.

Cody had called Sherrie to go directly to the kids' school to pick them up when he received a call from the police telling him that Lindsay had been shot. The neighbor who called the police after hearing the gunshots told the police that the kids rode the school bus home. The police officer warned Cody to get to the kids before they got on the school bus and got home to find their mother's blood in the driveway.

If Cody knew any details surrounding her daughter's shooting, he did not share them with Sherrie at the time. He simply told her that she had been shot, it seemed by Sha'Ron, but she was still alive. Sherrie did as he instructed and got the kids from the school. On the way to the school, she called Kevin who was sitting at the restaurant waiting on his sister to arrive, assuming she was just running late, to tell him the real deal. She then headed straight to the hospital, telling the kids once she got them exactly what Cody had shared with her.

"Mom, I'm sorry. I see I missed your call seven times, but I can't get a signal in certain places in the hospital, specifically right outside the operating room. I'm on my way down to the lobby to talk to you."

Kevin came barreling into the waiting area just before Cody arrived. He grabbed the front of his mother's coat. "Mama, how is she? I can't believe he shot my sister."

Kevin collapsed on the floor of the waiting room, almost pulling his mother down with him.

"Kevin Westbrook, don't you dare fall out on me. I demand that you hold it together. Put your faith and trust back in God. Your sister is still alive, and we have to believe she will stay that way. Please, baby, get up."

Cody came into the lobby just then and helped his mother-in-law get his brother-in-law to his feet and in a chair.

"It's okay, Uncle K.J. God won't let my mommy die. That's just too much death. My daddy died, then my grandma. I mean my daddy's mama, not yours. So he won't take my mommy too. That's just too much, and He won't give us more than we can bear. It says that in the Bible," Li'l Shaun said.

"Out of the mouth of babes come truth," said Sherrie.

"Thank you, Li'l Shaun. I needed to hear that," Shauntae said as she wiped tears from her eyes.

"Cody, what's going on upstairs? What are the doctors saying?" Sherrie asked.

Cody struggled to share with them what the surgeon told him, but he knew they deserved the truth. He considered sending the kids on a frivolous errand to avoid having to talk in front of them, but decided against it. They had stood through everything else, so they deserved to know this as well.

"She was hit three times. There is a bullet in her left shoulder that is pretty serious, but there should be no problem removing it. She was also hit in the right shoulder by a bullet that went in and out."

Cody paused to gather himself and make sure he didn't break down as he delivered the last piece of news. The family all seemed to be collectively holding their breath as they waited to hear the rest.

"The third bullet hit her square in the back." Cody had to pause again as he choked, but decided to push the truth out through the pain. "The bullet hit her spine and lodged itself too close for them to remove it. Lindsay is going to be paralyzed. The only thing we can hope for is that the paralysis is partial; from the waist down instead of from the neck down."

Cody lost it then. He broke down and cried. The rest of the family followed suit. They all cried as well while still trying to comfort one another. After a solid ten minutes of weeping, Sherrie stood.

"Come on now, y'all. We have just been sitting here wailing as if we have given up on my baby. Not once have we opened our mouths to God to pray and thank Him."

"What are we thanking Him for, Grandma? Mama was shot, and she won't ever be able to walk again. She might not even be able to sit up or move again. Why are we supposed to be thankful?" Shauntae screamed at her grandmother.

"We are going to thank the Master that my baby, your mama, is not dead. She's alive. The devil's plan was to kill her. Satan did not send Sha'Ron to simply paralyze your mama. He wanted her dead, but God stopped his plan. She's alive. Now let's pray."

Everyone gathered around and held hands. A few of the strangers in the waiting room who overheard Sherrie's speech also joined in the prayer circle as well.

"Father in heaven, we come right now to say thank you." Sherrie began to cry again right then, but she continued to pray and cry out to God. "We thank, you, Father, for sparing my child's, more important, your child's, life. Lord, the devil has an agenda and he was on his job, but you, Lord, said no. Father, we come right now as a family of believers, and we are believing that you, who can do exceedingly and abundantly above all we can ever think and ask, will do your very best for our daughter, wife, sister, and mother. Lord, we are asking that you touch the hands of the surgeons, Lord. Guide them the way that you will have them to go so that your plan and purpose is brought forth in Lindsay's life. The doctors say that the best that we can hope for is paralysis from the waist down, but we know you to still be in the miracle-making business. You, Lord, are bigger than the doctors, and we know it is you who have the final say.

And, Father, I come praying right now for the strength and courage for all of us to be able to handle whatever your will is. Help us, Lord, to support my daughter and to support each other. And, Father God, I also come praying for Sha'Ron. Lord, we know that the baby was just an instrument used by the devil. I pray, Lord, that you have mercy on him. Let this trauma be a wake-up call for him, Lord. Touch him, Father, and show him the way to you. Touch his family as well, Father, as they deal with all that will come from this. This is our prayer in Jesus' name . . . Amen."

In unison, everyone else said, "Amen."

"Frannie, there is definitely something wrong with Sha'Ron. I don't know exactly what it is, but it's not good. I have never seen anyone look the way he did when he came in here about an hour ago. Francine, honestly, he looked like the walking dead. He went in his room, and he hasn't been out."

"Have you tried to talk to him, Tameeka?"

"Yes, I've knocked on his door three separate times. He has not answered, and the door is locked."

"Tameeka, remember, Sha'Ron has been through a lot these past few weeks. He may just be having a delayed reaction to Mama's death. We're going to have to give him some space. If you couple that with Uncle Bobby more than likely being locked up for the rest of his life, Sha'Ron, just like us, has a lot to deal with. We have to cut him a little slack."

"Hold on, Frannie. Somebody's at the door."

"Oh my goodness. Nooooo!" Tameeka heard Francine's words just before she removed the cordless phone from her ear, but she would address them after she answered the door.

Tameeka looked through the peephole and saw two plainclothes police officers standing in the snow on the still unshoveled porch. She panicked. Her heart began to beat a mile a minute. Everything inside of her told her that the two detectives on her porch definitely had something to do with Sha'Ron's bizarre look when he came in a little while ago.

She put the cordless phone back to her ear. "Francine, there are two detectives at the door. I haven't opened the door, but I know this has something to do with Sha'Ron."

"Meeka, I just heard on the six o'clock news that Nay-Nay was shot in the driveway of her home in broad daylight. The news report says she's in critical but stable condition."

Tameeka nearly fainted. She let the phone fall from her limp hands. The police knocked again, more forcefully this time. The loud noise brought her out of her stupor.

Not exactly sure what she should do, Tameeka glanced in the back of the small house to see if Sha'Ron had emerged from his bedroom at the sound of the loud knocking. He had not. The door still remained closed.

"This is the Detroit Police Department. Please open the door," a loud voice exploded from the other side of the two doors that separated them and Tameeka.

Slowly and warily, Tameeka took the lock off the storm door and opened it. She didn't immediately open the screen door, however. She just stared at the officers outside without uttering a word.

"Ma'am, is this where Sha'Ron Taylor lives?" one of the officers asked.

Tameeka could only nod her head in affirmation.

"May we come in?" the second detective asked.

Tameeka slowly pushed open the screen. Beyond the two detectives on the porch, she now noticed four other uniformed officers, two marked and one unmarked police cars.

The detectives stepped in quickly and two of the four uniforms approached the porch, but stood just outside the door. The detectives identified themselves by name, but Tameeka did not hear their names.

"Ma'am, we have a warrant for the arrest of Sha'Ron Taylor. Is he here?" Detective One asked.

Still too stunned to speak, Tameeka simply looked in the direction of her nephew's bedroom. The detectives looked at each other. Detective One silently agreed to take the lead. He walked toward the bedroom with Detective Two following a few feet behind. Detective One knocked on the door and waited a few seconds for a response. Upon not receiving one, he knocked again.

"Sha'Ron, are you in there?" Still no answer. The detective tried the door to find it locked.

"Ma'am, do you have a key? If you don't, we'll have to kick it in," Detective One said.

Tameeka, still stuck on mute, shook her head.

Detective One stepped back and kicked the door in the vicinity of where the lock was. The door flew open easily from the force of the officer's leg.

On the inside of the room Sha'Ron sat on his bed facing the door with his hands folded in his lap, his head hung toward the floor.

"Sha'Ron Taylor, we have a warrant for your arrest for the attempted murder of Lindsay Vincini." Detective One advanced carefully toward Sha'Ron, who stood cooperatively as the officer got close enough to touch his shoulder. Detective Two entered the room. He turned Sha'Ron so he could place the handcuffs on him. After he was cuffed, the officers did a quick but thorough search of Sha'Ron's person to check for weapons. One of them then began to read him his rights as he led Sha'Ron out of the house without incident. . . .

When Sha'Ron saw Lindsay's blood begin to stain the white snow beneath her body, he felt complete terror and panic take over him. He stood in the middle of the street just staring as the sidewalk became more and more coated in crimson. It wasn't until he heard the voice of a neighbor who had come from inside his house to investigate the sound of the gunshots that he actually moved.

"Young man, do you know what happened out here?"

From the man's distance, he was unable to initially see Lindsay's body lying on the ground.

Sha'Ron turned and stared at the white man for several seconds. Now he was paralyzed in that position.

The neighbor began moving in Sha'Ron's direction until he got close enough to notice the large silver gun in his hand. Then he stopped moving, afraid now for his own life.

When Sha'Ron saw the stranger's hand go to his mouth to stifle any noise that threatened to come out, he was again propelled into movement. He quickly tossed the gun in the car, jumped behind the wheel, then sped off down the street at a dangerous speed.

He drove to his friend's house without even realizing how he got there. He jumped out of the Malibu and left the keys in the ignition even though he had the presence of mind to turn the car off. He was happy to see that his friend was home because his Mustang was parked in the driveway. He got in his car using his spare key and drove away.

Sha'Ron was not sure where he was going until he found himself parked outside of Uncle Bobby's house in West Bloomfield. He sat outside looking at the beautiful Tudor-style home, reminiscing about the wonderful times he'd had at this house before his father died.

Sha'Ron used to think this was the coolest house. His daddy and Uncle Bobby were the coolest men in the world. These two men seemed to have all the power in the world right in the palm of their hands. They would speak and grown men immediately moved into action.

There were always a lot of pretty women around too. The ladies would always tell Sha'Ron how cute he was. Those days held great memories for him.

But again, that was before his father died. Every time he had come to this house since then, all his uncle wanted to talk about was how he had to avenge his father's death by killing his stepmom. Now he had done it. Now the evil witch who killed his father and mother and who his family considered responsible for the failed health and death of his grandmother was also dead. And he had done it on his own without the help of his stupid uncle.

He sat in front of the house until a city police car came cruising by. The police officer got out of his car, came over to Sha'Ron's vehicle, and asked for his identification and insurance information. Sha'Ron told the officer that he had come by to pick up something from his uncle's home but just realized he had left the spare keys to the place at home. The police officer bought his story because of the similar names. The city police were well aware of who Robert Taylor was and that he was currently in custody.

After the scare with the West Bloomfield police officer, Sha'Ron subconsciously drove himself home, went to his bedroom, locked the door, and sat in the one position until the police came to take him into custody.

Chapter Nineteen

"Thank you, Officer. Yes, sir, we appreciate your prayers. I'll be in touch." Cody hung up after ending his phone conversation with the detective handling Lindsay's case. Cody approached his wife's hospital recovery bed. "That was Officer Jarvis Williams. They have Sha'Ron in custody, baby. He was arrested and charged with your attempted murder."

Lindsay lay flat on her back staring straight up. Cody had to stand over her for her to be able to see his face. She took a painful deep breath and released it extremely slowly.

Cody saw the strain it took for his wife to breathe and anger shot up so hot in his bones, he nearly screamed from his frustration. He watched her lie there, unable to move, fear covering her features, sadness radiating from her pores. He loved this woman like he loved no one aside from God before her. In fact, he actually loved her before he loved God, before he had enough sense to love God more.

Lindsay tried to speak, but her words initially came out in a faint whisper. Cody leaned in closer in an effort to hear her clearly.

She attempted to speak again, and Cody's ear was pressed near on top of her lips. But even though he was listening closely, he was certain he could not have heard her correctly.

"Baby, please repeat that."

"Cody, you heard me. I want you to forgive Sha'Ron for what he did. I want you to represent him in court."

Cody walked away from his wife's bed to collect himself before he cursed in front of her and God.

Lindsay had been out of surgery for about six hours and awake for about an hour. Cody had convinced Sherrie and Kevin to take the kids to her home after the surgeon had come to give his post-op report while Lindsay was still asleep.

"The surgery on Mrs. Vincini went as well as to be expected. In other words, we were able to remove the bullet in her shoulder with no complications. We were also pretty successful in maneuvering and repairing the area around the spine damaged by the bullet that hit her in the back. Right now, there is a lot of swelling around the spine. Once it goes down in about seventy-two hours we will be able to assess where she is physically and in her movements. But from the looks of things, the chances of her being mobile from the waist up are pretty good. So keep praying." The surgeon then left them in their private waiting area.

That was hours ago. Now Cody stood in the room alone with his wife wondering if they had accidently opened her head and worked on her brain instead of her back. He stared at her awkwardly, questioning if he should go find the doctor. She was obviously having a reaction to the medication.

"I see you don't believe me, but I'm serious."

Cody stared even more strangely at her because he now believed she was truly serious.

"Lindsay, I don't want you to wear yourself out. Otherwise, I would make you explain yourself. But my primary concern is your physical health. I'll deal with your mental stability later." Cody's voice was filled with agitation.

"Cody, I can talk, and I must say this while it's on my heart." Lindsay paused to catch her breath. "Can you give me some water," she rasped out.

Cody stood next to Lindsay's bed and placed the straw to the water cup in her mouth. She took several sips, nearly draining the cup. She then continued to plead her and Sha'Ron's case.

"Baby, I, of course don't like what Sha'Ron did, but I can relate to why he did it. Honey, I have walked in Sha'Ron's shoes. He hates me because I killed his father and mother. He probably feels that Shaun's death is what made his grandma sick. So inadvertently, I am responsible for Patricia's death also in his eyes. Remember, I killed Shaun because I blamed him for Shyanne's death. I snapped after all the trauma I suffered as a result of my relationship and marriage to him." Lindsay's voice began to fade. "More water."

Cody moved from over the bed where he stood listening to and watching Lindsay speak. He took the cup to the nurse's station to find out where he could refill it.

As he walked to where he was directed, he thought about what Lindsay had said thus far. While he didn't agree with her, it amazed him that she could be so forgiving and understanding. He returned to the recovery room hoping that Lindsay had fallen into a nap, but she was wide awake. He again held the straw to her lips while she took a few sips.

"Cody, do you remember trying to talk me into taking a temporary insanity plea? You said we had a good chance of winning considering my state of mind when I shot Shaun. You said I could have gotten a self-defense plea for killing Rhonda. Well, if you think I was crazy when I shot Shaun, how do you think Sha'Ron felt when he shot me? I killed *both* his parents."

Cody's admiration for his wife soared, but his animosity for her assailant had not lessened any. He couldn't understand how Lindsay could expect him to be in the same room with Sha'Ron and not end up charged with attempted murder himself at the very least.

"Lindsay, you are asking a lot of me. I know it's wrong to feel this way, but right now, I hate Sha'Ron. I'll pray that God removes this anger from my heart, but right now, it's there, wild and hot."

Cody lips said he hated Sha'Ron, but his demeanor and his attitude had softened somewhat. Lindsay remained silent. She was allowing her words to continue to work on her husband. The tone of his voice told her he was starting to give her idea some consideration, despite what he said. He just had not realized it yet.

Cody paced the room as he tried to come up with the words to explain to his wife that her desire for him to represent Sha'Ron would not come to fruition.

"Lindsay, listen, even though I don't want to defend Sha'Ron, no judge would allow it anyway. He or she would consider it a conflict of interest at the least, and perhaps even legal sabotage."

Whoa! Lindsay had not thought about that. It just might look crazy to a judge to have the husband of the victim defend her shooter.

Cody came back and stood over the bed. He could see the wheels turning in the head of his beautiful wife. His last argument had convinced her that it was not possible for him to defend Sha'Ron.

"Baby, look, I don't want you to worry about Sha'Ron right now. I just want you to concentrate on getting strong enough to get out of this hospital and back home to me and the kids." Cody leaned in and kissed the compassionate head of his wife. Unable to resist, he then kissed her dry, chapped lips.

Lindsay felt Cody's lips as they touched and melded with her own. She was very grateful to God for the ability to feel the intimate caress of her lover's mouth.

"Lindsay, I want you to know this. I heard your argument on behalf of Sha'Ron. Just knowing that you not only don't hate him, but you want to help him pulls deeply on my spirit. On the strength of your forgiveness, I want you to know I have given up the idea of personally harming him. As I said, I will work with God on forgiving him to the point you have, but I feel grateful to Him already for taking even just that much anger from me."

"Cody, I want you to talk to Tameeka and Francine. You are a great attorney. I know you can convince them to allow you to sincerely represent Sha'Ron. They're his guardians now, I'm assuming. Therefore, they can convince the judge to allow you to defend Sha'Ron. They are allowed to choose whatever attorney they want to, right?"

Cody bucked his eyes as his mouth fell wide open. "Are you still on this, woman?"

"I am, honey. I believe in this with all my heart. You said it yourself, if I can forgive him while lying here in my condition, then I know God can give you the heart to not only forgive him, but offer him the best defense any defendant has ever received."

"Lindsay, I don't know if I can do that."

"You can, Cody. You just have to work your faith. You believe in God, and you trust His Word. His Word says that faith without works is dead. This is an opportunity to truly put your faith to work. His Word says we are to forgive our enemies. It also says we are to feed our hungry enemies and by doing so, we will heap burning coals on their head. Honey, by our helping him, I think that means God doesn't want us to make Sha'Ron suffer. I think that means this can be an opportunity to show a soul who knows nothing or little about our God how wonderful He really is. Sha'Ron needs us, Cody. If I remember correctly, you are the one who told me it was our Christian duty to give him that help. This is not about us, but all about God."

Now that was a low blow. He was sure his wife had not done it intentionally, but she just tap-danced all over his guilt button. If he had not talked her into allowing the kids to reunite with Sha'Ron, she might not be in this hospital bed.

Lindsay realized what she said and how Cody may have interpreted it a second after it came out of her mouth.

"Cody, baby, I'm sorry. I did not mean to imply that this is in any way your fault. I was simply—"

Cody cut her off in the middle of her apology. "I already know that, love. I do. You were only trying to convince me that we do need to help Sha'Ron. The Holy Spirit was speaking through you. And I'm going to be obedient. I'm going to represent Sha'Ron."

Lindsay closed her eyes as her heart opened and expanded. She received such joy and relief from her husband's statement. When she again opened her eyes they were brimming with tears. "Thank you, Cody. Thank you, God."

"Lindsay, if this is going to work, I'm going to have to go see Tameeka and Francine tonight. I realize it's late, but I have to get their permission to represent Sha'Ron so I can be with him in court first thing in the morning. I just pray his street smarts made him remember to not say a word until he spoke with an attorney."

"Okay. Go, baby. I'm going to rest now."

"Good. I'll call your mom and the kids on my way out to tell them to wait until tomorrow to come back down here."

Cody kissed Lindsay's lips again, then left to take on what was probably going to be the hardest case of both his career and his faith walk.

"Hey, God never promised it would be easy. He only said He would be with us through it all," Cody said out loud to himself in the hallway.

When Cody left the hospital he headed straight to Sha'Ron's house. He prayed for two things. One, Tameeka was there, and two, that she would actually talk to him when she saw him. Her first thought may be that he was there for some type of revenge. She might very well think the offer to defend Sha'Ron was part of a revenge plot. He prayed and asked God to soften her heart and set this up if this is what He wanted him to do.

When he arrived, there was a car parked in the driveway and a car in front of the house. Cody had no idea what kind of car Tameeka drove, but he assumed the red Toyota Camry in the driveway was hers.

It was now after 10:00 P.M. This was not a visitor-friendly hour for people you liked. To have someone you despised show up on your doorstep at this time of night was downright dangerous. Cody, however, was on a mission from his wife and from God. So he got out of the car, walked up the snowy steps onto the snowy porch, and knocked on the door.

Tameeka and Francine were sitting in the living room of their mother's house, discussing Sha'Ron's situation when they heard the knock at the door.

"Are you expecting someone?" Tameeka asked her sister.

"No, of course not. Nobody even knows I'm over here except my children. I left them at home. Daiquan is in charge with strict instructions to call me if there's an emergency and to go next door to Mrs. Langley's if they must leave the house."

Both sisters got up and went to the door together. Tameeka looked through the peephole.

"Who is it?" Francine whispered as if they were hiding from whoever was on the other side of the door.

"You will *not* believe this. White Boy is on the porch," Tameeka screamed in contrast to her sister's whisper.

"Why are you yelling?" Francine asked again softly.

"Why are you whispering?" Tameeka countered. "This is *our* house."

Before Francine could say another word, Tameeka had snatched open the front door.

"What the heck are you doing here, especially at this time of night?"

"Tameeka, why did you open the door? He could be here to hurt us for what Sha'Ron—"

"Shut up, fool!" Tameeka hushed Francine before she gave White Boy evidence to use against Sha'Ron.

"Look, ladies, I'm glad you are both here together, and I'm not here to hurt you. I'm actually here to offer my help. I want to represent Sha'Ron in the case against him for shooting my wife."

Bitter acid boiled in Cody's stomach and rose to his throat as he spoke those last words.

"What! Do you think we're crazy, White Boy? You think we gon' let you represent our nephew so you can purposely jack up his case and get him life in prison? If this ain't the stupidest thing I ever heard. If I wasn't so mad at your suggestion I would laugh in your face." Tameeka slammed the door in Cody's face.

Cody seriously wanted to walk away from that house for good. He could go back to the hospital right now and tell his wife he tried, but they refused. However, he knew she would send him back and make him convince these two women that he was the best thing that could happen to Sha'Ron right now. So Cody knocked on the door again.

Tameeka again snatched open the door. "Are you freakin' kiddin' me, White Boy? Are you serious?"

"Tameeka, I'm very serious. This was not my idea at all. It was actually Lindsay's. She says she knows exactly what Sha'Ron is going through right now because she has worn his shoes . . ." Cody then went on to quickly explain Lindsay's strategy and reason to help Sha'Ron.

When he was done speaking, both Tameeka and Francine were standing in front of the still closed screen door.

"You know what, White Boy? If I were some naïve country bumpkin who just hit Detroit a few weeks ago I might believe you and your wife were sincere. You are actually a pretty good pay lawyer. I know you worked a miracle for my brother before you started sleeping with his wife. Then you pulled another Houdini act when you got her that crazy sentence for killing my brother and Rhonda. So, yeah, I know you got mad skills. But I'll be doggone if we let you use those skills against my nephew."

Tameeka was again about to slam the door in Cody's face, but Francine caught it when it was about halfway closed.

"Wait, Tameeka. Listen to me now. I heard Cody, and I actually believe him. I believe this incident with the evil witch could have really changed her heart. Look at how she and Keva have become such good friends."

"That's her and Keva. Keva only slept with her boyfriend and had a baby by him. She didn't sh . . . do what Sha'Ron is being accused of doing," Tameeka said.

"Okay. That's true. But think about this. If Cody isn't sincere we can always fire him and get the case declared a mistrial. The fact that he is who he is will actually work in our favor in this instance."

Wow. That was actually a very shrewd point Francine came up with, Cody thought. Perhaps this lady should consider a career in law.

"Francine what you just said makes a ton of sense because I'm actually thinking that's the way this is going to have to play out. I can't believe you are actually falling for this *Nay-Nay's sorry and truly wants to help crap.* I ain't buying it. Now I just want to know how do you think we should sell it to Sha'Ron, Frannie?" Tameeka's attitude changed from that of distrust to one of calculating and plotting.

"I think we should tell Sha'Ron the truth. I believe what Cody says is the truth. No attorney worth his salt wants to be kicked off a case. If Cody is trying to scam us, he can be disbarred. I don't think he's willing to risk it."

Tameeka shook her head at what she perceived to be her sister's naïveté. "You know what, Frannie? You can believe what you want. I'm only going along with this because this could be good for Sha'Ron either way." Tameeka then walked away and left Francine standing in the doorway with Cody who was still standing outside in the cold.

Francine considered letting him in but thought better of it. Tameeka would probably try to hurt him.

"Cody, it sounds like you will be representing Sha'Ron on this case against him. So what do we do next?"

Cody was cold but saw no invitation to come inside forthcoming so he made his statement quick.

"I will meet you and Tameeka downtown at the Wayne County Jail first thing in the morning. I need to get in to see Sha'Ron to make sure he doesn't make any statements to the police."

"You don't have to worry about that. Tameeka and I as his guardians have already told the police they are not to question him without an attorney present. But truth be told, I don't think it was necessary for us to tell the police anything. Sha'Ron has been in a sort of catatonic state since he came home from . . . since he came home today. He has not said a word."

"Really? Wow. That's very helpful information. I'll talk to Sha'Ron tomorrow to get a full assessment of things, but I'm pretty sure I'm going to plead him not guilty on the grounds of temporary insanity."

"Well, if that's what you think is best. Like Tameeka said, you seem to be very good at what you do. So we will give you free rein. But if I get even the slightest indication that you are trying to do my nephew dirty, I will work very hard at making you pay both professionally and personally. See you downtown tomorrow." With that Francine closed the door.

When Cody arrived at the hospital the next day, Shyanne's parents and Keva were in Lindsay's recovery room. The Kennedys looked like they had both been crying. Keva looked a little more pulled together, but there was a definite sadness in her eyes.

"Hello, everybody," Cody said as he entered the room. He went straight to his wife's bed and kissed her forehead.

"Cody, is it true? Are you actually going to be the attorney for the boy who shot Nay-Nay?" Mrs. Kennedy asked.

Cody looked at Lindsay a little surprised she had shared this with the Kennedys.

"When they arrived asking where you were I told them you were downtown at court," Lindsay said sheepishly.

"We assume that Nay is having some sort of strange reaction to her medication, but we figured you would be more sensible than this," Mr. Kennedy said.

"Cody, he tried to kill your wife. He tried to take away our other daughter. How can you both be so forgiving?" Mrs. Kennedy added.

"Mama T, this is what I have to do—what we have to do. This is what God expects of us," Lindsay responded.

Keva put in her two cents. "I totally understand what you and Cody are doing, Nay-Nay. I don't know if I would have the courage and the faith to do it myself under the circumstances, but I am sure proud of you two for being strong enough to do it. I am glad to be able to tell people I know you two."

The nurse came into the room just then. "I'm sorry, but I'm going to have to ask everyone except the husband to leave. We have to be very cognizant of our patient's strength. We want to give her a little something to make her sleep for a while. So you all have exactly five minutes. Then you have to leave." The nurse said her piece, then left the small room.

"Okay, baby girl, we're going to leave now, but we'll be back tomorrow. I just want to say this before we leave. Nay, Cody, this young lady makes a great point. What you two are doing for that child is remarkable. I think I speak for your godfather here when I say we may not agree with you, but we will support you both on this," Mrs. Kennedy said.

"Thank you, Mama T, Daddy. Cody and I appreciate your support," Lindsay replied.

The Kennedys came and kissed Lindsay's forehead, then left. Keva then came to stand at Lindsay's bedside. "I mean it, Nay-Nay. What you are doing can probably be considered miraculous. God is truly going to get the glory from this unselfish act of forgiveness and love."

"Thank you, Keva. Thank you for everything." Lindsay almost cried at Keva's encouraging words.

"Thank you, Nay. You have truly allowed me to see Jesus in action. I love you, girl. I'll see you tomorrow." Keva kissed Lindsay's forehead, then left the room.

"Well, it looks like you're a hero, baby," Cody said as he took up the spot Keva vacated. He gently lifted Lindsay's hand and rubbed his own hand across it.

Lindsay's smile was brilliant as she announced, "Cody, I can actually feel you touching my hand. I can't move my hand or arm, but I can feel the sensation of you rubbing my hand."

"That's great, baby! Do you want me to get the nurse?" Cody asked excitedly.

"No. I'll tell her when she comes back. I want you to tell me what happened with Sha'Ron this morning."

Cody pulled up to Lindsay's bed and began recounting what happened.

"Lindsay, when I saw Sha'Ron today, all the anger I felt for him drained away. All of his tough veneer and bravado were gone. What I saw today was a scared little boy who needed protecting. He looked so pale and helpless. If I had gone there with the intention to kill him, I would not have been able to do it after looking at him."

Lindsay allowed the pain in her heart for Sha'Ron to spill from her eyes. Cody got up and got her a Kleenex, then quietly dabbed her leaking eyes. He then finished telling her what happened.

"Frannie and Tameeka explained to Sha'Ron that I was going to be his lawyer because you wanted me to help him. They told him the story as you told it to me and as I told it to them."

Cody then sat back down in the chair as he told the next part. He sat because he knew he would need the chair's support.

"Once Frannie, who did most of the talking, finished telling Sha'Ron how you felt, he spoke the first words either of them had heard him say since yesterday. The police officers also informed us that he had still not spoken all night last night either."

"Well, what did he say?" Lindsay asked anxiously.

"He asked, *'For real? She wants to do that for me?'* It was really quite simple, but it was more about the tone of his voice and his demeanor versus the words he spoke. It was as if he could relate to you having sympathy for him. He really appreciated it. It was kind of like you said yesterday; you have walked in Sha'Ron's shoes. Today, it was if he felt that he had walked in yours as well."

Lindsay blinked her eyes to combat more tears threatening to spill out. Again, Cody got up to wipe her eyes. He stood as he told the end of the story.

"When we got to court and informed the judge that I would be representing Sha'Ron, she looked over the case file and chuckled out loud at all the names involved. By the time she came to the end, you could almost see the words *in total shock* run across her forehead.

"She gave me the normal warnings and cautioned Sha'Ron about allowing me to represent him. She then asked him point-blank if he was sure he wanted me as his attorney. And without hesitation, Sha'Ron said yes. So the judge proceeded. The judge asked how he pleaded, and Sha'Ron said not guilty. I then informed her that I would be seeking an insanity defense. The judge set his bail at $100,000, 10 percent cash. Tawanda and Francine were making preparations to bail him out when I left to come down here. He should actually be at home as we speak."

"So now what happens next?" Lindsay asked expectantly.

"The district attorney will have a psychologist examine Sha'Ron and give a report. I will also have a separate one do the same thing. They will both give a report on Sha'Ron's state of mind at the time of the shooting."

Lindsay asked one final question. "Cody, do you think you can help him? That is what I truly want. I want to help him the way you wanted to help him when we first started this thing."

Cody nodded his head, very happy to be able to give his wife such positive news.

"Lindsay, if you had seen the young man I saw today, you would be as doubtless as I am. We—you, me, and God—will definitely be able to help him. The best thing about this whole thing is he actually wants to be helped. . . ."

Epilogue

". . . In conjunction with your plea agreement, this court finds you guilty of assault with intent to do great bodily harm and sentences you to a five-year suspended sentence. You are also placed on probation until the time of your twenty-first birthday. In addition, this court orders you to receive biweekly counseling sessions with a therapist chosen by the court. If you fail to meet any of these conditions, you will be arrested and ordered to serve the full five years in prison, dating from the time of your arrest. Do you understand these conditions as the court has laid them out before you?" Judge Brandy Oliver asked.

"Yes, Your Honor. May I please address the court for a moment?" Sha'Ron respectfully petitioned.

"Yes, Sha'Ron, you may."

"Your Honor, I would like to say in front of everyone here today how very grateful I am for this second opportunity I have been given at life. I want to thank all of the people in this courtroom who have shown me love, forgiveness, and support." Sha'Ron turned to face the court. "You all have been very wonderful examples of Christ and how He forgives us over and over again. I could stand here all day and not be able to fully express how much I appreciate you."

In the courtroom was Sha'Ron's immediate family, which included his aunts, Tameeka and Francine, his sisters, Shauntae and Shauna, and his brothers, Shaun (he requested that the "Li'l" be dropped from his name as his aunt Tameeka suggested) and Kevaun.

In addition, his new extended family was also in court to offer their support. Keva, who held the rambunctious Shauna, was there. Tawanda was currently in custody awaiting trial on a serious drug possession charge. Shauna now lived with Tawanda's mom, who allowed the little girl to come to court with the family. Also in attendance were Kevin, Sherrie, the Kennedys, Pastor Adams, and Dr. Hooper.

All of these people rallied around Sha'Ron during his court proceedings, which initially began with a full-scale trial. The new overzealous district attorney was determined to make a name for himself with the press and the sensationalism this trial provided.

It made national news when it came out that Cody, a very reputable defense attorney, was going to defend the young man who shot his wife, leaving her paralyzed from the waist down. Several national newspapers, magazines, news shows, and talk shows had interviewed and written articles about Sha'Ron and Lindsay. Once enough media attention had been garnered and the DA figured his name had been heard enough times nationwide, he conceded by offering Sha'Ron a plea deal.

In the eight months since the whole ordeal started, Lindsay's entire family decided to stand behind her and show her their love by giving their love to Sha'Ron just as she had done.

Kevin, who did marry Brooke and was now the proud father of a baby daughter named Shyanne Renee Westbrook, became an uncle to Sha'Ron, teaching him things completely contrary to what he had learned from his uncle Bobby. Sherrie, who always expressed that she was not trying to replace Patricia, became his surrogate grandmother. Keva became his aunt and allowed him to spend a lot of time at her home with Kevaun and her husband, Cheval. Mr. and Mrs. Kennedy became another set of extended grandparents to him.

After witnessing the love and support of Lindsay's family who were all Christians, the Taylor family decided they too wanted to give their lives to Christ. Francine and her children, Tameeka, and Sha'Ron all joined Tribe of Judah Baptist Church. As a family, they began special counseling with Pastor Adams. Sha'Ron also started attending family counseling with Shauntae and Shaun with Dr. Hooper, paid for completely by Cody and Lindsay.

Uncle Bobby was sentenced to two consecutive life sentences without the possibility of parole. His entire drug organization collapsed under the weight of the local, federal, and international indictments. Everyone from his street soldiers to his lieutenants were arrested, charged, and sentenced in accordance with their crimes.

"I would like to especially thank Cody, my attorney, my friend, my mentor. I love you, and I thank you for loving me and for deeming me worthy of another chance. And Nay-Nay, I spent more than two years hating you more than I could ever truly express. That hate consumed all of my thoughts. It actually consumed my whole family.

"But you countered our hate with forgiveness and love. By you doing that for us, you taught us how to do it also. You are my hero. You have inspired me in ways unimaginable. I hear and see the skepticism of the people who hear our story, and it doesn't even faze me. I am living this love out with you every day. I know beyond a shadow of a doubt that it is real. You are my hero. I don't think you even realize it, but I believe you saved my life.

"Pastor Adams, I want to announce to you that when I graduate from high school, I will be attending college in pursuit of some sort of degree in religious studies. I will then go on to seminary school. I am announcing my call to ministry here at the end of my trial and the end of my criminal life."

At the end of his written speech, there wasn't a dry eye in the courtroom, including Sha'Ron's or the judge's.

Through her tears, the judge asked, "Are you done, young man?"

Sha'Ron nodded through his own tears that he was.

"Bailiff, please escort the defendant to where he needs to go to complete his paperwork. This case is adjourned."

Cody shook Sha'Ron's hand before he was led off by the bailiff. Tameeka and Francine walked with him to complete the paperwork that would begin his suspended sentence and probation. Lindsay followed them in her motorized wheelchair.

DISCUSSION QUESTIONS

1. I didn't realize that this novel had an overall theme to it until the very end. What do you think the theme is? Do you feel it is realistic?

2. Cody convinced Lindsay to allow Shauntae and Shaun to spend time with Sha'Ron, knowing he was selling drugs. Would you have allowed your children to spend time with a sibling or half sibling under the same conditions?

3. Pastor Adams really gave Cody what-for regarding his attitude toward Lindsay keeping the abortion secret from him. Do you believe that Cody was equally responsible, if not more, for Lindsay doing what she did?

4. Should Cody feel responsible in any way for Lindsay being shot by Sha'Ron since he was the one who insisted she allow him to reunite with the kids?

5. I know that many of you who read *His Woman, His Wife, His Widow* felt that Lindsay got off too easy for killing Shaun and Rhonda. Do you think she deserved what happened to her at the hands of Sha'Ron for what she did to his parents?

6. Lindsay was blessed with a great friend in Shyanne in *His Woman, His Wife, His Widow*. How do you feel about Keva and Lindsay's fast friendship? Is it realistic considering their history?

7. Give your take on all that Shauntae and Li'l Shaun had to endure from both *His Woman His Wife His Widow* and *Lindsay's Legacy*.

8. Were Tameeka and Francine justified in attacking Lindsay at the hospital? Do you think Lindsay is responsible for Patricia's illness and subsequent death?

9. Give your overall take on Sha'Ron.

10. If you could rewrite any part of the novel, which part would it be? How would you do it?

AUTHOR BIO

My name is Janice Jones. I was born July 6, 1966, in Detroit, Michigan. I lived in the great state of Michigan until August 2007, when I moved to Phoenix, Arizona. I am the mother of two sons, Jerrick & Derrick Parker, and grandmother to Jevon Jerrick Parker.

I went to church as a child and always enjoyed attending, but I never truly understood what it meant to have a real relationship with God. I fully accepted Christ as my Lord and Savior in May of 1999. Approximately one year later, I heard the voice of God instructing me to write my first novel, *His Woman, His Wife, His Widow*. Obediently but slowly, I wrote the book.

Since moving to Phoenix, I have become an associate minister at First Institutional Baptist Church under the leadership of Pastor Dr. Warren H. Stewart, Sr. As a member of FIBC, I work with the Women's Ministry and Ms. Jessie's Place, our church campus bookstore and coffeehouse. I also write and distribute a weekly message titled "Minister JJ's Midweek Message For The Soul." Back in Detroit, I was led and directed by two dynamic pastors, Dr. Nathan A. Proché of Tree of Life Missionary Baptist Church and Dr. Wilma R. Johnson of New Prospect Missionary Baptist Church.

It is my goal, and I believe God's true calling on my life, to be a successful author, novelist, and minister. I truly love to write, and I enjoy telling and creating stories that will prayerfully edify, uplift, and educate others about the benefits of living life as a Christian, a true follower, and servant of Jesus Christ. Everything that I pen is done to show the redeeming power of Christ's love and sacrifice, which is available to all who are willing to accept.

UC HIS GLORY BOOK CLUB!

www.uchisglorybookclub.net

UC His Glory Book Club is the spirit-inspired brain-child of Joylynn Jossel, Author and Acquisitions Editor of Urban Christian, and Kendra Norman-Bellamy, Author for Urban Christian. This is an online book club that hosts authors of Urban Christian. We welcome as members all men and women who have a passion for reading Christian-based fiction.

UC HIS GLORY BOOK CLUB pledges our commitment to provide support, positive feedback, encouragement, and a forum whereby members can openly discuss and review the literary works of Urban Christian authors.

There is no membership fee associated with UC His Glory Book Club; however, we do ask that you support the authors through purchasing, encouraging, providing book reviews, and of course, your prayers. We also ask that you respect our beliefs and follow the guidelines of the book club. We hope to receive your valuable input, opinions, and reviews that build up, rather than tear down our authors.

WHAT WE BELIEVE:

—We believe that Jesus is the Christ, Son of the Living God

Urban Christian His Glory Book Club

—We believe the Bible is the true, living Word of God
—We believe all Urban Christian authors should use their God-given writing abilities to honor God and share the message of the written word God has given to each of them uniquely.
—We believe in supporting Urban Christian authors in their literary endeavors by reading, purchasing and sharing their titles with our online community.
—We believe that in everything we do in our literary arena should be done in a manner that will lead to God being glorified and honored.

We look forward to the online fellowship with you. Please visit us often at *www.uchisglorybookclub.net*.

Many Blessing to You!
Shelia E. Lipsey,
President, UC His Glory Book Club